Jan, 2013 - DK
(Good)

P.K.
2012

D1563078

A STRANGE SHADOW PASSED OVER HIM . . .

His pallid face became a mask of horror. Two black dots wheeled in the brassy sky. . . . The buzzards floated downward and touched the ground thirty feet away, flapping their jagged black wings. They were directly in front of him, turning their repulsive red necks. The smell of his fresh blood was in their nostrils.

Finch had never felt so helpless. Those carnivorous predators would pick his flesh to pieces. . . . The loathsome birds hopped closer. His eyes bulged in terror. He tried to cry out, hoping to scare them off. But he had lost too much blood; his strength was totally gone. No sound would come. And the hideous creatures were closing in. . . .

Other Books in the
DAN COLT WESTERN SAGA

LAST STAGE TO ETERNITY

Morgan Hill

A DELL BOOK

Published by
Dell Publishing Co., Inc.
1 Dag Hammarskjold Plaza
New York, New York 10017

Copyright © 1983 by Morgan Hill

All rights reserved. No part of this book may be
reproduced or transmitted in any form or by any
means, electronic or mechanical, including
photocopying, recording or by any information storage
and retrieval system, without the written permission
of the Publisher, except where permitted by law.

Dell ® TM 681510, Dell Publishing Co., Inc.

ISBN: 0-440-14806-5

Printed in the United States of America
First printing—January 1983

DD

LAST STAGE
TO ETERNITY

CHAPTER ONE

Tumbleweeds bounded across his path, helpless before the blustering August wind. The sun-bleached streets of Taos, New Mexico, lay undisturbed in the noonday brightness. Only swirling dust devils moved between the faded buildings.

Narrowed against the glare, the pale blue eyes of the lone rider darted from side to side. The citizens of Taos had deserted the town's main street in search of shade. That was all right with Dave Sundeen. At this moment he was not looking for people. He was looking for a horse. *His* horse.

Some contemptible thief had stolen the big buckskin gelding from the livery stable in Creede, Colorado. Steal a man's woman on the raw frontier, you'd better prepare to fight. Steal a man's horse, you'd better prepare to *die*.

Sundeen had bought a bay mare and set out tracking the thief two weeks ago. He was immediately aware that the skunk who had stolen his horse was riding in a group. Observers along the way had remembered seeing the horse, ridden by a man traveling with eight or ten other riders.

The trail had led south over Cumbres Pass on the Colorado–New Mexico border, through the town of Tres Piedras. From there Sundeen had tracked the men down the long parched hills to the Rio Grande. He had found their campsite on the river's bank at ten o'clock this morning. They were no more than an hour ahead of him. Hope ran high within him that they had stopped in Taos.

Dave Sundeen had the look of a man who had ridden a long time. His grim, angular face was leathered by the wind and tanned by the sun. His medium-blond hair and mustache stood out in bright contrast to the mahogany of his skin.

Riding slowly up the dusty street, the tall, muscular Sundeen studied each horse at the hitch racks. Most stood heads dropped, hip-shot, tails swatting at pesky flies.

Suddenly he focused on the big buckskin.

The animal stood between two smaller horses, head down, ears lowered. He was tied in front of the Silver Spur Saloon on Dave's left. Angling the bay across the street to the right, Sundeen dismounted and tied her to a rack. Sweeping the bright street with his gaze, he strode across to his horse. Squeezing between the buckskin and the next horse, he patted the buckskin's rump and said, "Howdy, big boy!"

Instantly the animal's head came up, ears erect. He nickered in recognition of the familiar voice. Dave ran an experienced hand over the horse's body, looking for any sign of mistreatment. Satisfied that the big animal had not been abused, he released the reins from the rail and backed him into the street.

The buckskin nickered again, bobbing his head.

"Glad to see me, boy?" asked Dave. Rubbing the soft muzzle, he said, "I'm glad to see you, too."

The tall, broad-shouldered man cast a quick glance toward the bat-winged door of the saloon. His forehead knitted into a hard frown. Sooner or later the man who had stolen Dave Sundeen's horse would be coming out. Sundeen would be waiting for him.

He led the buckskin up the sun-struck street toward an alleyway that ran between Harrel's General Store and Mike's Barber Shop. Reaching the alleyway, he turned in and guided the horse to the rear of the buildings.

While Dave Sundeen looked for a shady place to tie his horse, another rider rode in from the north. He stopped at the livery stable, took a quick look in the barn, then the corral, and continued into town.

His pale blue eyes scrutinized the horses that lined both sides of the street. He swung the huge black gelding to the water trough in front of Mike's Barber Shop. Dismounting stiffly, the tall, blond man adjusted the twin Colt .45s on his narrow hips, then removed his hat. While the black slurped eagerly at the water, the muscular rider sleeved sweat from his brow and worked the handle on the water pump.

Dropping his head under the spout, he let the cool water drench him, then drank his fill. He tied the gelding to the hitch rail and crossed the boardwalk to the barber shop.

When Dave Sundeen came out of the alley and looked around, he saw the tall man passing into the barber shop. Otherwise the street was still deserted. He crossed the street and took refuge from the burning sun under a slanted canopy in front of an empty shop. The faded sign on the door said Wilson's Clothiers. Dave assumed Wilson had gone out of business. With his back to the wall, he set his eyes on the door of the Silver Spur. It wouldn't be hard to identify the thief. He would be the only man without a horse.

While the wind whipped tumbleweeds down the street, the tall, blond man who had just entered the barber shop hung his hat on a wall peg and sat down in a straight-backed chair. The barber was already working on a customer.

"Howdy, stranger," said the barber with a smile. "Be with you shortly."

"Fine," said the tall man, rubbing his stubbled chin.

A portly man in his mid-fifties studied the blond stranger's suntanned features from the barber chair. When their eyes met, he looked away.

Moments passed. The wind slammed dust against the building. The only sound in the shop was the metallic scrape of the barber's shears.

The tall stranger picked up a day-old copy of the Santa Fe *Gazette* and scanned the front page. He could feel the portly man's eyes on him. Slowly he raised his pale blues to meet the stare. Again the man looked quickly away.

The tall man who wore the tied-down .45s spoke up. "Do we know each other, mister?"

"Uh, no," said the man, clearing his throat. "That is . . ."

"What?"

"Well, you don't know me, but . . ."

11

"You think you know me?"

The man blinked and squinted. "I . . . I'm not sure without my specs. Naw . . . it couldn't be. He's dead."

"Who's dead, mister?"

"Fastest man I ever saw draw a gun. Except he always drew two." The portly man's line of sight lowered to the twin .45s that seemed to be part of the stranger's body. "I'm talkin' about *Dan Colt*," he said, lifting his gaze to the ice-water eyes. "But, like I said, he's dead."

"You think I look like Dan Colt?" queried the blond man.

"Just a minute," said the rotund man in the barber's chair. Looking up at the barber, he said, "Mike, hand me my specs."

Mike Otero reached behind him and produced Oscar Berry's glasses. Berry took them and quickly put them on. Otero lowered his scissors and comb, waiting.

"I don't believe it," gasped Berry. "It's just not possible!"

The suntanned stranger smiled, exposing a set of white, even teeth. "I know," he said dryly. "You heard that Dan Colt had been ambushed by a yellow-bellied gunman and shot in the back. You heard that he'd been buried in an unmarked grave in western Kansas."

"That's the gist of it," said Berry.

"Well, sir, it ain't so. You are correct. I *am* Dan Colt and as you can see, I'm very much alive."

Berry bounded from the chair, reaching around the striped apron. As he shook Colt's hand, hair clippings dropped to the floor. "Well, I'm mightly glad to know you're still alive, son!"

Standing up, Dan towered over the man and said, "Where have we met, sir?"

"Well, we haven't really met, son, but I saw you in a gunfight once in El Dorado. You shot it out with two gunslicks who were trying to prod a young man named Ken Berry into a shoot-out."

Dan thought a minute. "Oh, yeah," he said, eyes brightening. "Ken was a nice young feller who had no business wearin' a gun."

"Right," said the rotund man. "He had the foolish idea of becoming a gunfighter. You saved his life by challenging those two killers. You left them both dead in the street."

"I remember," said Colt, nodding.

"Ken is my son, Dan," said the man. "I'm Oscar Berry. I'm

12

president of the Taos National Bank. What you did eleven years ago in El Dorado not only saved my son's life but turned him from the dead-end direction he was headed."

Colt smiled. "I'm glad."

"The crowd was heavy that day, Dan. By the time the smoke cleared and I got Ken calmed down, you were gone. I've always wanted to thank you. Now I can do it properly."

With the apron still dangling from his neck, Oscar Berry stepped to where his coat hung on a peg. Reaching to an inside pocket, he produced a fat wallet. Slipping ten one-hundred-dollar bills from the fold, he extended them to the tall man. "Here, I want you to have this."

Dan Colt's hands came up, palms forward. "Oh, no, Mr. Berry," he protested. "You don't owe me anything. I can't take—"

"Oh yes you can," insisted the banker, jamming the bills into Dan's right hand.

"But—"

"No buts," said Berry. "Thanks to you, my son is alive today and happily pursuing a banking career. Please don't refuse the money."

"If he don't want it," spoke up the barber, "I'll take it!"

The three men laughed, and Oscar Berry returned to the barber's chair. A bit flustered, Dan pushed the folded bills into his shirt pocket and buttoned it down. He groped for words of gratitude but was cut short as Oscar Berry said, "What *did* happen, Dan? Where were you all that time you were supposed to be dead? What are you doing in Taos?"

Dan Colt relaxed back into his chair. "I don't want to bore you."

"If I wasn't interested," said Berry, "I wouldn't ask."

Oscar Berry listened intently as Dan explained how he had given up his gunslinging to marry beautiful Mary Jordan of Wichita. He had bought a ranch some twenty miles west of Fort Laramie, Wyoming. He and his bride settled there and lived a quiet life for five years. It was during this time that some glory seeker took advantage of Dan's disappearance to make up the story about shooting him in the back and dropping him in an unmarked grave.

Mike Otero stopped clipping the banker's hair as he became

engrossed in Dan's story. When Berry snorted at him, the barber halfheartedly returned to his task.

Dan told them of the day he drove the wagon home from Fort Laramie and found Mary brutally murdered. His hired man was also mortally wounded, but he lived long enough to describe three saddle tramps who had robbed and shot them. Dan had met them earlier on the trail—had even stopped to talk with them. He left the ranch in care of friends and rode out to track the killers.

He explained how he tracked the killers to Holbrook, Arizona. There he confronted two of them on Holbrook's main street. The third one was absent. When the gunsmoke cleared, the two murderers were dead.

Dan told the banker and the barber of his arrest by Holbrook's town marshal, Logan Tanner. His gunfight with the two killers had been fair, and he was surprised to find Tanner holding a shotgun on him as he turned to leave. The marshal arrested him as one Dave Sundeen, a wanted outlaw who had resisted arrest and shot Tanner in the process a few months previously.

"Logan Tanner?" broke in Mike Otero. "He's a US marshal now. Works out of the office over in Raton."

"I know," said Dan. "He's still on my trail."

"Still on your trail?" echoed Berry with surprise. "You mean you didn't clear yourself?"

"Nope."

"Well, why—?"

"Before the trial," spoke up Colt, "Tanner showed me a Wanted poster with an artist's sketch of Sundeen. It was *my* face."

Berry's jaw slacked. "*Your* face?"

"Mmm-hmm."

"Some horrible mistake?" queried Berry with a confident tone.

"Well, yes and no," replied Colt.

The banker's face furrowed. "I don't get it."

"You will in a moment," said Dan, shifting his position in the hard wooden chair.

Before Dan could continue, Mike Otero said, "You're all finished, Mr. Berry," and removed the apron.

"Oh," said Berry. "All right." With that he stepped out of the barber's chair and looked in the large mirror on the wall. Otero brushed him off with a whisk broom and accepted Berry's half dollar.

"Okay, Mr. Colt," said the barber.

Dan stood up and eased into the big padded chair. "I guess you can see I need a haircut," he said, smiling. "I thought I'd better stop and get one before somebody mistakes me for Farmer Jones's sheepdog."

The banker and the barber laughed.

"You can give me a shave, too," continued Dan Colt. "Leave the sideburns the same length and just touch up the mustache."

"Give him the haircut first, Mike," put in Berry. "I want to hear the rest of the story. He can't talk while you're shaving him."

Otero nodded and dropped the large apron over Colt, pinning it around his suntanned neck.

Oscar Berry sat down in the chair Dan had recently occupied and said, "So your face was on the Wanted poster with Sundeen's name. Go ahead."

As the barber began snipping at his blond locks, Dan told how he had stood trial in Holbrook. Eyewitnesses had identified him positively as the man who had shot Logan Tanner. The jury found him guilty, and he was sentenced to five years in the territorial prison at Yuma.

Oscar Berry shook his head in disbelief.

"At this point," said Colt, "I'll have to go back and tell you about my childhood."

Oscar Berry mopped sweat with a large handkerchief and nodded.

"When I was about three years old," continued Dan, "my parents were traveling in eastern Arizona. I don't even know where we were headed. A gang of cutthroats jumped us. They killed my parents and took everything of value. I vaguely remember watching a terrible scene from some brush or bushes. Apparently I had been playing away from the wagon. The gang never saw me."

"Sounds like your guardian angels were looking after you," commented Berry.

Dan nodded, smiled and said, "A man named Ben Mason and his wife, Katie, were traveling from California to Texas. They happened on the dead bodies of my parents and also found *me*.

They took me with them to Texas and raised me. I learned I had a natural knack for guns when Ben Mason was murdered. I was just a kid, but I strapped on a gun and went after his killers. After I avenged Ben's death, I fell into gunfighting."

"So how long were you in Yuma?" asked Berry.

"About five months," replied Dan.

The tall man went on to explain that in Yuma Prison he met a convict who had ridden with the gang the day they robbed and killed his parents.

Oscar Berry's jowls hung down unevenly when Dan said, "That convict told me they carried away a little blond-headed boy about three years old."

The banker's eyes widened. "Your *twin*!" he exclaimed.

"Really?" asked Mike Otero.

"Yep," sighed Dan. "He ended up with a family named Sundeen."

"So you broke out of Yuma to find your twin brother!" said the banker.

"Yessir," replied Colt. "He's not only wanted in Holbrook but Texas, too. Robbery. So he's constantly on the move. I've been trackin' him since I got out of Yuma."

"Does he know it?" asked Berry.

"Huh-uh. He doesn't even know I exist."

"You don't think he remembers you?"

"I didn't remember him," Dan said flatly. "Had a vague recollection of a little blond playmate, but nothing more. No doubt it's the same with him."

"Couldn't you take Marshal Tanner back to Yuma and let the convict tell his story?" queried the barber.

"Nope. Convict's dead. Big guard beat him to death."

"Oh."

"So the only way you can clear yourself," put in the banker, "is to capture your own twin brother and turn him over to the law."

"That's right."

"You think he's near here?"

"Yep. He cleaned a couple gamblers out of their bankrolls in a poker game up in Tres Piedras. Told them he was going toward Taos. Had to catch a man who was on the move. Didn't say what for. Could be he's bounty huntin'."

"How far you figure you're behind him?" asked Berry.

"Not much," said Colt. "Expected he might even be in Taos."

"Maybe he is."

"Wasn't when I came in. I checked the street from stem to stern. He rides a big buckskin. Everyone that's seen it says you can pick the horse out easy. No buckskins on the street."

"How about the livery?" asked Mike, knocking blond hair from a comb.

"I already checked there," said Colt.

"Is he as fast as you on the draw?" asked the banker.

"Don't know," said Dan in a level tone. "They tell me he's got invisible hands."

"How you planning to capture him?"

"No plan. Just gonna take it as it comes."

"What if it comes to a shoot-out? You going to be able to draw on him?"

Dan's face stiffened. "That's a good question, Mr. Berry. It has haunted me ever since I started after Dave."

All was quiet for a long moment.

Then Dan spoke again. "Tell you one thing . . ."

"What's that?"

"I'm not goin' back to Yuma."

CHAPTER TWO

Less than a hundred feet from where Dan Colt sat in Mike Otero's barber shop, Dave Sundeen waited in the shade across the street from the Silver Spur Saloon. An angry silence hung over him like a black cloud. The man who had stolen his horse had to come out sooner or later. When he did . . .

Inside the saloon ten men sat huddled together around two tables they had slid side by side. Several whiskey bottles were strewn on the tables among numerous shot glasses.

"I suppose you're right, Harry," said a hatchet-faced man with a blue sheen of stubble on his cheeks.

"You know I'm right, Lefty," said Harry Doyle, his own ugly face a fixed and unpleasant scowl. "It'll be much easier to jump that stage and bust Jake loose from Tanner than to try breakin' him outta that jail. Blasted thing's built like a fortress."

"We're all in agreement, Harry," spoke up a third man. "We'll hit the stage somewhere between here and Los Alamos."

Lefty Winn nodded reluctantly. "Okay, but it sure would be fun to wade in there guns blazin' and blow that marshal and his deputy to kingdom come. We'd show this stupid town that Jake Finch's boys are somep'n to be reckoned with."

"Yeah," said Doyle, still scowling, "but some of us would get cut in two by them sawed-off shotguns. Wouldn't be worth it when the risk is a whole lot less catchin' the stage in open country."

Outside, Dave Sundeen watched a wagon pass, its wheels

lifting clouds of dust which were carried away swiftly by the hot wind. His attention was drawn to the south end of town, where a rider pulled to a stop in front of the stone-walled building that served as both jail and marshal's office. As the rider dismounted and went inside, a slender form detached itself from between two buildings near the jail and headed north up the street.

Sundeen watched as the skinny man scurried past the barber shop and Harrel's General Store, eventually darting through the bat wings of the Silver Spur. An old man dressed in bib overalls had almost collided with the skinny man as he exited Harrel's door. He threw the skinny man a dirty look, watched him until he dissappeared into the saloon, then moved down the board side-walk. Dave saw him enter the barber shop.

Inside the Silver Spur, Skinny Mulligan spoke breathlessly to Harry Doyle. "He just rode in. He's at the jail right now."

A cynical smile twisted Doyle's lips as he looked at the other hard cases around the tables. "Tanner's here, boys. Right on schedule. Now if the stage is on time, he'll be headin' out with Jake in exactly two hours."

"Might be best if we sorta scatter ourselves up and down the street," put in Lefty Winn. "Don't wanna attract too much attention."

"Good idea," agreed Doyle.

" 'Sides that, I wanna take my new buckskin down to the livery and chuck him full o' oats," added Winn.

Lefty Winn had the mark of the gunfighter. He was lithe, mean and eagle-eyed. The big iron on his left hip was slung low and thonged to his thigh.

"Yeah, Lefty," spoke up one of the gang, "beauty of an animal like that shore oughtta be tooken good care of. Haw! Haw! I bet the dude that owned him was plenty mad when he knowed you'd stole him!"

A wicked light danced in Winn's eyes. "He'll git over it."

"Let's have one more round, boys," said Harry Doyle, lifting a whiskey bottle. "Then we'll hit the street and wait fer the stage to show up."

While whiskey gurgled into the shot glasses, Lefty Winn scraped his chair back and ambled toward the bar. Narrowing his eyes menacingly, he spoke to the bartender. "You need to forget everything you heard, mister. Understand?"

The bartender swallowed hard. "Y-yes, sir."

"If one word of our conversation gets to the law, you're a dead man. Understand?"

"I . . . I didn't hear nothin', mister," said the man behind the bar. "Nothin'."

"Good," said Lefty. "You'll live longer that way."

United States Marshal Logan Tanner eased stiffly out of the saddle and tied his horse to the hitch rack. He lumbered across the boardwalk and knocked on the door of the marshal's office. The face of deputy Al Kelly appeared in the narrow, barred window.

"Yeah?" said Kelly.

"I'm Logan Tanner," drawled the big man in his heavy voice.

"Oh, yessir!" said Kelly. The big lock rattled and the door swung open. As Tanner entered, the deputy turned toward the back and hollered, "Marshal! Mr. Tanner's here!"

The heavy door swung shut. The room was hot and stuffy. Footsteps echoed from the cell area. The rear door came open and town marshal Bob Zachary emerged into the office. A wide smile formed on his face when he saw the leathery features of Logan Tanner.

"Tanner!" exclaimed Zachary. "It's been a long time!"

"Sure has, Bob," smiled Tanner.

The two lawmen shook hands. Zachary introduced Tanner to his young deputy, then said, "Tanner, you want to see him?"

"Yeah," came the big marshal's booming voice. "I'm proud of you, Bob. Made me mighty happy when your wire came. How'd you do it?"

"Well," replied Zachary, a bit flustered, "Finch rode into town alone. He's usually got his gang around him, but he got bit by a love bug and came by himself to see a woman staying over at the hotel. It just happened I saw him go into the hotel about eight o'clock Sunday night. Recognized him from the posters."

Zachary turned warm eyes toward his deputy. "Al and I crept into the hallway in the hotel and got the drop on him when he came out of his girl friend's room."

"Ain't the first time a female paved the way for a man's downfall," said Tanner idly.

"Yeah," said Al Kelly with a chuckle, "like Bathsheba and Delilah in the Bible!"

"Let's take a look at him," said Logan Tanner, moving toward the rear door.

Zachary stepped around him and led the way.

Jake Finch was the only prisoner in the Taos jail at the moment. As the two lawmen appeared in front of the cell, Finch eyed them coldly from his prone position on the bunk.

"Howdy, Jake," said Tanner. "Been over five years, ain't it?"

Jake Finch looked the US marshal up and down. Logan Tanner was a broad-shouldered, thick-bodied man in his late forties. He was handsome in a rugged sort of way. He stood just under six feet, with a muscular frame and the beginning of a middle-aged paunch. He wore a heavy mustache that was salted with gray, as were his temples and bushy sideburns.

Finch's narrow-set, dark, watery eyes flickered evilly at the federal man. "So you're a big-shot United States marshal now," he rasped.

"Mmm-hmm," responded Tanner tightly.

A sneer came over the prisoner's dark face. "You'll never do it, Tanner," he said with a biting edge to his voice. "You'll never get me back to Yuma."

Tanner pinned Finch with his steely eyes. "I'll do it, all right. You'll soon be right back where you belong."

"It's a long way across Arizona, lawman," retorted the dark-skinned outlaw.

"We ain't goin' in saddles this time, Finch," snapped Tanner. "We're goin' to ride the Butterfield stage to Gallup and catch Wells Fargo all the way to Yuma."

"I already know about that, Tanner," Finch said, tight-lipped. "The big city marshal here told me all about it. Don't make no difference. Like I said, it's a long way across Arizona."

"If you're thinkin' that some of your pals are gonna spring you, Jake," lashed Tanner, "you can forget it. You're gonna be shackled to me."

"Oh, mercy," said Finch in a mocking tone. "Just look at me

tremble all over. You can be disposed of, Marshal. Even if you are gettin' fat."

Logan Tanner turned casually to Bob Zachary. "Shall I tell him the rest of it, Bob?"

"Might as well," agreed the marshal of Taos.

Tanner's formidable features hardened. "There's Apache trouble, Finch. The army's gonna escort us in relays all the way to Yuma."

Jake Finch's face blanched. He sat up, dropping his booted feet to the floor. "You're lyin'," he said angrily.

"Ain't lyin', my boy," said Tanner. "Your boys want to tangle with the US Army?"

Finch leaped to his feet and approached the bars. He swore at Logan Tanner vehemently. "You're lyin', Tanner!" he shouted with anger. "Don't try to bluff me!"

While Jake Finch shouted at Logan Tanner in the jail, Dave Sundeen watched the old man in the bib overalls come out of the barber shop. At the same instant the bat wings squeaked at the Silver Spur. Sundeen's eyes flicked to the spot as men began to file out the door.

The man in the bib overalls crossed the street and entered the blacksmith shop. The big doors were closed to keep the dust from blowing in.

With an easy, professional motion the tall blond man lifted both Colt .45s up in their holsters, then eased them back into leather. With a keen eye he watched the scruffy-looking crew head for their horses at the hitch rail.

Eventually there was one man left standing on the boardwalk, looking up and down the street. The man had a big iron on his left hip. He scanned the street again, swearing.

The broad-shouldered Sundeen stepped off the boardwalk and walked with determined steps across the street. While the rest of the gang sat astride their horses, Dave paused at an empty place in front of the hitch rack. Setting his ice-blue eyes on the horseless man, he rasped, "Missin' somethin', cowboy?"

Lefty Winn threw Sundeen a petulant glance. "Who are you? What business is it of yours?"

"Name's Dave Sundeen," the tall man said in a biting tone. "It's my business because what you're lookin' for is *my* horse. You stole him in Creede."

Winn's wicked eyes widened. A mixture of surprise and anger framed his hard features. "You accusin' me of bein' a horse thief?" he hissed maliciously.

"You're lookin' for the buckskin you were ridin', aren't you?"

Lefty Winn did not reply. His silence was Dave's answer. Without taking his dark, vitriolic eyes from Sundeen's face, Winn stepped from the boardwalk into the street.

"Man doesn't steal my horse and walk away scot-free, mister," snapped Dave heatedly.

"I'll have him back in a minute," retorted Winn.

One of the gang members spoke up, "Better back down quick, Sundeen! That's Lefty Winn you're facin'. He's as fast as Bat Masterson, Dan Colt or Wyatt Earp!"

The three names sifted through Dave Sundeen's brain. Only one found a lodging place. *Dan Colt.* Dave had lost count of how many times he had been compared to Dan Colt. Many had said that they even resembled each other. Eyeing Lefty Winn, Dave doubted that he could be ranked with gunfighters of such distinction.

"Let him prove it," said Sundeen icily.

The wind had suddenly stopped. Sundeen's challenge hovered like a dust cloud in the still-hot air.

A curse spewed from Winn's lips as his left hand snaked toward his hip. Dave Sundeen's twin Colts roared. One bullet tore into Winn's chest. The other ripped through his throat.

Just as Lefty had started to draw, one of the other outlaws was having trouble with his skittish horse. The horse backed into the line of fire. The bullet that tore through Winn's neck hit the horse in the flank. With a wild scream the animal pitched his rider off and stumbled against another horse. Both animals went down in a cloud of dust. The one with the bullet in his flank fell on top of Lefty Winn's lifeless body.

Pandemonium prevailed.

Hoofs flailed. Dust stirred. Men cursed.

People began coming out of nearby buildings, gawking at the commotion. Mike Otero had just placed a hot towel over Dan

Colt's face in preparation for his shave. Leaving Dan in the chair, he and Oscar Berry stepped out the door to see what was going on.

Dan looked up and said, "Hey! Let's get on with the shave!"

Both men returned quickly. "Looks like a couple cowboys got into it and one of their horses caught a bullet," said Berry.

Otero began to lather Dan's face.

At the jail Marshal Bob Zachary heard the roar of Sundeen's guns from up the street. He eyed Logan Tanner and said, "Sounds like trouble."

Tanner was on his heels as Zachary dashed into the office and grabbed a sawed-off shotgun. Looking at his deputy, Zachary said, "Al, you button the place up tight when we go out the door. This may be a trick to get us out of the office. Don't you open the door for anybody but Marshal Tanner or myself."

"Yessir," snapped Kelly.

While the lawmen were coming out the door, the dust settled in front of the Silver Spur. Harry Doyle looked at Lefty Winn's corpse underneath the wounded horse. Gun in hand, he looked for the tall, blue-eyed gunfighter who had just killed Lefty. "Where's Sundeen?" he shouted.

The rest of the outlaws were out of their saddles, guns drawn. The dying horse ejected a painful wail.

Dave Sundeen was gone.

"We gotta find that dirty killer!" bellowed Doyle. "We'll blow his blond head off!"

"You say the man who did this was blond?" asked an old man on the sidewalk. He looked at Doyle, then the bleeding horse lying on top of Lefty Winn.

Doyle's gaze swung to the man. He was dressed in bib overalls. "Yeah, mister," said Doyle. "He was tall. Blond hair. Pale blue eyes."

The old man in the bib overalls said, "I seen him over at the barber shop!"

"Let's go, boys!" shouted Doyle. "He's at the barber shop!"

Inside the shop Mike Otero stropped the straight-edge razor. Oscar Berry was preparing to leave when he looked out the window and said, "There's a bunch of men comin' this way, Mike. They got their guns drawn."

The old man in the bib overalls circled around the gang and hurried toward the marshal's office.

As the gang reached the barber shop, one of them said, "You wait here, Harry. Me 'n' Ralph'll go in after him. Lefty 'n' us go back a long way."

Doyle nodded and waved at the others to stop.

The two outlaws charged through the door. They eyed Dan Colt sitting in the barber chair and raised their guns. Two black holes appeared instantly in the apron on Dan's neck as his twin .45s boomed.

Down the street the old man met the two lawmen and blurted out, "Marshal Zachary! There's been a shootin' up by the Silver Spur. Bunch o' men got a killer named Sundeen cornered in the barber shop!"

The name Sundeen hit Logan Tanner's ears like a tornado. "Did you say Sundeen?" Tanner asked, gripping the old man's bony shoulders.

"Yeah," came the answer. "Tall, blond, blue-eyed fella!"

Logan Tanner swore and started running just as gunfire erupted at the barber shop.

The shop was filled with blue smoke as bullets began smashing through the windows from outside. Dan Colt was bellied down, blazing away at the gang through the door. Amid the fracas, Dan did not hear the back door of the barber shop being broken open.

Suddenly there were shouts outside, then the diminishing thunder of hoofs. The shooting stopped as fast as it had started.

"Sundeen!" came a familiar voice from the board sidewalk. "Throw down your guns and come out!"

Logan Tanner!

Dan's heart sank. How had Tanner found him? Who were the gunmen who had come to kill him? What was the shooting about up the street?

"Sundeen!" came Tanner's voice again.

Colt's eyes searched the rubble from his position on the shop floor. The two men he had shot through the apron were sprawled in the doorway, one on top of the other. His eyes widened as he saw

25

Mike Otero slumped against a small wooden cabinet. The barber was dead, riddled with bullets.

Dan began crawling. The broken glass underneath him made a grating sound. He looked around for the banker. Oscar Berry was nowhere in sight. Dan was trying to remember. Where was Berry when the shooting broke out?

"Sundeen!" came Tanner's booming voice the third time. "You can't get away! Give it up!"

Dan Colt's mind was spinning. If he gave up to Logan Tanner, he would be sent back to Yuma. *There must be some way—*

Dan's thoughts were interrupted by a strange voice behind him. "Drop the guns, Sundeen!"

Colt whirled, lifting his line of sight toward the sound of the voice. He saw two black muzzles of a sawed-off twelve gauge. There was an ominous, dry clicking sound of two hammers being cocked.

Behind the shotgun was the grim, determined face of Marshal Bob Zachary. "Drop 'em!" the lawman repeated.

Reluctantly Dan Colt laid his guns on the scattered broken glass.

CHAPTER THREE

"I got him, Marshal!" shouted Zachary.

Instantly the figure of Logan Tanner filled the door. Tanner stepped over the bodies of the two outlaws. "Well, Dave," said the US marshal, "we meet again. On your feet."

Zachary's shotgun and Tanner's revolver remained on Dan as he stood up, glass crackling under his boots. The entire front window of the shop had been knocked out. A few shards clung tenaciously to the window's edge.

"I'm not Dave," said Dan with a sigh. Pulling off the apron and wiping lather from his stubbled face, he said, "I'm Dan Colt."

"Yeah," said Logan Tanner dryly, "I've heard you sing that song before."

A cold wave of despair washed over Colt as Tanner said, "Pick up his guns, Bob. Sundeen here is going back to Yuma."

A man burst through the door, almost stumbling on the inert forms lying in the doorway. "Marshal," he said to Zachary, "there's been a shootin' up by the Silver Spur and—" His eyes locked on Dan's face. "Uh . . . you got him, I see."

"Is this the man that did the shootin' up at the saloon?" asked Zachary.

"Shore is, Marshal," said the man, eyeing Dan warily.

"You positive?" said Logan Tanner.

"I was right there when it happened," nodded the man. "Saw his face as good as I'm seein' it right now. He shot and kilt thet man deader'n a doornail."

Logan Tanner's steel-gray eyes bored into Dan Colt. But the big marshal was far from the tall man's mind at the moment. Dan's blood had turned to ice water. *His outlaw twin had been right there in the street only moments ago!*

"It wasn't me, Tanner," said Dan emphatically. "I was right here in the barber chair when the shootin' started up the street." Stepping closer to the man who had just entered the shop, he said, "Take a real good look, mister. Are you positive beyond a shadow of any doubt that it was *me* you saw?"

"Absolutely," retorted the man. "I've got perfect eyesight."

Whirling to face the US marshal, Dan said excitedly, "Tanner, don't you see? I was here in the barber shop. You saw the lather on my face. It was my twin out there! He can't have gotten far yet. Go after him, Tanner! Let me go with you. We can clear my name once and for all!"

Doubt crept into Logan Tanner's steely eyes. "Wouldn't be hard for you to run down the street, charge in here, throw a gun on the barber and slap lather on your face. What was that bunch shootin' at you for?"

"I didn't know at first, Tanner," said Dan. "But I do now. The man Dave shot by the saloon was no doubt one of that bunch. Somehow Dave slipped away from them. Somehow they found out I was in here. Mistaking me for Dave . . . just like you've been doing . . . they came in here shootin'."

"That's a lot of somehows," Tanner said coldly.

Dan lunged at the eyewitness and grabbed his shirt. "How about the clothes, mister?" he said through his teeth. "Am I wearin' the same clothes you saw on the man who did the shootin'?"

The man blinked his eyes and looked Dan up and down. "Well . . . I . . . uh . . . ."

"C'mon!" hissed Colt, "speak up!"

"I . . . uh . . . didn't pay no attention to the clothes, mister," the man replied nervously.

"How about the hat?" said Dan, releasing him and yanking his hat from the wall. Shaking it in his face, Dan said, "Is this the hat?"

The man looked at Bob Zachary pleadingly.

28

"Well?" demanded Dan.

"Take it easy, Sundeen," said Zachary, voice level.

"I'm not Sundeen," lashed Colt. "That's what I'm tryin' to prove." Turning back to the man, he said, "Is this the hat?"

Bob Zachary made his way to the large shop window and looked past the clinging shards to the boardwalk.

The man swung his gaze to Zachary, then back to Colt. "Yes, it is," he said firmly. "That's the hat."

Dan threw his hands up in despair. He looked around at the corpse of Mike Otero on the floor. Suddenly he thought of Oscar Berry. "Wait a minute, Tanner," he said, a faint ray of hope in his voice. "I can still prove I was right here in the shop when the ruckus started up the street. The banker. Mr. Berry. He was here all the time. He can tell you!"

Bob Zachary spoke up from his position by the window. "Not unless dead men have learned to talk."

Glass crackled under Dan's boots as he stepped to the window. Oscar Berry was lying crumpled and twisted amid broken glass on the boardwalk. A crowd stood in the hot sun, glaring at Colt's face. It was evident that during the shooting, Berry had been hit and plunged through the plate glass.

"Looks like all your aces were left out of the deck, Dave," said Logan Tanner in a mocking tone. Motioning with the revolver muzzle, he said, "Let's go."

A hubbub lifted in the crowd as the two lawmen appeared, guns trained on Dan Colt.

"Good work, Marshal," came a male voice from the crowd. "That's one gunhawk that didn't make it far."

"Yeah," came another. "Blamed fool shoulda run for it. Sure was stupid to try hidin' in the barber shop!"

While Dan was ushered toward the jail, two well-dressed men in vested pin-stripe suits rode into town from the north and dismounted in front of the Silver Spur Saloon. They watched with interest as a group of citizens labored to pull a dead horse off the body of a hatchet-faced man.

Dan Colt was relieved of his holsters and locked in a cell next to that of Jake Finch. He had argued all the way to jail that Logan Tanner should go after Dave Sundeen, but to no avail. As far as Tanner was concerned, he had Dave Sundeen in custody.

As the cell door clanked shut, Tanner looked through the bars and said, "My lucky stars are twinklin' beautifully. The two men I wanted most. All locked up together. And I'll have the privilege of personally escorting them back to Yuma."

Dan peered through the bars at his neighbor, a sinking sensation spreading over him. From the bunk where he sat puffing on a cigarette, knees drawn up to his chin, Finch eyed Colt without expression.

The two lawmen left the cells. Dan slumped on his bunk, pursed his lips and let his breath out slowly.

"You been to Yuma before, too?" came Finch's callous voice.

"Yep," said Dan, looking into the adjoining cell.

"Well, don't worry, pard," said the narrow-eyed outlaw. "Tanner will never get us there. My boys'll spring us before we even get close enough to smell the place. Guess you know we're leavin' soon's the stage gets in."

"You mean today?" asked Dan with surprise.

"Yep."

"On a regular stagecoach?"

"Yep," said Finch. "Last time it was me 'n' Tanner by horseback. When he was tinhorn at Holbrook."

"I went from Holbrook, too," said Colt. "Only I didn't have the privilege of doin' it in a saddle with Tanner's company. I rode in one of those bone-killin' barred-up wagons."

Finch swore. "I've seen them horrid things." Without moving from his bunk, the dark-featured outlaw said, "I'm Jake Finch."

"Dan Colt," responded the blond man.

Finch was quiet for a long moment. Finally he spoke. "Hey, man. I'm one of your kind. You don't have to pretend with me. What's your *real* handle?"

"I'm Dan Colt."

Finch laughed and stood up. Walking to the bars and eyeing Dan sardonically, he said, "What'd Tanner get you for? Climbing out of a Kansas grave?"

Dan knew it was no use to try convincing Jake Finch that it was only a rumor that he had been ambushed and killed in Kansas.

"Anyway," said Finch, "when my boys bust me out of that stagecoach, you'll be free to go along."

Heavy footsteps brought Logan Tanner into the cell area. Eyeing Dan harshly, he said, "Coupla gents out here, Dave. They say you cheated them in a poker game up in Tres Piedras. They want their money back."

"Wasn't me," snapped Dan. "I met those same men there myself. They told me Dave had won the money from them. Didn't say anything about him cheatin'. Why don't you ask them if I didn't come through Tres Piedras trailin' Dave."

"They told me about it," said Tanner flatly. "Said they believed the twin stuff at first. Then they got to thinkin' about it. Said they'd decided you cheated and made up the twin thing, changed clothes, then doubled back to check on yourself."

Dan popped a fist into a palm. "It's asinine, Tanner," he said heatedly. "Dave may have cheated them. I don't know. But I don't have their money."

"They say you've got eleven hundred dollars of it."

Colt's face went red. The muscles in his jaws corded. "Well, why don't you just search me, Marshal? Huh? Why don't you—?" Suddenly Dan remembered the ten one-hundred-dollar bills in his shirt pocket. Hot knots formed in his stomach. His chest went tight. He felt a raging, helpless anger rush through him. There was no way Logan Tanner was going to believe that Oscar Berry had given him that money. And there was no way to prove it. Berry and Mike Otero were both dead.

"You were readin' my mind, Sundeen," rasped Tanner. Turning his face toward the office door, he said loudly, "Hey, Bob! Bring me the key!"

Zachary entered and handed the key to the cell door to Tanner.

"Hold your gun on him, Bob," said Tanner. "I don't trust him. I'm gonna search him."

The lock rattled and the door creaked dryly on its hinges. Dan backtracked quickly, saying, "Before you do, Tanner, tell me somethin'."

The big marshal paused, brow furrowed. "What?"

"Did these gamblers tell you what the denominations were?

31

What kind of bills made up the money Dave took from them?" It was a long chance, but Dan Colt was grasping at straws. The hideous thought of Yuma Prison was straining him to desperation.

"They didn't say," said Tanner with a chuckle. "You got the money on you, don't'cha?" His eyes sparkled triumphantly.

"I have a thousand dollars in my shirt pocket, yes," admitted Dan. "But it's not their money!"

"Honestly, Dave," said the marshal, "why don't you just come clean? Admit that there is no twin brother? Admit that it's been a hoax all along?"

Desperately Colt said, "Tanner, do you remember that day in Welcome, Colorado, when Tate Landry had his gun between your eyes?"

Logan Tanner nodded with guarded reluctance.

"There was nobody there but us," breathed Dan. "I could have let him kill you, then killed him. No one could've ever proved that I let you die."

Tanner's jaw squared.

"If this was all a hoax," continued the tall man, "why didn't I let Landry kill you?"

The face of the United States marshal crimsoned. "You'd be good at chess, Dave," he said tightly. "But I've never had any concrete evidence that says you aren't an outlaw."

"Isn't your life concrete evidence?"

"I don't have time for this rag-chewin'," snapped Tanner. "Turn around and put your hands on the wall."

Tanner relieved Dan Colt of the ten large bills plus over sixty dollars he found in a pants pocket.

Moments later Al Kelly let Tanner out the front door. Squinting against the glare, Tanner eyed the two gamblers.

"Well," said one, "did he have the money on him?"

"What denominations was the money in?" asked the marshal.

The gamblers looked at each other. Then one said, "How are we supposed to remember that?"

"I would think it would stick in your minds, gentlemen."

The two eyed each other again. "Mostly hundreds, wasn't it, Morey?" said one.

"Yeah," said Morey, eyes brightening. "Mostly hundreds and a few fifties."

Logan Tanner looked puzzled.

"What's the matter, Marshal?" asked the one called Morey.

"He had a thousand dollars on him, but it was all in hundreds."

"So what?" spoke up the other one. "He could have changed the fifties at any bank."

"Not too many banks between Tres Piedras and Taos, gentlemen," countered Tanner. "Wouldn't be hard to check it out."

"True, Marshal," agreed the nameless one. "But he also could have been in more poker games since then."

The US marshal scratched his head next to his hat brim. "Guess that's possible, too," he said. "You boys better be glad he didn't lose this thousand in a game, huh?"

"The way he cheats, he *can't* lose," said Morey.

Tanner gave them the thousand, plus sixty-three dollars. The gamblers mounted and rode away. The thick-bodied marshal turned and rapped on the jail door. Al Kelly's face appeared. "I'm goin' over to the stage office," said Tanner. "Got to make arrangements for carryin' *two* prisoners."

Kelly nodded.

Inside the jail Dan Colt flopped disgustedly on the bunk. All was quiet for a few minutes. Then Jake Finch said, "If your name's Dave Sundeen, how come you try to pass yourself off as the famous gunfighter? I'd think you'd have gunhawks challengin' you everywhere you go."

"Happens on the average of twice a week," said Colt evenly.

"Man hasta be made outta lightnin' to last long at that rate," mused Finch.

"I'm still here, ain't I?" said Colt.

"Can't argue with that."

"Reason is because I *am* Dan Colt."

"Then who is Dave Sundeen?"

"It's a long story, Finch. I won't bore you with it except to say that he's my identical twin brother."

Finch was quiet again.

The sound of the Butterfield stage thundering into town met the ears of the two prisoners. "There's our sweet chariot," said Finch. "We won't have to ride it long. My boys will figure out a way to stop the stage. They'll blow the driver and shotgunner to kingdom land. Tanner, too. You can throw in with us, Sundeen . . . or Colt . . . or whoever you are."

It was Dan's turn to be silent. He did not want to go back to Yuma. But if he sided with the outlaws, he would be considered one of them. Even when he found Dave, it wouldn't help. He would be considered an outlaw on his own if he took part in Finch's escape.

There was another problem. He could have no part in killing the driver and the shotgunner, or in killing Logan Tanner.

Dan shook his head. Certainly Tanner was aware that Finch had a gang. *Gang! Wait a minute*, he thought. *Maybe that was Finch's gang that came after me today. Dave must've killed one of Finch's men! If Finch's men stop the stage and see me, they'll think I'm Dave. Just like they did today. Finch doesn't believe my story any more than Tanner does. When they tell Finch I killed his man—*

Dan's thoughts were interrupted by the office door opening. The big federal man appeared through the bars. "It's gonna be a coupla days, boys," Tanner said.

"What's gonna be a couple days?" asked Jake Finch.

"The start of our trip," Tanner said blandly.

"How come?"

"I've decided not to try it alone with two of you. I wired Raton for a deputy to ride over here. Like you said, Jake, it's a long way across Arizona."

"Well, what about the army?" asked Finch cynically. "Isn't that enough for you? What do you need a deputy for?"

"Army?" said Colt, looking at the outlaw.

"Yeah," said Finch. "The marshal here tried to feed me some cock and bull about the army gonna escort us all the way to Yuma."

"They are," snapped Tanner. "But not until we get into Arizona. They'll come up from Fort Apache and meet us at Eternity. The Apaches haven't shed any blood east of there. We'll take the

Butterfield stage to Gallup. Then it's Wells Fargo all the way from there. I've wired the army about our delay."

"What's this *Eternity*?" asked Jake Finch in a mordant tone.

"You don't know much about Arizona, do you?" said Tanner.

"Thought I knew most of the territory," remarked the outlaw, "but I ain't never heard of no place called *Eternity*."

"It's the halfway point between Gallup and Fort Apache," spoke up Dan Colt. "Those hundred and fifty miles seem like they go on forever. That barren stretch seems to take an eternity to cross. So somebody stuck a way station and a tradin' post there and called it *Eternity*."

Finch swore. "How many people live there?"

"About thirty," said Dan. "The Little Colorado River peters out a few miles north of there and goes underground. The water surfaces there in Eternity as a bubbling spring. It's a real genuine desert oasis."

"You boys enjoy your stay," said Logan Tanner. "This nice cool jail will seem good to you when you get back to Yuma."

Dan stood up and walked to the bars. "Tanner," he said, forcing a friendly tone, "I gotta do somethin' about my horse."

"I already did," said the big lawman flatly. "He's at the livery. I told the hostler to sell him."

Dan felt his neck turn hot. "*Sell* him? You have no right to do that! That's *my* horse. You—"

"Sundeen, you broke out of Yuma. Once you're back there, the judge who commuted your original sentence will decide how much to add on for the prison break. Time you get out, that black gelding will be too old to ride."

Hot temper flared in Dan Colt's eyes. Gripping the bars, he said passionately, "You send that hostler over here right now! You hear me, Tanner? Right now! If you hadn't stolen that thousand dollars off me, I could have him boarded somewhere for a long time!"

Logan Tanner's face grew rigid. "You don't order me to do nothin', Sundeen. You got that? As a lawman, all I did was give those two men what was rightfully theirs."

The veins in Dan's temples distended. His jugular vein took on the form of corded rope in his neck. "That money was given to me by Oscar Berry, Tanner, and that's the truth. But then you wouldn't know the truth if it stood up and spit in your eye. You stole my money and gave it to those gamblers. There's nothin' I can do about it. But at least you can let me take care of my horse properly."

Marshal Logan Tanner was uncomfortable under Dan Colt's frosty blue stare. Swayed by the man's intensity, he blinked and said, "Okay, Dave. I'll send the hostler over in the morning."

"I said *now*!" Colt hissed. "He might sell him by morning."

"Okay, okay," said the marshal resignedly. "I'll go after him right now." Tanner walked to the office door, then paused and looked over his shoulder. "You might just as well sell the horse, Dave," he said with a tight grin. "You'll be ten years in Yuma."

CHAPTER FOUR

Dan Colt lay on the hard bunk in the darkness and stared into the gloom. *Why?* he asked himself. *Why would the hand of fate allow Dave to come within arm's reach, then slip away?*

Now the nightmare would begin all over again. The Arizona Territorial Prison at Yuma was the closest thing to hell on earth. It would be bad enough to go there knowing you were guilty. But to be impelled through those foreboding gates knowing you were innocent was more than most men could stand.

Dan had no doubt that Jake Finch's gang would attempt to stop the stage and free their boss. They would probably kill everybody on the stage, including himself. Once they identified him as the man who had killed one of their own, his life wouldn't be worth a nickel.

The thought crossed Colt's mind, as Jake Finch snored, that he should tell Finch about one of his men being gunned down by Dave Sundeen. Maybe the outlaw leader would give him the benefit of the doubt. He could play along as if he were going to join up, then hightail it. If Logan Tanner and the other occupants of the stage were all dead, they couldn't testify that he had left with the gang.

Dan shook his head. *What are you thinkin' about, Colt?* he asked himself. *If your corpse wasn't found with the others, anybody would guess it was because you had thrown in with them.*

*You'd be a fugitive the rest of your life, and never be able to prove
your innocence.*

Dan Colt knew that there was but one thing to do. He would
have to find a way to warn Logan Tanner of the gang's plans. Even
if it cost him his life, he couldn't let the two lawmen ride into a
trap. The driver and shotgunner would also die. He determined
that he would find a way to talk to Tanner alone before they started
on the trip.

Dan let his mind rest on the promise of the hostler to take care
of the big black gelding until he could make better arrangements.
He had no idea what those arrangements would be, but somehow,
some way, Dan Colt would get away from Logan Tanner on the
long trek across Arizona. He would come back to Taos, reclaim
his horse and go after Dave again.

As the night wore on, time slid back for the tall, blond man. He
could see Mary. Beautiful, captivating, vivacious Mary. She was
standing on the porch of their ranch house in Wyoming. The wind
teased her long, dark hair as she waved at him. The love light was
in her eyes, reflected from her heart. A heart that belonged to only
one man. *Her* man.

Dan could see himself dismounting and Mary dashing into his
arms. Her fingers dug into the thick hair on the back of his head.
Her velvet lips were on his—

Suddenly the tall man shook himself and swung his long legs
over the edge of the bunk. Standing, he groped his way to the
open, barred window at the rear of the cell. He eyed the twinkling
stars through the wire mesh that covered the window. As the
crickets played their nightly song, Dan Colt thumbed away a tear
that ran its course down his wind-burned cheek.

Morning came to New Mexico with the flush of sunrise tinting
the eastern sky a brilliant orange. Clusters of high clouds were
fringed the same color on the underside, fading to cottony white at
the top.

Southwest of Taos about ten miles, the Jake Finch gang was
holed up in an abandoned shack. The aroma of hot coffee
permeated the air as six of the remaining seven men sat around a
wobbly old table.

Biting off a chunk of beef jerky, Harry Doyle fingered the

makeshift bandage on his arm and ejected a string of curse words. "I'd feel better about this," he said bitterly, "if I knew we'd plugged that blond hawk."

"We threw a lotta lead in that place, Harry," piped up an outlaw named Dink Perryman.

"Yeah," said one called Tommy Elbert, "there's a good chance we hit him. Did you see that fat slob come crashin' through the window?"

Light laughter made the rounds.

"I won't feel right till I know that blue-eyed dude is as dead as poor ole Lefty," said Doyle with grating voice. "I'll get over this hole in my arm, but Lefty's gone forever."

"Yeah," spoke up another, whose name was Pat Lewis, "and so's Ralph and Lon."

A big ugly one called Jess Richards poured himself a second cup from the blackened coffee pot and growled, "Lefty got what was comin' to him. He shoulda never stole that dude's hoss."

"How was he to know the animal belonged to a hawk with hands like a rattler's tongue, Jess?" snapped another of the gang, Frank McCarthy.

Richards was a swarthy giant with a full beard and greasy, matted hair that dangled to his massive shoulders. He was an impatient man with a flinty temper. His left eye was blind. It was centered with a large white spot, which gave him a mean look and added to his fearsome countenance. He wore a dirty, sweat-stained hat and grease-shiny buckskins. They were stiff, and a crusty ring edged his collar and the ends of the sleeves.

"One thing a man oughta pay for in life is his horse," said Richards in a dismal tone. "Winn was a jackass fool."

McCarthy's eyes flashed fire. "You shouldn't talk about the dead like that, Jess! Lefty was my friend. It ain't right you should stomp on his grave!"

Jess's one good eye zeroed in on McCarthy's face. "If I want a sermon, Frank," he said, baring a mouthful of yellow teeth, "I'll go to church. Don't you be preachin' to me. Lefty'd be sittin' here right now if he'd had a brain in his head."

Frank McCarthy filled his cup with steaming coffee, his temper rising as Richards continued. "Lefty was stupider'n a retarded mule for thinkin' he was in the big leagues as a gunfighter. All he ever drawed against was clumsy, horny-fingered saddle tramps. I tried to tell him more'n once thet he was slower'n sick molasses, but the dumb jack wouldn't lis—"

McCarthy jumped to his feet, face flushed. "Now you look here, big man! I—"

Harry Doyle broke in, his voice pitched high. "Now you two stop it! We're all uptight. Let's not fight amongst ourselves."

"There ain't no need in him runnin' Lefty down, Harry!" retorted McCarthy angrily. "Lefty saved my life once!"

"That proves he was a jackass fool!" snapped the big hairy Richards.

Instantly Frank McCarthy seized his cup of steaming coffee and flung the hot liquid in Jess's face. Like a savage animal, Richards roared and sprang from his chair. The table careened across the room, pot, cups and coffee flying. Men were knocked off balance as Richards lunged for McCarthy.

Dink Perryman called Jess's name and made an attempt to stop him. For his effort he caught a sledgehammer elbow in the mouth and went down like a rotten tree in a high wind.

McCarthy clawed for his gun but barely lifted it from the holster. The huge man slapped it out of Frank's hand. As the revolver clattered across the floor, McCarthy swung a hard punch and connected with Jess's bearded jaw. The giant shook it off. A big, meaty fist caught McCarthy on the jaw, lifted him off his feet and sent him across the room. The smaller man slammed into a corner and lay still.

Harry Doyle rushed to McCarthy and knelt down, rolling him over. Doyle's face grayed as he laid a hand on Frank's neck. "He's dead, Jess! You killed him! His neck's broken!"

Jess Richards spoke in an ominous, deep-throated voice. "Man pulls a gun on me, he don't live to pull one on nobody else."

The rapid beat of hoofs drummed outside, slowed, then came to a halt. Footsteps thumped on the hollow porch and Skinny Mulligan came through the door. Instantly his gaze fell on the two men sprawled on the floor. "What the—?"

Harry Doyle stood up, his face still gray. Dink Perryman was stirring.

"Little ruckus, Skinny," said Doyle. "Frank's dead."

Skinny Mulligan didn't have to ask who had killed Frank McCarthy. The stance of Jess Richards told the story.

"What'd you find out?" Doyle asked Mulligan.

"Man at the Butterfield office says the US marshal ain't leavin' Taos till day after tomorrow."

"How come? There's a stage to Gallup every day."

"Seems the yellow-haired gunnie that took out Lefty is a escapee from Yuma, too. Tanner's got a depitty comin' from Raton. The two of 'em's gonna escort the boss and the yeller-haired dude to Yuma together."

Harry Doyle's mouth pulled into a thin line. "So we didn't get him, huh? Well, we *will*. When we spring Jake, the blond dude will die."

"Uh . . . there's more, Harry," said Skinny.

Doyle's brow furrowed. "Whaddya mean?"

"Agent says the Apaches are on a killin' spree over in Arizona. Army's gonna meet Tanner's stage and go along as a escort."

"Where they meetin' the stage?" demanded Doyle.

"Dunno. Neither does the agent. Tanner hasn't told him."

Doyle swore. "One thing for sure," he said with a hiss in his voice, "we gotta stop that stage before it meets up with the army."

On the third day after Logan Tanner had captured Dan Colt, the sun was lowering in the western sky. A lone horseman rode into Taos from the north and dismounted in front of the jail. He stretched his long arms and legs and knocked on the door. Deputy Al Kelly peered at him through the barred window.

"Steve Proffitt," said the tall man. "Deputy from Raton. Marshal Tanner is expecting me."

The lock rattled and the heavy door swung open. Kelly extended his hand. "Howdy, Proffitt," he said with a winsome smile. "C'mon in. Mr. Tanner is over at the saddle shop. He'll be back shortly."

Deputy Proffitt spotted Bob Zachary sitting behind the desk as Kelly closed the door and shoved home the bolt. Zachary stood up and reached across the desk. "I'm Marshal Zachary, Proffitt," he said, gripping the federal man's hand.

"Glad to meet you," said Proffitt.

"Sit down," said Zachary, motioning to a wooden chair with a worn green cushion resting on the seat. Zachary eased back into his seat as Proffitt did. Al Kelly plunked into a chair next to the wall.

"So you're going to help Mr. Tanner take these bad boys to Yuma?" said the Taos marshal.

"That's what I'm here for," replied Proffitt. "Couple mean hombres, eh?"

"Guess so," said Zachary. "Least one of 'em is."

"Oh?"

"Real mean one is Jake Finch. Has narrow, beady eyes like a diamondback. Just about as deadly."

"Sounds like he'll be good company," said Proffitt cynically.

"Other one's got a pretty bad reputation. Even shot up Tanner when he was marshal of Holbrook. But he doesn't seem to have the mean streak like a Yuma bird. He—"

Zachary's statement was cut short by a heavy knock at the door. Al Kelly glided across the room and glanced through the small window. He slid the bolt and opened the door. Logan Tanner shouldered his big frame through and entered the office. In one hand he carried a sawed-off double-barrel twelve-gauge shotgun. In the other was a strange-looking leather harness.

"Ah, Steve," said Tanner pleasantly. "You made good time."

"Had a good animal under me," said Proffitt with a smile.

Steve Proffitt was thirty years old. He stood six feet tall and was fast with the Colt .44 that rode his right hip. He had proven his abilities as a lawman while he was sheriff of El Paso County in Colorado, and he had been appointed a US deputy marshal just a year previously. He had been chosen for this trip because of Logan Tanner's utmost confidence in him.

Proffitt eyed the strange harness affair in Tanner's hand. "What's that thing?" he asked.

"I'm wonderin' that myself," said Al Kelly.

"I had to find a way to play my trump card against Finch's gang," said Tanner. Holding up the leather contraption, he said, "You're lookin' at it."

Puzzlement was on Marshal Bob Zachary's face. "Well, don't hold us in suspense. What is it?"

"Little invention of mine," said the big US marshal. "I told Hugh Rains over at the saddle shop what I wanted and he put it together." Turning his big head, he looked at Proffitt and said, "C'mere, Steve. You're gonna be handlin' this thing, so I want you to get a close look." Tanner then eyed Kelly. "Al, we'll let you stand in for Jake Finch."

Logan Tanner laid the short-barrel shotgun on Zachary's desk and held the harness with both hands. "Turn around, Al," he said.

The others watched as the thick-bodied marshal lifted the harness over Kelly's head. "Put your arms through those two square openings," he said.

As Kelly obeyed, Tanner settled the strange leather contraption on his shoulders. There were four straps on the back with corresponding buckles. Tanner cinched the strap tight in the buckles.

On the right side of the chest, in front, was a heavy leather square with a rounded, raised piece of leather riveted to it. Tanner grasped the shotgun and broke the action. He pulled out the two shells and snapped the fearsome weapon shut with a flick of his wrist. Moving to Kelly, he lowered the stock and vertically inserted the double muzzles of the eleven-inch barrels into the rounded piece of leather. They fit perfectly. He slid the barrels upward until the muzzles rested under Kelly's chin. As the cool metal touched his skin, the young deputy winced.

There was a half-inch leather strap dangling down Kelly's chest. Looking at Steve Proffitt, the big marshal said, "Wrap that loose strap around my wrist twice, then fasten it with that buckle under his arm." Proffitt complied.

Logan Tanner eased back both hammers. Sweat beads formed on Deputy Al Kelly's forehead.

"Now you can see," said Tanner, "with the wrist strap in place, there is no way my hand can fall away from the triggers. If someone was to shoot me in the head, the shotgun would still be fired." Looking at the faces of Proffitt and Zachary, he said, "If you were Jake's boys and you saw him in this fix, would you start trouble?"

"Huh-uuuh!" said Al, lifting his chin off the muzzles.

"You're gonna man this thing, Steve," said Tanner. "You'll also have your left wrist handcuffed to Jake's right wrist."

"How come me?" queried Proffitt.

A stony look captured Logan Tanner's steel-gray eyes. "Because I'm gonna have Dave Sundeen shackled to me," he breathed heavily. "He's been a thorn in my hide ever since he busted out of Yuma. If he gets away on this trip, it'll be by draggin' my dead body."

"You're the boss," said Steve Proffitt resignedly.

Tanner eased the hammers down, and Al Kelly sighed with relief. "What's the matter, boy?" said the husky marshal with a chuckle. "It ain't loaded. You saw me pull the shells out."

"I know," breathed Kelly, "but those two muzzles put the shivers down my spine. I'm sure glad I'm not Jake."

"I figure," said Tanner, motioning for Proffitt to unbuckle the wrist strap, "that Jake's boy will nose around the stage office and find out that the army's gonna meet us on the trail. Only they won't know *where*. So you can bet your boots they'll hit us early."

Tanner slipped the shotgun loose and laid it on the desk. As he unbuckled the back straps, he continued. "They're not gonna come in shootin', 'cause they might hit Jake. So they'll have to figure a way to stop the stage . . . or hang close and jump us when we've stopped of our own accord. All we need is for them to get a gander of Steve pushin' those muzzles against their boss's Adam's apple." Eyeing Proffitt with slightly narrowed lids, he said, "Of course, Steve, if they should play stupid and try something, you better be prepared to blow Finch's head off."

"Ugly thought," said Proffitt, "but that's why I'm wearin' a badge."

CHAPTER FIVE

The last rays of sunlight were fading on the western horizon as Deputy Al Kelly left the Empire Café carrying two trays of food. The Butterfield stage from Alamosa rolled in from the north end of town and stopped at the stage office in a cloud of dust.

As Kelly approached the stage, balancing the trays, the driver was opening the door. "Hey, Al," said the driver, "you bringin' supper fer me and Pete?"

The young deputy stopped on the boardwalk adjacent to the coach. "Sorry, Norm," he said, smiling. "This is supper for a couple prisoners we got in the jail. In fact, they'll be—" Al Kelly's gaze was drawn to a young woman who was alighting from the stage. She was petite and dazzingly beautiful. She had long, dark hair, which was done in an upsweep and topped with a tiny hat, under which Kelly caught a glimpse of fair skin, a lovely little upturned nose, full red lips and large brown eyes. Her powder-blue full-length dress matched her hat.

Behind the woman appeared a portly man in his fifties. He wore a black derby hat and a vested black suit. There was a large diamond stickpin in his necktie.

"The hotel's right down there," said the driver of the stage to the portly man, pointing.

"I know where it is," snapped the man curtly. "I stayed there last week on my way to Alamosa." With that he grasped the young lady's arm and said, "Let's go, girl. I'll send the hotel porter for our luggage."

Al Kelly stood holding the food trays, his eyes fastened on the girl.

"You were saying something about the prisoners, Al," said the driver, his voice filtering into Kelly's thoughts.

"Oh, yeah," answered the deputy, blinking. "I started to say that our two prisoners will be taking the Gallup stage in the morning. Coupla US marshals are takin' them to Yuma."

The shotgunner finished unloading the boot and lowered himself to the ground. Eyeing the deputy, he said, "Hey, Norm, did you see how Kelly's tongue laid on the ground when he got a gander at Miss Kates?"

"Yeah," chuckled Norm. "Fer a minute I thought he was gonna stumble on it!"

"What's her first name, Pete?" Al asked the shotgunner.

"Don't rightly know, son," answered Pete. "All the old goat ever calls her is *girl*. He signed her on as Miss D. Kates."

"His name is Samuel Kates," spoke up Norm. "So I s'pose he's her dad. Seems there's bad blood 'tween 'em, though. She's real quiet, and he yells at her a lot."

Kelly looked down the street just as the man and girl entered the hotel. "Man oughtn't yell at a pretty little thing like that," he said firmly. "She sure is somethin' to salve sore eyes with."

The young deputy dismissed himself and carried the food to the jail. Bob Zachary let him in, commenting on the length of time he had been gone. Kelly went to the cell area, slid the trays under the cell doors and reentered the office. With a sheepish look on his face he said, "Bob, the reason I took longer'n usual was because I just saw the most gorgeous female creature that these peepers have ever had the privilege to land on."

"Really?" said Zachary with casual interest.

"She got off the Alamosa stage with her father and went over to the hotel. I tell you, Bob, she will make your eyeballs jump out and switch sockets!"

"Well," said the marshal, "maybe I'll get a look at her in the mornin'."

At that instant a loud crash and clattering noise came from the cells. Bob Zachary bounded through the door, Kelly on his heels.

Jake Finch was standing in the center of his cell, his face florid with anger. Food, coffee, dishes and tray were scattered on the floor.

"What's goin' on, Finch?" demanded the marshal.

Jake Finch swore vehemently. "Food's cold! That's what's goin' on!" bellowed the dark-eyed outlaw.

"What do you think jail is, Jake?" rasped Zachary. "You think it's a resort hotel?"

Finch kicked the tray, sending it sailing against the wall. It clattered noisily to the floor. "I want some hot food!" he shouted.

"Well, maybe you can breathe on it and warm it up," said Zachary evenly. "Because that's all you're gettin' tonight!"

Jake Finch went into a rage, yelling, kicking, shaking the bars. While he carried on, Dan Colt took advantage of the moment to motion for Al Kelly to come to his cell door. As Kelly warily moved close, Dan said in a subdued voice, "Tell Tanner I need to talk to him before we leave in the morning. It's important. Tell him to make it look like it's his idea. I need to talk to him away from Jake."

Kelly nodded as Finch continued his tirade.

When the outlaw paused to take a breath, Bob Zachary said, "When you get it all out of your system, you can eat what you can scrape off the floor, Jake." With that he and Deputy Al Kelly walked away.

The Gallup stage arrived on schedule at nine thirty the next morning. The driver unhitched the sweating team and drove them to the livery.

"But it's too dangerous," Marshal Logan Tanner was saying to the portly man inside the Butterfield office. "Certainly you can wait until tomorrow."

Sam Kates swore. "Look, Marshal," he said with irritation. "I've already been away from my business too long. I've got to get back to Tucson."

"You may be in for a delay once you get to Fort Apache, Mr. Kates," said the Butterfield agent.

Kates whirled, scowling. "What do you mean?"

"There's Apaches on the warpath south and east of the fort."

Sam Kates swore again. "The army will have them under control," he said impatiently. "Probably already have." Turning back to Logan Tanner, he barked, "Now I'm not afraid of your prisoners, Marshal. If you've got them in shackles, what danger is there?"

"There's always potential danger in transporting criminals, sir," retorted Tanner. "If it was just you, I wouldn't say anything. But I'm thinking of your daughter."

"She's not my daughter," snapped Kates. "She's my dead brother's daughter. I inherited her when her parents were killed by Indians. She's been nothing but a headache. Little brat took off and ran away from home. I had to chase her all the way to Alamosa." His face was beet red. "Should've let her go, but I promised my brother if anything ever happened to him I'd finish raising her. She'll be twenty-one in eight months. Then my job will be done. Then she can go wherever she wants to. And I hope she does."

"It's gonna be crowded, too," argued Tanner. "There'll be six of us."

"I've been on crowded stagecoaches before," retorted Kates.

Logan Tanner took a deep breath and let it out through his nose. "It's only fair to warn you, Mr. Kates," he said, tight-lipped. "One of the prisoners I'm takin' to Yuma is the leader of an outlaw gang. I fully expect the gang to try to stop the stage and spring their boss."

"I'm sure you and your deputy can handle the situation, Marshal," said Sam Kates.

"I don't like to put that girl in danger," rasped Tanner.

"She's been in danger since she left her mother's womb, Marshal. Life is full of it." Kates's face was rigid. "If she hadn't run off, she wouldn't be in this particular fix. So she'll have to take her chances. I have *got* to get back to my business in Tucson."

US Marshal Logan Tanner shrugged his shoulders. "Okay, Mr. Kates. There's no way I can stop you." Turning to the agent, he said, "Go ahead. Let them on the stage."

A smug look spread over Sam Kates's face. To the agent, he said, "I'll go to the hotel and send the luggage over. The girl and I will be here at ten thirty." With that he was gone.

Logan Tanner waited until the driver returned with a fresh team of horses. He watched while the driver and shotgunner hitched the six horses to the coach, then approached them. "Mornin', gentlemen," he said, running his fingers over his mustache.

"Mornin', Marshal," replied the driver, eyeing the badge on Tanner's vest.

"I'm US Marshal Logan Tanner. Gonna be ridin' with you gentlemen to Gallup."

"Glad to have you aboard, Marshal," said the driver. "My name's Zeke Collier. My partner here, is Hector Mann."

Tanner shook hands with the two men and said, "I have a deputy with me. He and I are taking two prisoners to Yuma. Just thought I should tell you."

"You'll have 'em trussed up good, won'tcha?" asked Collier.

"Yep," said Tanner. "But you should know that one of the prisoners is the boss of a gang that's lurkin' around near. They'll probably try to jump us before we reach Gallup. I've made some extra preparations for the occasion, as you shall see, but I just wanted to alert you."

"Thanks, Marshal," said Collier. "Appreciate it."

"There's one serious complication," added Tanner.

"What's that?"

"There's a Tucson businessman and his niece going, too."

"Maybe they oughta wait till tomorrow."

"I tried to talk the man into it," said Tanner, "but he won't listen."

"He knows 'bout the prisoners and the gang and all?"

"Yep."

"Well, every man to his own poison, I always say."

"See you in a few minutes," said the marshal and headed down the street toward the jail.

Al Kelly was watching for him. Logan Tanner was spared the trouble of knocking. The heavy door swung open as he approached. Tanner moved inside. With furrowed brow he looked at Steve Proffitt and said, "All set."

"What's troublin' you?" asked Proffitt.

"We're gonna have two passengers on the stage with us. A man and his niece."

Al Kelly's eyes lit up. "Is she a tiny little thing? Big brown eyes? Long dark hair?"

"I haven't seen her," answered Tanner. "But the man is about fifty-five. Stout. Rich."

"That's him!" said Kelly. "Steve, I'll trade jobs with you! I'd love to be on that stage with *her*!"

"Somethin to look at, eh?" queried Proffitt.

Grinning from ear to ear, Kelly said, "Brother, you ain't gonna believe your eyes!"

Steve Proffitt looked at Logan Tanner. "Wouldn't it be better if they took another stage?"

"Mmm-hmm. I tried to tell Kates that. But he's in a big hairy hurry to get back to Tucson. Insists on going today. Nothin' I can do. It's a free country."

Bob Zachary pushed his chair back and stood up behind the desk. Lifting a small box from the floor and placing it on the desk, he said, "Here's some extra shotgun shells, Tanner, in case you need them."

"Thanks." Tanner nodded. "Will you bring 'em along to the stage for me?" Looking at his deputy, he said, "Steve, did you get the handcuffs out of my saddlebags for me?"

"Yessir," replied Proffitt, producing two pairs of jingling cuffs from his hip pocket. "Hostler said to tell you he'll take good care of your horse."

"You have a key to the cuffs, don't you?" queried the marshal.

"Yessir."

Logan Tanner moved to the wall where his special leather harness hung on a nail. Taking it in hand, he said, "All right, Steve, let's get you and Mr. Jake Finch hooked up."

All four lawmen shuffled into the cell area. Bob Zachary unlocked Finch's cell door. Finch stood up as Logan Tanner moved into the cell. He eyed the harness warily. "What's that thing?" he demanded.

"Little precaution for your friends," said the big marshal dryly. "Turn around."

"Oh no you don't!" snapped Finch, backing up. "You ain't wrappin' me up in no contraption like that!"

Dan Colt was on his feet, peering through the bars with interest.

"You're gonna wear this, Jake," said Tanner through his teeth. "I'll put it on you while you turn around, or after I put a knot on your head. Choice is yours."

The determined look in Tanner's steel-gray eyes convinced Finch. As he slowly turned around, he said over his shoulder, "What is it, Tanner?"

"Lift up your arms," said Tanner, lowering the harness over Jake's head. "Put your hands through those openings."

"What's this thing for?" said Finch, repeating his query.

"It's a little invention of mine," said the federal lawman, buckling the harness tightly.

"It's gonna be hot," snapped Jake. "The thing will make me sweat like a work horse."

"It'll feel cool compared to the rock pit at Yuma," said Tanner heavily.

"What's it for?" asked Finch heatedly.

"You'll see," clipped Tanner. Turning to his deputy, he said, "Now, Steve, the cuffs."

Proffitt handed the marshal both sets of handcuffs. Tanner jammed one set into his hip pocket. Fishing in a vest pocket, he produced a small key. Inserting the key in both cuffs, he pulled them open. None too delicately he grasped Jake's right wrist and snapped on a cuff, pinching it tight. Finch winced but said nothing.

Steve Proffitt moved next to Finch, extending his left wrist. Gently the thick-bodied US marshal closed the cuff over Proffitt's wrist and said, "I pronounce you man and wife until death does you part. Or Yuma Prison. There's not much difference. *Wherever* you're goin', Jake, it's hot."

A glum look washed over the outlaw's face.

"Oh, don't look so sad, Jake," said Tanner. "The best part is yet to come." With that Tanner slipped the key back where it had come from and turned to Dan Colt. "I'll be back for you in a minute, Sundeen."

Tanner had not acknowledged Dan's request for a private conversation. From the marshal's statement about Finch's friends, Dan knew now it would not be necessary.

Jake Finch donned his hat as Steve Proffitt led him from the cell. In the office Logan Tanner moved to the gun rack under the watchful eye of the outlaw. Finch's beady eyes widened as the marshal picked up the sawed-off double-barrel twelve-gauge.

Flicking his eyes to the looped piece of heavy leather on his chest, he understood the picture.

With dramatic, forceful movements Tanner broke the action of the shotgun and showed Finch the gleaming heads of the shells in the chambers. Snapping it shut with a flourish, he lowered the stock and shoved the muzzles upward through the leather loop. Jake Finch felt his scalp tingle as the cool muzzles pressed against the underside of his jaw.

"Now look, Tanner," Finch protested, "this is no—"

"Shut up!" bellowed Tanner with his booming voice. Wrapping the strap around Proffitt's right wrist and buckling it securely, he said, "Jake, when your boys show up, you'd better tell 'em to hightail it to China. Both of these triggers are touchy as a coyote trap. When Steve cocks the hammers, the slightest motion will splatter what brains you've got all over the desert."

Jake Finch swallowed hard. The defiant look on his face began to fade. It disappeared completely when Logan Tanner said, "The reason Proffitt is my deputy, Jake, is because he's cold as ice with a shotgun. He and I shot it out with a gang up in Colorado once. I saw him ram a twelve-gauge into an outlaw's belly and pull both triggers. They buried the dude in two pieces."

Cold sweat beaded Jake Finch's brow.

"Let's get the other one," said Tanner, nodding to Zachary.

In less than a minute Tanner returned to the office with Dan Colt shackled to his left wrist. Dan eyed the shotgun under Finch's chin and shuddered.

Turning to Al Kelly, Tanner said, "Open the door." Flicking his glance to Zachary, he said, "Bob, go out and take a gander at the street."

Kelly slid the heavy bolt and pulled the door open. Taos's marshal stepped out into the bright sunlight. Slitting his eyes, he slowly probed the length and breadth of the wagon-rutted street. Several of the town's citizens were moving about, but there was nothing unusual. Looking over his shoulder, Zachary waved them out.

"Now, gentlemen," said Logan Tanner, "we're going to take us a nice walk up to the stage." He nodded to Proffitt.

Steve nudged the muzzles tight against Jake's lower jaw and

thumbed back both hammers with a portentous, dry clicking sound. Finch did a fast intake of breath.

"Mr. Finch will walk slow, Marshal," Proffitt said slyly.

Proffitt and Finch went first, followed by Tanner and Colt. The office door snapped shut. Zachary and Kelly brought up the rear.

Dan Colt looked at the azure sky, took a deep breath and moved in rhythm with the US marshal. People stopped on the street and gawked, mouths agape. The eyes of all four lawmen raked the street and the rooftops. There was no sign of the outlaw gang. Tensely they approached the six-up stagecoach. One of the horses stamped and blew. Jake flinched. Sweat was running into his eyes. He blinked against the smarting fluid.

Standing on the boardwalk in front of the stage office was Sam Kates and his niece, along with the Butterfield agent. They watched in silence, as did Zeke Collier and Hector Mann, who stood in the street next to the coach.

"Get a gander of that female, Steve!" said Al Kelly from behind.

"You just watch where you're walkin'!" said Jake Finch nervously.

"Open the door," Logan Tanner said to Collier.

The stagecoach door swung open. It was on the right side of the vehicle.

"How you want us, Marshal?" asked Steve Proffitt.

"You two ride facing forward," said Tanner. "Sundeen and I will sit katty-corner on the opposite side. You two get in and slide all the way over. We'll put the girl next to you. She's small. That'll give some room for the shotgun . . . and the muzzles will be pointing away from the girl."

"Now look, Tanner," protested the dark-faced outlaw, "you're not gonna make me ride all the way to Yuma with this shotgun under my chin!"

"Steve'll plant the hammers, Jake," lashed the big marshal. "But the shotgun stays!"

Deputy Proffitt eased the hammers down. "Get in, Jake," he said.

When Proffitt and Finch were in place, Tanner looked at Dorianne Kates and said, "Now, miss, you will ride next Deputy Proffitt."

Fear etched itself plainly on the girl's lovely features. Slowly she inched her way through the door, set her large brown eyes on the face of Steve Proffitt, then lowered her small frame onto the seat.

Proffitt's heart skipped a beat. Looking through the door to Al Kelly, he said, "You were right, Al!"

"Told you . . . you lucky stiff!" responded Kelly.

Logan Tanner eyed Sam Kates. "Now, Mr. Kates," he said in a congenial tone, "you get in next."

Kates hoisted his corpulent body into the vehicle and slid across the seat. His eyes met those of Jake Finch. The outlaw gave him a hard look, and Kates threw his gaze toward his niece. The girl was obviously petrified.

At the same instant that Dan Colt and Logan Tanner were entering the coach, Skinny Mulligan slid out of his saddle between two buildings a block to the south. He peered around the edge of the building in time to see the last two men climb in. He waited and watched while his heaving horse caught its breath.

Logan Tanner dropped his huge frame next to Sam Kates. Dan Colt looked at the small space that was left and said, "If you want me to go along, Tanner, you're going to have to make me more room than that."

Tanner eyed Kates. The stout man grunted, pressing himself tighter against the side. The big marshal scooted over some more, and Colt stepped in and sat down.

Dorianne Kates fixed her gaze on the handcuffs that bound Tanner and Colt together. Trying to ease her tension, Dan smiled and said, "Really, miss, I hate to travel like this, but my big Saint Bernard here chases cats if I let him loose!"

The girl's face muscles relaxed. A smile tugged at the corners of her perfectly formed mouth. Logan Tanner grunted.

The driver stuck his head in the open window. "Just wanted to introduce myself," he said, smiling. "I'm Zeke Collier, your driver, and this feller with the shotgun in his paw is Hec Mann. We'll have you to Los Alamos by mid-afternoon. You can stretch your legs while we change horses there. We'll grab a bite to eat and move on to Parker Flats. In case this is your first trip, Parker

Flats is a way station where we'll spend the night. It's situated right on the Jemez River." Looking at the beautiful girl, he said, "Now, ma'am, if you need to stop anywhere along the way, you just have one of these gents give a holler. Okay?"

Dorianne tried to smile. "Okay."

Collier and Mann climbed into the seat. Collier took the reins in hand and cried, "Hee-yaah!"

The Butterfield stagecoach, bound for Gallup, New Mexico, lurched and rolled toward the south end of town. Raising dust, it moved past Skinny Mulligan. The outlaw caught a glimpse of his boss through the window. That was all he needed. Just to make sure Jake Finch was on the stage.

Mulligan watched the vehicle move out of town, swinging, swaying and throwing up dust. Then he mounted up.

CHAPTER SIX

Swaying with the movement of the stagecoach, Dorianne Kates watched the rocks and sagebrush move rapidly by the window.

Dan Colt studied the girl's face. She was afraid. That was obvious. But there was more than fear in those large, lovely eyes. Dan couldn't put a word to it, but she had the look of a puppy that had been whipped without knowing why.

"Well, I suppose," said Logan Tanner, breaking the silence with his grizzly-bear voice, "we ought to get everybody acquainted. It's going to be a long ride." Pointing to the man on his right, he said, "This gentleman is Mr. Sam Kates. Businessman from Tucson." Moving the finger toward the girl, he said, "And this is his niece, Miss . . ."

"Dorianne," she said quietly.

"Miss Dorianne Kates," said Tanner, completing his statement. "My deputy here is Steve Proffitt. The gentle—the man next to him who is snuggling the shotgun is the noted outlaw, Jake Finch. This blue-eyed wonder next to me is another noted outlaw, Dave Sundeen. Both of these men are escapees from the Arizona Territorial Prison at Yuma. Proffitt and I are returning them to their proper home."

The tall, blond man waited a moment, then said, "The truth is, Miss Kates . . . Mr. Kates, I am not Dave Sundeen. He is my identical twin brother."

Dan immediately captivated the attention of Dorianne Kates.

"Shut up," clipped Tanner, looking at Colt fiercely.

Ignoring him, Dan continued, "My name is Dan Colt. I went to Yuma for crimes committed by my twin. I escaped so I could find my brother and prove my innocence. But Marshal Tanner has never believed that Dave exists. The reason that our names—"

"I said *shut up!*" broke in Tanner.

"The reason that our last names are different is because we were separated as little children when our parents were killed, and he took the name of the people who raised him."

Tanner's face reddened. "Sundeen—"

"If Marshal Tanner would get off my back and leave me alone, I could find Dave and bring him in. Fact is, he was right back there in Taos three days ago. I could've had him if Marshal Tanner had not been so pig-headed."

"One more word, Sundeen," warned Tanner, "and I'm gonna clout your head with my gun."

Turning to look at the lawman, Dan said, "Only wanted to set the record straight with these nice people, sir. Just because you won't believe my story doesn't mean it isn't true."

"Like I told you, mister," growled Tanner, "you've never given me any concrete proof that you aren't Dave Sundeen."

"And like *I* told *you*, sir," snapped Dan, "your own life ought to be evidence enough. I didn't have to save you, you know."

Jake Finch bolted Dan with a hot look. "If you saved Tanner's life, you deserve to go to Yuma!"

"Both of you clamp your traps!" hollered Tanner. "Or I'll put knots on your heads!"

Steve Proffitt adjusted the shotgun in his right hand, easing it down from Finch's neck, and said, "Mr. Kates, what business are you in at Tucson?"

"Land development. Real estate," responded the rotund man, lifting his derby and palming away sweat.

Proffitt nodded. "You and your niece on a business trip . . . or pleasure?"

A scowl claimed Sam Kates's face. He threw Dorianne a petulant glare. "Neither."

Steve saw he had touched a sore spot. From the corner of his eye he could see Dorianne looking out the window. When he heard her sniff, he knew she was crying.

A woman's tears had always touched Dan Colt deeply. He watched Dorianne dab at her eyes with a small handkerchief. She turned her head to the side, trying to conceal her tears. Dan wanted to comfort her but didn't know what to say.

Steve Proffitt turned to look at Dorianne, then spoke. "I . . . uh . . . I'm sorry, Miss Kates. I didn't mean to upset you."

Dorianne sniffed. "It's not your fault, Deputy. You were just making polite conversation."

Sam Kates spoke in a crusty voice. "No, it's not your fault, Proffitt. It's *her* fault. If she hadn't run away, I could be at my office running my business and we wouldn't be riding a stagecoach across this dusty inferno." Kates lifted his hat and wiped sweat again.

With quivering lip Dorianne looked at her uncle and said, "You didn't have to come after me. You don't care whether I live or die. All you want to do is be self-righteous and noble. You'll look after me till I'm twenty-one so you can polish your halo. You will stand over my father's grave and boast that you kept your promise. Well, Uncle, there's more to looking after a person than food, clothes and shelter. There's a four-letter word that starts with *l* and ends with *e* and it rhymes with *dove*. But you wouldn't know what I'm talking about."

Sam Kates glared burning daggers at the girl as she broke into sobs. "You shut your mouth, girl!" snapped Kates angrily.

"What do you think killed Aunt Laura?" retaliated Dorianne. "She was sick and needed her husband's love and understanding. But you bellyached and badgered her until she got out of that sickbed and worked herself to death!"

Kates's face was livid with rage. "You shut your filthy mouth, girl!" he bellowed, spraying saliva. "You shut up right now or I'll stop this stage and shut you up!"

The hair stood up on Dan Colt's neck. His blood ran hot. Leaning forward and looking past Logan Tanner, he fixed his ice-blue eyes on Sam Kates. "If you lay a hand on that girl, mister," he said, lips pulled tight over his teeth, "I'll use Tanner as a club and knock you to the Gulf of Mexico!"

Kates stared wordlessly at the eyes that seemed to look through him instead of at him.

"Sounds to me like Dorianne has needed to say a few things for a long time," said Colt. "If you've got any more, honey, let it out."

"It wouldn't do any good, Mr. Colt," said Dorianne. "You and this other man are not the only prisoners on this stage. But thank goodness I've only got eight more months of his abuse. Then I'll be free.".

"Yeah," rasped the fat man, "free to run around with men and make the name of Kates look cheap!"

Dorianne's tiny face pinched. "I've never done anything to shame my father's name, Sam Kates, and you know it! All I have wanted is to have normal relationships with young men, as any girl does. But you make me out as something cheap if I take a walk with a man or sit on the porch in the moonlight."

"How about Wilbur Martin?" lashed Kates. "I caught you then, didn't I? You *hussy!*"

"Wilbur Martin is a fine young man, Uncle! He's good and kind and decent." Having found in Dan Colt an ally, she said, "I ask you, Mr. Colt, does holding hands with an army sergeant make a girl a hussy?"

"Not in my book," said Dan levelly. "I even *kissed* my wife before we were married."

"Well, if I hadn't caught you and Wilbur, it would have been worse," hissed Sam Kates.

Tears spilled down Dorianne's cheeks. "Uncle, you have no grounds to say that," she said, her voice breaking.

"You're worse than a hussy, girl," taunted Kates. "You're a *slut!*"

The word carried a blow like a fifty-caliber slug. Dorianne seemed to shrink in size. Her countenance went white. Her hands lifted to her face.

Dan Colt fumed. "Tanner," he said through his teeth, "you shut that bird's mouth or I'll go through you to do it myself."

Logan Tanner turned to Kates and said, "That's enough. Save your family squabbles till later."

The portly man looked hard at his niece, then set his gaze out the window.

The sun climbed higher and grew hotter. The stagecoach rocked on. The wind was picking up and throwing dust through the open windows.

Dorianne Kates dried her tears and gave Dan a warm smile, which he returned.

Jake Finch felt the muzzles touch his neck every time the vehicle bounced. He thought about Harry Doyle and the rest of the gang. What would they do when they saw the shotgun pressed to his jaw? What *could* they do? No matter what they did, the shotgun would be there to blow his head off. Finch experienced a cold, sinking feeling. The thought of Yuma Prison gave him a touch of nausea.

As the dust and the heat rose, Dan Colt also thought of Yuma. The five months he had spent there had seemed like an eternity. It just *couldn't* happen again. There had to be some way out of this . . .

On the south crest of a deep draw, six horsemen sat outlined against the sky. A seventh horse stood riderless on a lead rope. As they peered northward with squinted eyes, they saw a rolling sea of sun-bleached hills spotted with cactus and sagebrush. Off to the west stood long, flat plateaus, and just beyond them, tall, shaggy mountains pushed upward against the blue.

The rough and patchy road ran down the steep draw, up the other side and threaded its way north among the rocks, hills and gullies. A cloud of dust appeared in the distance, preceded by a black dot.

"There it is," observed Skinny Mulligan. "Should hit the draw here in about twenty minutes."

"Okay, boys," said Harry Doyle, studying the crest just before him. "When the coach comes up this side of the draw, it has to follow the road between these boulders. If it swerved to go around them, it would never make it over that sharp climb. So we'll pile the tumbleweeds between the boulders. We'll set 'em on fire about the time the stage is halfway up this side."

"That's good," put in Jess Richards, observing the road in the draw. "Once they're that far up, they can't turn around. There's too many big rocks on the sides of the road."

"It's a perfect spot, Harry," said Tommy Elbert. "We got 'em cold. The boss'll sure be glad to see us."

"Now, no shootin' unless it's necessary, boys," said Doyle. "We could spook them horses. If they went wild, they could turn the stage over and maybe injure or even kill the boss. If Jake wants to kill ever'body after he's off the stage, that's his decision."

"If we time it right," put in Jess Richards, "one man can torch the weeds here at the crest while the rest of us hide behind the rocks right where the coach is gonna stop. I doubt the shotgunner or anybody inside will start gunplay with five guns trained on 'em."

"Right," agreed Doyle. "We'll hide the horses back over in that arroyo."

The outlaws dismounted and went to work. The wind gave them a little trouble with the tumbleweeds, but finally they were able to pack them tightly between the boulders. Just before taking their positions, they sighted the approaching object, which had taken the shape of a six-up stagecoach, bobbing and weaving along the dusty, bumpy road.

Inside the coach talk had dwindled to a minimum. Dorianne Kates had dried her tears. The dust continued to sift through the open windows. Periodically the girl brushed it from her clothing. At one point the vehicle swerved and rocked, sending additional dust into the coach.

Dorianne began to choke and cough.

Dan Colt looked around and said, "Collier should have left one of those canteens inside." Setting his gaze on the girl, he said, "We'll get you some water, ma'am." With his free hand Dan reached behind and rapped hard against the wooden panel. "Hey! Driver! Stop!"

Immediately the vehicle began to slow. Dorianne continued to cough.

Sam Kates looked at Logan Tanner. "You lettin' that dadburned criminal run this show, Tanner?"

The big marshal eyed Kates blankly. "Your niece needs water. Even a criminal can see that."

The stagecoach slowed to a halt. Collier and Mann stepped down as the desert wind carried away the dust.

Collier stuck his grimy face through the window on Kates and Finch's side. "What is it?"

"Miss Kates needs some water," spoke up Colt.

Quickly the driver appeared on the other side with a canteen, while Hector Mann circled the coach, peering against the glare in all directions.

Dan took the canteen, wiped dust from around the spout and worked the lid loose, all with his free hand. Removing the lid, he cupped it in his hand and extended the canteen to the girl. With a grateful smile, she took it and drank deep. Her coughing subsided immediately.

Finished, Dorianne handed the vessel back to Dan Colt with a smile. "Thank you, Mr. Colt," she said warmly.

"His name's Sundeen," interjected Logan Tanner in a flat tone.

A spark of indignation flashed in Dorianne's brown eyes. "I don't think so, Marshal," she said.

"Don't let his smooth ways fool you, miss," Tanner retorted. "He pulled a gun on me when I was marshal of Holbrook. Shot me here in the right shoulder. Might 'near crippled me for life."

"If it'd been me," piped up Jake Finch, "I'da shot you in the head." Looking at Dan, he said, "Gimme the water."

Dan passed the canteen to Tanner, who grudgingly shoved it into Finch's left hand.

"How do you know it wasn't Mr. Colt's twin who shot you, Marshal?" asked Dorianne.

"It was this man right here who shot me, miss," the marshal said defensively.

"If they're identical twins, it could have been the other one," she argued.

"Jury found this man right here black-and-white guilty, ma'am. Eyewitnesses pointed him out in the courtroom. Judge sentenced him."

"Now just what would you, the judge and the jury have done if the identical twin had walked into the courtroom at the precise moment the judge was pronouncing sentence? What if both twins claimed they were innocent. Both accused the other of shooting you. Which one would you have sent to prison, Marshal?"

A broad smile worked its way across Dan Colt's mustachioed mouth. *Hey, that's good!* he thought to himself. *I never thought of that! Heh, heh. That would've dropped a hot potato in their hands!* Dan Colt found himself liking this girl. She had spunk.

The marshal's gray eyes were fixed on Dorianne Kates. She had just presented him with a notion that had never crossed his mind.

What *would* they have done? There was no way the law could allow both men to be sent to prison for *one* man's crime. There would be no means of proving which one was guilty. *Good gravy!* thought Tanner. *Would both men have walked out of that courtroom scot-free?*

After Finch, Sam Kates took a long pull from the canteen, then handed it to Tanner. The marshal put it to Steve Proffitt's lips, since both of the deputy's hands were occupied. Tanner drank, then passed it to Dan Colt.

The blond man took his fill, then said to Collier, who waited, "Just leave it in here, driver. Miss Kates may get thirsty again." Dan set the canteen on the floor.

Collier nodded and disappeared. Dan was proud of Dorianne's clear thinking. He flashed her a winsome smile. The girl blinked and blushed, her skin turning a dark warm color.

The coach lurched and soon the wheels settled into their usual monotonous hum. Dust rose through the floorboards and blew through the windows. Dorianne Kates was not through with US Marshal Logan Tanner. She liked Dan Colt. Something deep inside told her that he was no criminal. He was telling the truth. Somewhere north, south, east or west of Taos, New Mexico the real Dave Sundeen was riding free.

Setting her large, probing eyes on the big lawman, Dorianne said, "You haven't answered my question, Mr. Tanner."

Tanner threw her an empty stare. "Huh?"

"If Dave Sundeen had shown up at the trial and both twins had claimed innocence . . . which one would you have sent to Yuma?"

"The question isn't valid, young lady," said the marshal curtly.

"Why not?"

"There is no twin."

"Are you sure?"

"I'm sure."

"Are you positive?"

"I'm positive."

"Are you *sure* you're positive?"

"Young lady, this is senseless jibber-jabber!"

Sam Kates butted in. "Girl, button your lip! Leave the marshal alone."

Ignoring her uncle's command, Dorianne prodded Tanner. "What are you going to do, Marshal, when someday you find out there really *is* a twin? How are you going to feel when you realize you have put an innocent man in prison, stolen years from the only life he'll ever have?"

Logan Tanner fidgeted under the fiery female's gaze.

Dan Colt was elated. Dorianne Kates had Logan Tanner in checkmate. She continued. "I thought under the law a man was innocent till proven guilty, Marshal."

"He *was* proven guilty," retorted the lawman.

"Not if there's the least possibility that Dan Colt has an identical twin."

Sam Kates leaned forward. "Girl," he snapped, "I told you to button your lip."

Jake Finch reached over and kicked Kates's shin. As the fat man winced, sucking air throught his teeth, Finch said, "Let her talk, man. She's takin' the boredom out of this trip."

Kates bent over, face twisted with pain, rubbing his shin.

"Dan Colt is dead," Tanner told the girl. "He was a famous gunfighter. Faster'n a weaver's shuttle with a pair of .45s. But he was shot in the back by a bushwhacker in Kansas. Buried in a hidden grave."

"Rumor," said Dan. "I *am* Dan Colt, whether you choose to believe it or not. I *do* have an identical twin brother who goes by the name of Dave Sundeen."

"Why can't you believe him, Marshal?" asked Dorianne.

"Why are you so quick to believe him, Miss Kates?" parried Tanner. "You never saw him before today. Why do you take his side against me? I'm the one wearin' the badge, in case you hadn't noticed."

"I can't explain it, Marshal," replied the girl. "It's his face . . . his eyes . . . his mannerisms . . . I don't know. I just have this feeling. This man is no criminal."

"Even if I believed like you do, Miss Kates," said Tanner, "there's nothing I can do about it."

"You could let him go."

"Not and wear this badge."

"But how is he ever going to track down his brother if he's locked up in prison?"

The marshal gave her a sour look. "That's his problem. First thing he'll have to do is convince me there *is* a twin."

"But how can he do that if he—"

"Look, miss," cut in Tanner. "I have five senses. Sight, smell, taste, hearing and touch. I have never *seen* this alleged identical twin brother. I have never *smelled* him, *tasted* him, *heard* him, or *touched* him. Therefore, as far as I'm concerned, he *has* no twin."

"Some logic," said the beautiful Dorianne, with asperity. "Let me ask you something, Marshal."

"What's that?"

Eyes flashing, she said, "Have you ever *seen* your brain?"

Tanner looked at her curiously. "No."

"Have you ever *smelled* your brain?"

"No."

"Have you ever *tasted, heard* or *touched* your brain?"

The big man blinked. "No."

"Then by your own logic, *you have no brain!*"

Jake Finch broke into hoarse laughter. "Hey, little girl!" he said jubilantly, "too bad you ain't a man. You'da made a terrific lawyer!"

"Yeah," said Dan Colt with a laugh, "or a mighty persuasive preacher!"

Steve Proffitt joined in the laughter as the stagecoach started down a steep grade. Even Logan Tanner began to laugh. Sam Kates sat with marble face.

The coach bottomed the draw and started to climb. Suddenly it came to a halt. The passengers, still laughing, looked out the windows. Zeke Collier's voice cut the desert air. "Marshal! We got trouble!"

CHAPTER SEVEN

The laughter died quickly as five men appeared, guns drawn, closing in on both sides of the stagecoach.

Instantly Steve Proffitt thumbed back both hammers of the shotgun and pressed the muzzles under Jake Finch's jaw.

"Everybody stay cool," said Logan Tanner. "Nobody panic."

"All right!" bellowed a deep-throated bull voice. "Everybody out!"

The smell of smoke filled the air as Dan Colt flipped the latch and pushed the door open. The big man giving orders was dressed in greasy buckskins. Long, matted hair fell to his wide shoulders from under a sweat-stained hat. The man had a full beard, and Dan wondered if he smelled worse than he looked.

Colt and Tanner came out first, handcuffs shining in the sun. The marshal's gun hand was raised.

Dink Perryman said, "Well, lookee who we have here!" As billows of smoke were carried down the draw from its southern crest, Perryman hollered, "Hey Harry! C'mere!"

Dropping over the low embankment next to the boulders where the tumbleweeds were blazing, Harry Doyle ran down the steep slope. Siding Jess Richards, he raised his line of sight to the face of Dan Colt.

"That's the gunslick that plugged Lefty!" blurted Richards.

A look of contempt formed on Harry Doyle's face. "Well, I'll be . . ." he breathed. "Let's get Jake out, Jess."

"Come on!" bellowed Richards. "Everybody out!"

Next was Dorianne Kates. A catcall pierced the air. Sam Kates squeezed out the door behind the girl, who now stood beside Dan Colt.

Zeke Collier and Hector Mann sat on top, hands raised.

"Hey, Harry!" came the voice of Pat Lewis from the other side of the stagecoach. "We got a problem!"

Jake Finch's voice came from inside the coach. "You guys be careful! You'll get my head blown off!"

Harry Doyle ran to the coach and looked in. His jaw sagged. He said something no one could distinguish.

"Back up!" came Steve Proffitt's voice.

Doyle stepped back, eyes bulging.

Inside, Proffitt said, "We're goin' outside, Jake. I want your boys to get a good look at the fix you're in. Remember, these are touchy triggers."

Jake Finch was breathing hard as he and the deputy slowly inched their way out the door. The outlaw's face was gray. His head was bent sideways from the pressure of the muzzles. As they moved gingerly out into the harsh sunlight, every man in the gang uttered an oath.

Logan Tanner eased his gun hand down.

All six of Finch's men had gathered on the right side of the coach. They stood like statues, transformed by the awesome sight.

Proffitt halted the outlaw leader in front of the stagecoach door. "One move outta you birds and Jake's head goes!" hollered the deputy. "Tell 'em, Jake!"

"Do whatever they say, boys," said Finch with a whining voice. Jake looked sick. His knees felt weak. His heart fluttered with fear. "Those are hair triggers, Harry! Don't let any of 'em do somethin' foolish!"

"Throw your guns in the dirt," commanded Tanner.

"Now, look!" rasped big Jess Richards. "We ain't—"

Jake Finch's voice cut the air, "Back off, Jess!"

"I can shoot that stupid deputy," snapped Richards. "Put a hole right through his head!"

"No, you fool!" bellowed Finch. "His hand's strapped to the gun! He'd pull the triggers just by fallin'!" Proffitt could feel

Jake's whole body trembling like an aspen leaf in the autumn wind.

Hotheaded and stubborn, Richards raised his gun. If Steve Proffitt had not seen Harry Doyle take aim at Richards, Jake's head would have been blown off in the next instant.

Doyle's revolver boomed. The slug caught the huge man in the side. A frantic outcry escaped Jake Finch's lips. Steve Proffitt held steady. Richards staggered but did not go down. Dorianne Kates screamed and dug her fingers into Dan Colt's arm as the big, hairy man whirled and fired at Doyle. The bullet went wild. Doyle fired again. Richards took the slug in his massive chest and staggered toward Doyle, eyes wild. Harry shot him two more times. Jess's gun slipped from his fingers, but like a wounded grizzly bear, he closed in.

Just as Doyle fired again, another gun roared. Dust puffed from Richards's big dirty hat. The slug tore through the huge man's head. He dropped like a rag doll. All eyes were fixed on the smoking gun in Logan Tanner's steady hand.

"Now you whelps drop your guns in the dirt like I said!" barked the US marshal. "Reach for the blue!"

Five pistols plopped to the hot sand. Quickly Hector Mann grabbed his shotgun from up on top and trained it on the five outlaws.

"Where are your horses?" demanded Logan Tanner.

"Over the top of the hill in an arroyo," answered Doyle with disdain.

Throwing his glance to the top of the stagecoach, Tanner said, "Zeke, you and Hec go get their horses. There'll be seven of them. Bring them down here. These boys are gonna see the inside of the jail at Los Alamos."

Within thirty minutes the five outlaws were aboard their horses, their wrists laced together with short lengths of rope. Logan Tanner rode behind them on Jake Finch's horse. Jess Richards rode his own horse, draped over the saddle. The stage followed.

Inside the stagecoach Dan Colt sat uncomfortably, his hands extended through the side window and the door window, cuffed together, the vertical doorpost between them. Steve Proffitt was now more relaxed, but the shotgun remained in place. Sam Kates sat in sullen silence.

As the coach rolled along slowly behind the column of horses, Dorianne Kates looked at Dan Colt with compassion. "You mentioned your wife earlier, Mr. Colt. Where is she? Do you have children?"

A twinge of pain registered in Dan Colt's sky-blue eyes. "No, there are no children," said Dan, trying to disguise his reaction to her questions. "My wife is dead."

"Oh," said the girl, dipping her chin. "Please forgive me. I'm sorry."

"That's all right," Dan said with a smile.

Changing the subject, Dorianne said, "Did you really save Marshal Tanner's life?"

"Mmm-hmm."

"Where did it happen?"

"Up in Colorado. Town called Welcome."

Dorianne smiled unbelievingly. "There's really a town in Colorado called *Welcome*?"

"Sure is. It's on the western side of the Continental Divide. Near Ouray. I trailed my brother through that rugged country. Stopped in Welcome. Tanner was trailin' me. Got himself shot in the leg by a murderous gunhawk. A gunfight was goin' on all around us at the time. A gang had tried to take over the town. Gunhawk's name was Tate Landry. He had an itch in his gut . . . er . . . I mean . . . a burning desire to draw against me. He shot Tanner and had him on the ground with a gun muzzle between his eyes when I came on the scene."

Dorianne was leaning forward, hanging on every word.

"Landry said he'd let Tanner live if I squared off with him," continued Dan. "Miss Kates, if I was the outlaw Tanner says I am, I would have let Landry kill him to get him off my back."

"Of course," she said, still leaning toward the handsome man. "But you put your own life on the line for him."

"I guess you could put it that way," said Colt.

"Oh me, oh my," cut in Jake Finch, "somebody get me a violin. This sob story needs a little music."

"Nip it!" rasped Steve Proffitt. "He was only answering Miss Dorianne's question."

Whirling toward the deputy, who sat beside her, Dorianne said,

"Do you believe he's telling the truth, Mr. Proffitt? Do you believe he's Dan Colt and that his twin is the real outlaw?"

Proffitt's face flushed.

"Well . . . *do* you?" she pressed.

Steve Proffitt parted his lips, but no sound came forth.

The girl popped her hands together. "You *do* believe it, don't you?" she exclaimed.

"Well, ma'am," said the deputy. "It seems to me that if this man was Dave Sundeen, the outlaw, he'd have let this Landry feller kill Mr. Tanner. Of course if this Landry thing is a made-up story . . ."

"Ask Tanner yourself," said Colt.

"See there," spoke up the girl. "Dan—I mean Mr. Colt has told you the truth. He's no outlaw. I just know it!" Squeezing Proffitt's arm, she said, "Why don't you help him escape? He needs to find his brother!"

"Ma'am, I can't do that," said Steve nervously. "I took an oath to uphold the law when they pinned this badge on me."

"But—"

"Miss Dorianne, this man was convicted in a court of law," Proffitt said defensively. "I can't go against the court."

Dorianne leaned back in the seat. Looking at Dan, she said, "If I were a lawman, Mr. Colt, I would turn you loose."

"I wish you were a lawman," said Dan with a slight grin.

Leaning forward again, the girl looked past Steve Proffitt to Jake Finch. "What about you, Mr. Finch?" she asked. "You're an outlaw. Do you think he's Dan Colt?"

"That's a good question, girlie," responded Finch. "My boys say he drew on Lefty Winn and killed him. It would take a Dan Colt–caliber gunfighter to outdraw Lefty."

"I didn't do it, though, Jake," said Dan. "I was in the barber shop at the time Lefty was killed. The man your boys saw outdraw Lefty was my twin. Dave has gone up against some of the fastest guns in the west and taken 'em out."

"Well, if you're Dan Colt and he's your twin brother, it must run in the family," mused Finch.

"Looks like it," said Colt.

"If you ever catch him," said Jake, "I guess you two will find out which one's fastest."

70

"That's possible," said Dan. "But I'm hopin' it'll be such a shock for Dave when he finds out he has a twin that I can get the drop on him."

Dorianne's large eyes grew even larger. "Are you saying that your twin doesn't even know you exist?" she gasped.

Dan Colt soon found himself starting at the beginning and telling Dorianne Kates the whole story. When he finished, she was more convinced of his innocence than ever, exclaiming that no man could make up a story like that.

The Butterfield stage pulled into Los Alamos three hours late. Marshal Logan Tanner deposited Jake Finch's five men in the Los Alamos jail under the care of Marshal Rex Chase. Jess Richards's body was turned over to the local undertaker.

Tanner returned to the stage office, where the driver, gunner and passengers waited. Speaking to Zeke Collier, he said, "Zeke, it's nearly six o'clock. What do you think?"

"Well," drawled the driver, "it don't get dark this time o' year till nine o'clock. We got a fresh team and the heat's gonna ease off. If we git right with it, we can make it by dark . . . or mighty close to it. Parker Flats is just about thirty miles." Zeke rubbed his chin. "If we stay here for the night, the army escort will be arrivin' too early at wherever they're supposed to meet you."

"Well, let's light out, then," said Tanner.

Ten minutes later the stagecoach bounded out of Los Alamos, headed southwest toward Parker Flats on the Jemez River. The heat began to subside as the sun lowered behind the western peaks. Dorianne Kates had been quiet for some time. Dan Colt was once again shackled to Logan Tanner. Now that the danger of Finch's gang attacking had been eliminated, Jake Finch had been relieved of the harness and shotgun and was merely handcuffed to Deputy Steve Proffitt.

As dusk hovered over the earth, Dorianne spoke. "Marshal Tanner . . ."

"Yes'm."

"Did Dan Colt save your life in Welcome, Colorado?"

Tanner looked at Colt from the corner of his eye. "Dave Sundeen did," he said evasively.

"Let me ask it this way," she said. "Did the man who is

71

handcuffed to you at this moment go into a gunfight with a Tate Landry at the risk of his own life in order to save yours?"

The big lawman cleared his throat. All eyes except those of Sam Kates, who was asleep, swung to the face of Logan Tanner.

"Well?" said the girl.

Tanner nodded his big head. "Yes."

"Then you owe him, don't you?" asked Dorianne.

"What . . ." Tanner cleared his throat uneasily. "What do you mean?"

"Doesn't his life mean more than all this badge and valor stuff?"

"He's not being executed, miss," retorted Tanner. "He'll be out in a few years. It would've been five, but the judge who sentenced him will probably double it because he escaped."

"Can't you see," said the girl, squinting at Tanner in the near-darkness, "if Dan was what you say he is, he would have walked away and let Landry kill you?"

Logan Tanner inserted a heavy, gruff tone into his voice. "The matter is closed, young lady. I will not discuss it anymore."

"You know what your problem is, Marshal Logan Tanner?" said Dorianne indignantly. "*Pride!* You are going to slam an innocent man into prison over your stubborn pride! Well, we'll close the matter at your command, sir, but let me close it with some words from the Good Book . . . *Pride goeth before destruction and a haughty spirit before a fall!* You'll find that in the book of Proverbs, chapter sixteen and the eighteenth verse."

Jake Finch stomped his feet and shouted, "Bravo! Bravo! You were right, Colt! She'd make an even better preacher than a lawyer!"

Logan Tanner eyed Finch coldly through the gathering gloom.

CHAPTER EIGHT

The six horses began to nicker at the smell of water just as the stagecoach topped a rise and the winking lights of Parker Flats came into view.

Ten minutes later the coach crossed a bridge and pulled to a halt in front of a cluster of squat adobe buildings. "Here we are," came the voice of Zeke Collier from the seat up top. "Parker Flats!"

The Butterfield way station was run by a man named Chester Thompson and his wife, Ophelia. The elderly couple appeared in the door of the main building. The light from inside cast a yellow rectangle on the dusty ground.

Thompson carried a lantern.

"Howdy, Chester!" said the driver, climbing down.

"Welcome, Zeke," responded Thompson. "You're a little late."

"Complications," said Collier.

The elderly woman's eyes widened as Colt and Tanner stepped from the stage. Her gaze was fixed on the handcuffs that joined the two men.

"Good evening, ma'am," said Tanner, touching his hat brim. "We have a couple of prisoners here on their way to Yuma. Nothing to be alarmed about. They're shackled."

Dan turned toward the coach as Dorianne Kates appeared in the door. With his free hand, he helped her out. Ophelia Thompson stepped up immediately and said, "Hello, my dear. I'm Mrs.

73

Thompson. Are you traveling alone, or is there someone in there with you?"

"My uncle, Samuel B. Kates, is traveling with me," said Dorianne, gesturing toward the rotund figure that was now filling the stagecoach door. "My name is Dorianne Kates."

As soon as Proffitt and Finch were out of the coach, the driver and shotgunner unhitched the team and put them in the corral next to the barn.

Chester Thompson showed his guests to their quarters while his wife prepared a meal. Dorianne had a room to herself. Sam Kates reluctantly accepted a bed in the same room with Logan Tanner and Dan Colt. Steve Proffitt shared the remaining room with Jake Finch. Collier and Mann occupied their normal quarters.

Colt and Finch were handcuffed to metal beds while the lawmen washed up. Then the prisoners did their washing at gunpoint.

The dining room was part of the kitchen. The room was hot, but the food smelled so good that no one minded. As the men filed in for the meal, Dorianne was waiting. She had combed her hair and looked beautiful in spite of her tiring day.

The Butterfield passengers stood around while Mrs. Thompson was putting the last touches on the meal. She tried not to look at the shackles that held the prisoners to the lawmen.

Jake Finch was standing near a corner of the table where Mrs. Thompson had been slicing tomatoes. The teakettle had suddenly started to whistle. Inadvertently she had left her paring knife lying beside the plate of sliced tomatoes. The shiny six-inch blade caught Jake's eye. Steve Proffitt was talking to Logan Tanner.

Taking advantage of the split second while no one was looking at him, Finch grabbed the knife and palmed it against the inside of his wrist.

Turning back to the table, the elderly woman said, "Go on, everybody. Sit down. I'll just finish these tomatoes and you can eat." Jake Finch eased down in the chair at the corner of the table. He saw the puzzled look on Mrs. Thompson's face as she picked up a partially cut tomato and ran her eyes over that section of the table.

Jake's heart froze.

Without saying anything the woman turned to the cupboard and produced a knife identical to the one in Finch's left hand. She finished slicing the tomato and scooted the plate toward the center of the table. "Okay, everybody," she said, "dig in."

Jake Finch slipped the paring knife into his boot.

The lawmen and the prisoners found it a bit awkward eating with one hand, but they managed to keep their mouths full.

Dan Colt ate and wondered how he was going to manage an escape without anyone getting hurt. He was not going to rot in that horrible prison. There had to be a way . . .

Jake Finch pondered the best time to make his break. Logan Tanner had already taken the precaution of having Chester Thompson ready to lock the room doors from the outside. Even if the prisoners somehow got free of their handcuffs, they could not get out of the rooms. The windows were long, narrow slits, built for defense against Indian attack. There was no way in or out of the rooms except through the doors.

Jake would have to make his break before they went to the rooms. It was a long way anywhere from Parker Flats, he thought, so he might as well escape on a full belly. While he ate, he planned.

Mrs. Thompson was filling coffee cups around the table after the food had been devoured. Talk was at a low ebb. As the coffee was slowly consumed, Jake reached into his boot. Slipping the knife into his hand, he got a firm grip on the handle. Just as Steve Proffitt was tipping his coffee cup back to finish it off, Finch swung the knife, touching the sharp point to his jugular vein.

"Everybody freeze!" shouted Finch.

Mrs. Thompson gasped. Logan Tanner started to move.

"I said *freeze,* Tanner!" bellowed the outlaw. "I've got nothin' to lose." Pushing his chair back and slowly rising to his feet, he said, "I'd rather die than rot in Yuma. So don't push me. I'll kill this stupid deputy as sure as any of you make a false move."

Dorianne's face lost its color. Logan Tanner's angry breathing filled the room. Collier and Mann eyed Finch warily.

Finch threw a glance at Chester Thompson, who stood near the outside door. "Grampa," he said evenly, "you get over there by Gramma and stay put."

The old man moved to where his wife stood by the cupboard.

"Now, Deputy," said Finch gruffly, "you dig out your key *real* careful-like and unlock the cuff. You so much as flinch and you'll have the full length of this blade through your neck."

While Proffitt obeyed, Logan Tanner glanced at his gun hand resting on the table.

"Don't even think about it, Tanner," lashed Finch, his narrow eyes wild.

The lock clicked, and Jake twisted his wrist free. Dropping the key on the table, he pressed the knife point closer against Proffitt's neck and said, "Now, Deputy, you reach down and get ahold of your gun with your fingertips and give it to me."

Steve lifted the Colt .44 above the table as it dangled from his fingertips. "Now gently lay it on the table," said Finch, "and lower your hand to your side."

As the deputy obeyed, Jake snatched the revolver from the table, thumbed back the hammer and threw the knife across the room. Sticking the muzzle in Proffitt's ear, he said with a triumphant tone in his voice, "Now, Logan old boy, you put your gun in my other hand. Quick! Butt first."

With deep reluctance US Marshal Logan Tanner eased his gun out of its holster and let it slide through his grip until his fingers closed around the barrel. He begrudgingly handed it to the smiling outlaw. Jake jammed the weapon under his belt and flashed a look at Hector Mann. "Now *you*, mister. Bring your own gun and your partner's over here and lay 'em on the table." Cautiously Mann obeyed, laying his own gun and Collier's in front of Finch.

With his free hand Jake stuck both guns under his belt, alongside Tanner's. He glared momentarily at Sam Kates, whose round, flabby face was dripping with sweat. Swinging his evil gaze to Chester Thompson, he said, "All right, Grampa, you go saddle me a horse."

Thompson shuffled toward the door.

"And don't get any cute ideas, old man," barked the outlaw. "You show up with help or come back totin' a firearm and I'll start shootin'. First one I plug will be your old lady. You understand?"

"Y-yessir," replied Thompson, pulling open the door.

"You've got exactly three minutes, Grampa. If I wait four minutes, Gramma dies. And I'll kill one person per minute after that. You'd better cinch that saddle right, too. Now git! You got three minutes."

Thompson disappeared like a frightened rabbit.

Finch looked at Dan Colt. "If I thought you were Dave Sundeen, I'd take you with me. We'd make a great team. But I'm with Dorianne. You're Dan Colt, all right. I can feel it in my bones. The only one too stupid to see it is this meathead marshal."

Tanner scowled at the outlaw.

Finch looked down at Steve Proffitt. The muzzle was still in his ear. "How does it feel, Deputy . . . havin' a cold muzzle next to your skin? Not as bad as that shotgun, but at least you get a little of the same sensation."

Proffitt did not comment.

Finch threw an impatient glance toward the door. "Where's that old man?" he said testily.

"Hasn't been three minutes yet," said Logan Tanner.

"How would you know, Tanner?" rasped Finch. "You ever have to mark time behind the prison walls?"

"You chose the life you're livin', Finch," said Tanner. "Don't blubber on my shoulder."

Finch swore. "Only difference between your kind and mine, Logan, is we're honest crooks and you boys are crooks with tin stars on your chests."

Ignoring the outlaw's insult, Tanner said coolly, "I'll catch you again, Jake. Sooner or later you'll be back at Yuma where you belong. Either that or you'll stretch a rope."

"Don't count on it, bub," lashed Finch.

At that instant hoofbeats sounded softly outside the door. Presently Chester Thompson entered. "Okay," he said to Finch, "your horse is saddled."

"Thanks, Grampa," responded Jake. Quickly he lifted the gun in his hand and brought it down hard on Proffitt's head. The deputy slumped in the chair, his face slamming the table.

Logan Tanner jerked, rising from his chair. Finch swung the gun in a savage arc. It met Tanner's head with a meaty, sodden sound. The big man rolled from the chair, taking Dan Colt to the floor with him.

The outlaw stepped to where Dorianne Kates sat frozen with fear. He seized her arm and pulled her from the chair. She ejected a tremulous whimper. "C'mon, honey," he snapped. "You're goin' with me."

77

Dan Colt was up on his knees. "Finch!" he said with fire in his eyes. "Leave her alone!"

Jake pulled Dorianne's back to him, fitting her neck in the crook of his arm. She began to weep. Raking the paralyzed faces with his dark eyes, Jake Finch snarled, "Anybody follows, I'll kill 'er!" With that he dragged the girl out the door in the silver moonlight and hoisted her to the waiting horse's back.

Suddenly Finch remembered Hec Mann's shotgun on the seat of the stagecoach. He ran to the coach, seized the shotgun and hurled it into the river. Swinging up behind Dorianne, he goaded the animal into a gallop. The hollow sound of hoofs on the bridge floated through the air, then disappeared.

Instantly Dan Colt's fingers went to the unconscious marshal's vest pocket. While he inserted the key into his handcuffs, he looked at the old man and said, "Have you got a gun?"

"Just a rifle, mister, but it ain't workin' too good. I've got a new one on order, but it ain't arrived yet. 'sides, I wouldn't give you one, anyway."

"I'm goin' after that girl, old man," rasped Dan. "I'm not an outlaw, but I don't have time to explain. Have you got another horse?"

"Yessir, but she ain't broke to a saddle. She only pulls a wagon." A sly look framed the old man's face. "You really won't need a horse. You can catch them on foot."

"Huh?"

A glint came into Thompson's eye. "That horse I saddled for the outlaw is old. She has rheumatism. She takes off like a house afire, but by the time they ride her a half mile, she'll go lame on them. They're probably afoot by now."

Colt looked at Collier and Mann. "You got any spare guns on the stage?"

"No," said Collier, "but that sawed-off shotgun is in the boot where the marshal had me put it."

Dan's eyes brightened. "I forgot about that. Would you get it for me?"

"You're a fool, Collier," spoke up Sam Kates. "This blood-thirsty killer will murder us all now!"

Ignoring Kates, Zeke bounded out the door.

Dan grasped the unconscious deputy, eased him out of the chair and laid him beside Logan Tanner. As he handcuffed them together, he said half to himself, "These two will want to join in on the chase, and they'd just get in the way."

Using Tanner's key, Dan unlocked the handcuffs dangling from Steve Proffitt's free arm. Quickly he yanked off one boot from each man and clamped the cuffs on their ankles. "Whew!" he gasped. "One of these two has dirty socks!"

Shoving Tanner's key in his pocket, Dan retrieved Proffitt's key from the table and put it in the same place.

Zeke Collier came through the door with the shotgun. Grabbing it, Dan broke it open and checked the loads. As he snapped it shut, Zeke said, "I'll go with you."

"No thanks," said Colt. "Too many cooks spoil the broth. That's why I immobilized the lawmen. I can handle it easier by myself."

The door swung open and Dan was gone.

"What was that he said about cooks?" asked Thompson.

"Too many cooks spoil the broth," said Collier.

"Imagine that, Ma!" exclaimed the old man. "Outlaws quotin' Scripture."

Dan Colt was glad for the bright moonlight. It would make his job of tracking easier. He bounded over the bridge. The Jemez looked like a silver ribbon winding through the desert. He hoped Chester Thompson was right and that the old mare would give out quickly.

The hoofprints were easily readable in the soft dirt of the road. Dan paced himself at an easy trot, reading the hoofprints and periodically looking up for any sign of Finch and the girl. He had no plan. He would have to adapt to the situation when he found them. One thing for sure—he would do his best to make sure Dorianne Kates did not get hurt.

As he ran up the moonlit road, a plan began forming in his mind. Once he delivered Jake Finch back to Tanner and returned Dorianne to her uncle, he would borrow one of Butterfield's horses and head for Taos. Back on his own horse, he would pick up Dave's trail. By the time the two lawmen got themselves out of those handcuffs, Dan Colt would be long gone.

Suddenly Dan noticed a change in the hoofprints. Sure enough, the horse had stumbled, and from that point on the prints were irregular. Chester had been right. Looking behind him, Dan judged he had come over half a mile. Then the trail veered off the road, to the right.

Up ahead were some tall rocks and a stand of mesquite trees and snakeweed. The tracks were headed straight between the two giant rocks about two hundred yards off the road. Further to the right was a shallow gully that circled the rocks and trees.

Dan looked down and saw the spot where the couple had dismounted. At first there were two sets of footprints, then one: Jake's. The old mare had been led into the trees. Descending into the gully, the blond man bent low and followed it around the collection of rocks and trees. Abruptly he heard a horse blow. Stopping in his tracks, he listened. Above the night breeze he heard Jake Finch's voice.

Dan crept toward the voice. Coming out of the gully, he looked through the brush. Finch was standing over Dorianne, who sat on a rock in an open area, rubbing her bare ankle. Her shoes lay in the sand.

"Why don't you go on without me?" Dorianne asked pleadingly. "You don't need me anymore."

"You're stickin' with me, honey," said Finch, "till I'm positive I'm in the clear. I know we passed a ranch north of here a mile or two. We'll snatch a couple horses and light a shuck outta these parts."

The girl's voice quivered. "But I'll only slow you down. My ankle is starting to swell."

"Once you're on a horse you'll be all right," countered the outlaw.

Slowly Dan made his way toward the mesquite trees, testing each foot before he let it take his weight. There were bound to be twigs underneath the trees. The tall man was now directly behind Jake. He inched his way to the edge of the brush. The outlaw was forty feet away. Dan would have to take him without firing the shotgun. From this distance the charge would spread wide and Dorianne would be hit with some of the buckshot.

Dan was waiting, studying the situation, when his chance came. Dorianne said, "I can't walk a mile or two. Please, just go and leave me alone."

"Why, honey," said Jake in a singsong manner, "there's all kinds of wild animals runnin' loose out here."

"I would rather be with them than you!" said the girl icily.

"Now, sweetie, you don't mean that," Jake said, bending down. "Now let's try again with that kiss."

Dorianne cried out as Jake pressed his stubbled face to hers.

Dan was on the move as the girl raked the outlaw's temple with her fingernails. Jake swore and responded by slapping Dorianne with his open hand. Just as she crumpled from the blow, Dan lifted the shotgun with both hands and brought it down violently on Finch's head.

The outlaw pitched headlong into the sand and lay still. Dan vaulted the rock and reached for Dorianne, who was lying on the ground trying to clear her senses. Seeing the dark figure coming at her, she screamed.

"It's all right, Dorianne," Dan said hastily. "It's Dan Colt."

Recognizing the voice, she gasped, "Oh, Dan! Dan!" and broke into tears. She felt herself being lifted. Clinging hard with both arms around his neck, the girl sobbed and spoke incoherently.

"Don't try to talk, honey," said the tall, muscular man. "Just calm down. You're safe now."

Dan eyed Jake Finch in the bright moonlight. He lay in a heap, out cold. As Dorianne's crying subsided, Dan lowered her to the rock where she had sat before. She squeezed his neck tighter, ejecting a fearful moan.

"I have to take care of Jake before he comes to," explained Dan.

Dorianne released his neck. Dan yanked the revolvers from under Finch's belt. Striding to the old mare, he deposited two of them in a saddlebag, jamming the third under his own belt. He stuck the sawed-off shotgun butt first into the saddlebag on the opposite side. The two muzzles protruded from the bag, pointing skyward.

While Dan whipped Jake's belt off, turned him over and bound his hands behind his back, he spoke to the girl. "How did you hurt your ankle?"

Attempting to bring her voice under control, Dorianne said, "When the horse stumbled, Jake whipped her, but she just couldn't seem to carry us anymore. Jake got off first. He lifted me down . . . and tried to . . . to kiss me. I got away from him and started running. Somehow I turned my ankle. He brought me in here to let it rest. Oh, Dan," she said, drawing a quivering breath, "I knew you'd come. I just knew it!"

Dorianne Kates was especially beautiful in the moonlight, Dan thought. Someday some lucky Prince Charming would come along and sweep her off her feet.

"Did the slap hurt you?" asked Dan tenderly.

"Stunned me a little, but I'm all right," she replied, touching the reddened cheek with her fingertips.

Jake Finch moaned, moving his legs.

Dan stood over him like a towering cedar. "Okay, Jake," he said briskly, "wake up!"

Slowly the outlaw returned to consciousness, looked up at Dan Colt and blinked. Suddenly he realized that he was bound. He began to swear.

"Shut up, Jake!" said Dan curtly. "There's a lady present!" Roughly the tall man sank his fingers into the outlaw's shirt and jerked him to his feet. "Okay, mister. You're walkin' back to the way station."

Turning to the girl, he said, "Grab your shoe, little lady. I think the old gray mare can carry *you*."

CHAPTER NINE

"Are you sure you don't have *something* that'll cut these off?" Marshal Logan Tanner asked Chester Thompson impatiently.

The old man looked down at Tanner and Proffitt, who were sprawled awkwardly on the floor, handcuffed wrist to wrist and ankle to ankle. "I'm sorry, Marshal," said Thompson apologetically, "but I just don't. My old wood saw would never cut those chains and I don't have a chisel. My ax might do it, but it'd be mighty dangerous tryin' it. One slip and . . ."

"Best thing, Marshal," suggested Zeke Collier, "you and your deputy try and get some sleep tonight. I'll bet by sunup Dan Colt'll be back acarryin' that pretty little gal in one arm and adraggin' that outlaw by the hair with the other one."

Logan Tanner's face contorted as if he had just smelled rotten eggs. "You're kiddin' yourself, Zeke," he said sourly. "Colt's not comin' back. He's gone and he'll just keep on goin'."

"If you'll pardon my saying so, Marshal," said Steve Proffitt, "you just called him *Colt*."

"Aw, you know I meant to say Sundeen, Steve. It's just with everybody else around here thinkin' he's Dan Colt, it slipped off my tongue. But one thing I'm right about. He isn't comin' back."

"If he does," spoke up Sam Kates, "it won't be to stay. You can bank on that. The way he mother-hens my niece, he'll probably deliver her to the door and cut out lickety-split."

Logan Tanner swore. Angrily he said, "I wish we had a gun, in case Kates is right." Eyeing the old man quizzically, he said, "How come you don't have guns on the place, Mr. Thompson? What are you gonna do if the Apaches come around?"

" 'paches ain't been this far east fer many a moon, Marshal," responded Thompson. "Don't expect they *will* be, either."

Sam Kates started to say something, then he checked himself and stood up.

"What is it, Kates?" asked Chester Thompson.

"I thought I heard—" Kates scurried to the door, pulled back the curtain and peered toward the moon-drenched road. "It is!" he exclaimed.

"What?" demanded Tanner from the floor.

"I thought I heard a horse crossing the bridge," replied the fat man, still looking past the curtain. "It's that Dave Sundeen. He's pushing Finch this way on foot and leading the horse. The girl is in the saddle." Whirling, Kates faced Logan Tanner. "Marshal, I started to tell you. I have a Derringer." As he said it, Sam pulled a pearl-handled, nickel-plated pistol from his inside coat pocket.

"Good!" exclaimed the marshal. "Give it to me!"

"Huh-uh," said Kates, shaking his head. "I want to put this on him myself."

"Kates," said Tanner brusquely, "he's a hardened criminal. Not only that, but he's lightning with a gun. I was holding a gun on him in Holbrook with the hammer cocked. He drew and shot me down before I could squeeze the trigger."

"He's only mortal," said Kates, his eyes wild with excitement. "There are no eyes in the back of his head." Quickly the obese man darted out the back door. Tanner called his name but to no avail.

Footsteps thumped outside the door. The knob turned. There was a slight pause, then the door squeaked open and Jake Finch entered sullenly. His hands were tied behind his back. His bare head was disheveled and there were claw marks on the left side of his face.

Presently Dan Colt appeared, carrying Dorianne Kates. Mrs. Thompson was quickly front and center. "Oh, my dear," she said, eyeing the girl's bare foot, "what happened?"

"I sprained my ankle," said Dorianne. Dan placed her gently on a chair next to the big dining table.

84

Logan Tanner's face flushed as he said stiffly, "Sundeen! You'll do another ten years in Yuma for this! You unlock these cuffs this instant!"

Ignoring him, Dan said to Ophelia Thompson, "Could you heat some water so Dorianne can soak her ankle, ma'am?" With that he turned and went out the door.

"Sundeen!" bellowed the US marshal. "You come back here!"

Dorianne looked around the room as Ophelia Thompson began preparations for soaking the foot. "Where's my uncle?" she asked.

"He had to go out back," spoke up Tanner.

"Oh," said Dorianne, assuming her uncle had gone to the privy.

Outside, Sam Kates lurked in the deep shadows and watched Dan Colt lead the limping mare to the barn. As soon as he had gone inside, the fat man crossed the open yard and flattened himself against the side of the barn.

Dan had left the big door open, allowing the silvery moonlight to shine inside. Kates peered through a knothole and watched Colt pull the sawed-off shotgun and the two revolvers from the saddlebags. The third revolver was still under his belt.

The tall man moved further into the barn and passed from Sam's line of sight. When he returned to view his hands were empty. He unsaddled the mare and slipped off the bridle. Moving back outside, he closed the barn door, bridle in hand.

The sweating fat man peered around the corner, waiting for Dan to turn his back toward him. He was poised to move when the tall man threw a glance in Sam's direction. Kates jerked his head back, his heart pounding inside him like a trip-hammer. Had the gunfighter seen him? If so, Sam Kates was a dead man.

Kates waited, breathing heavily. A full minute passed. Venturing a look around the corner, he saw Dan in the corral, slipping the bridle on one of the Butterfield horses. He led the animal through the gate and crossed the yard to the main building. Tying the reins to a hitching post, he moved back inside.

Dorianne looked up and smiled warmly as the tall man ducked his head and entered the room. In contrast, the face of Logan Tanner was livid with rage. Dan stood just inside the room, his broad back to the door. Sweeping the room with his blue gaze, he said, "Where's Kates?"

"My uncle had to go to the privy," said Dorianne before Tanner could speak.

Looking down at the marshal, Colt said, "Tanner, I really don't like leaving you like this, but you give me no choice."

Logan Tanner swore vehemently, eyes bulging. "Sundeen! You leave us like this, I'll see that you go to Yuma and *never* get out!"

"Ta ta now, marshal," said Dan. "Temper, temper! You oughtta be glad I brought Jake back to you."

Jake Finch was seated on a straight-back chair next to the wall. His hands were still tied behind his back. His vision had still not cleared from the crack on the head Dan had given him. He had a splitting headache and felt sick to his stomach.

Swinging his gaze to Zeke Collier, Dan said, "I'm takin' one of your horses. I'll leave him with the hostler in Taos."

Collier nodded.

Looking back at Tanner, Colt said, "I left all the guns in the barn but yours, Marshal." Patting the butt of Tanner's revolver where it lay next to his flat belly, he said, "I'll leave it with the hostler in Taos."

"Sundeen!" hissed the big lawman, "don't you do it! You get us out of these things right now!"

"Sir," said Dan, "when I find my twin and rub your noses together, I'll accept your apology for the wicked thoughts you're having about me right now. I've hidden the keys to the cuffs somewhere in the barn. Time these fellas find them, I'll be a safe distance down the road."

"Oh, Dan," said Dorianne, "take me with you! Please! I don't want to go back with my uncle."

"Little lady," said Dan, eyeing her tenderly, "you're young. Another few months with your uncle won't be so bad. Somewhere in the very near future there'll be a fine young man walking into your life. You'll get married and live happily ever after."

Dorianne Kates wanted to tell the tall, handsome man that she had fallen in love with *him* but could not bring herself to do so in front of all the spectators. Her lower lip quivered as tears filled her eyes.

"Good-bye, Dorianne," said Dan. "Maybe we'll meet again someday." Fixing his gaze floorward, he said, "Proffitt, you take good care of Mr. Tanner for me. I want him alive and well so he can rub noses with the *real* Dave Sundeen."

Dan backed through the door, ducking his head. As his boots touched the dusty ground, he felt cold metal thrust against his neck. "Hold it right there!" shouted Sam Kates. "It's a Derringer, Sundeen. And don't think I won't use it! I'd be a hero if I shot you, isn't that right, Marshal Tanner?"

Logan Tanner was craning his neck, trying to see out the door. "You sure would, Kates!" yelled the marshal. "If he moves, shoot him!"

Dorianne's mouth hung open as she thumbed away tears to clear her vision.

"Now, mister, you just lift your hands real high," commanded Kates.

Colt hesitated. The fat man screamed, "I mean it! I'll kill you!" The threatening weapon trembled against Dan's neck.

Going cold inside, Dan lifted his hands. Kates reached around and slipped Logan Tanner's gun from under Dan's belt. "One of you men come take this gun!" hollered Kates.

Hector Mann stepped up, took the revolver, eared back the hammer and leveled it on Dan Colt. "Okay, I've got him covered," he said, taking two steps back.

Sam gave the tall man an unfriendly shove. "Inside," he said through gritted teeth.

Logan Tanner was ecstatic. "Good work, Kates! You'll get a commendation from the governor for this!"

As Dan stepped back in the room, Sam Kates flung his derby onto the table. His face was streaked with sweat. Sleeving away the moisture, he waved the Derringer and said, "Sit down, Sundeen, and don't you move."

Dan dropped onto a chair near the door.

"All right, Dave," said the thick-bodied marshal from his uncomfortable position on the floor, "where are the keys?"

"With the guns in the feed bin," answered Colt resignedly. "I dropped them down the barrels of the shotgun."

Chester Thompson struck a match and touched it to the wick of a lantern. "I'll go get 'em," he said.

Zeke Collier followed Thompson outside, concerned with returning the horse to the corral.

Dorianne Kates set a pair of burning eyes on her rotund uncle, who still pointed the small handgun at Dan Colt. "I hope you're happy, Sam Kates!" she screamed. "You're helping to send an innocent man to prison!"

The fat man gave her a cold, hostile look.

Jake Finch stood up, fixing his dark, murderous eyes on Dan Colt. "You're gonna be sorry for what you did, Colt," he said through tightly drawn lips.

"Sit down, Jake!" barked Tanner.

"You'd have a hard time makin' me at the moment, Logan," Finch said, eyes hard on Colt.

Hector Mann swung his gun toward Finch. "Do like the marshal says, Jake," he said firmly.

"I owe him one!" shouted the outlaw, twisting his arms against the belt that held his wrists. "He nearly busted my skull!"

"You ever touch that girl again," warned Dan, "I'll knock your head clear off!"

Jake Finch stared at Dan Colt with open hatred. Suddenly his fury overtook his good sense. With an animal cry, he charged across the room, head down like an angry bull. Dan stood up to meet the oncoming outlaw, and the force of Jake's weight drove Colt against the wall. Knickknacks fell off a shelf and a glass-framed picture fell to the floor, glass shattering.

Tanner, Kates and Mann were all yelling as Dan, his blood up now, seized Finch. Spinning him around, he sent a savage fist to the outlaw's jaw. Sam Kates had retreated to stand next to Hec Mann. Dan's punch drove Finch into both men, legs flailing. All three crashed to the floor, Jake's body smothering Mann.

The Derringer slipped from Kates's fingers and slid across the floor toward the spot where Dorianne sat, favoring her swollen ankle. Forgetting her pain, the girl bounded from the chair and seized the small weapon. Instantly she swung it on Hector Mann, who was struggling to work his gun hand free.

"Hold it right there!" shouted Dorianne, eyes wide, face set in grim lines of ragged determination. She held the gun steady. "Get his gun, Dan!" she said loudly.

Ophelia Thompson, face white, moved along the cupboard away from where Dorianne stood.

"Miss Kates," spoke up Logan Tanner from where he lay

shackled to Steve Proffitt. "If you aid Sundeen's escape, you become an accessory. There are two law officers to witness your actions."

Dorianne shifted her weight to the good foot. Breathing heavily, she remained steadfast. "Get the gun, Dan!"

Jake Finch was out cold. Sam Kates was afraid to move, for fear of getting in the line of fire.

Hector Mann lay motionless, staring into the two vertical barrels of the Derringer. His own gun was totally out of play. The determined girl could shoot him before he could raise the muzzle.

Dan had not moved. He wanted to escape but could not involve the girl. He started to speak.

"Miss Kates!" roared Tanner, hating his helpless position. "You'll go to prison! Sundeen isn't worth it!"

Unflinching, she kept the Derringer trained on Hec Mann. "He's not Dave Sundeen, Marshal. You know it. I know it. Dan Colt has got to be free to be able to prove his innocence. Hurry, Dan, get the gun!"

Dan spoke softly. "Dorianne, I can't let you do this. Tanner's right. You—"

"You bet I'm right!" cut in the big marshal. "No matter who this man is, the fact remains. He was convicted in a court of law and sentenced to prison. As far as the law is concerned, he is a wanted criminal. As a federal marshal, I am returning him to prison. If you aid in his escape, you will be a wanted criminal, too. By holding that gun, you are already guilty."

Dorianne held her position. "Mr. Tanner," she said, her eyes still on Mann, "when a woman loves a man, she doesn't think about herself. I'm no child. I'm twenty years old. It doesn't make any difference what you or anyone else in this room thinks or says. I'm in love with Dan Colt and I don't care who knows it. I'll do anything for the man I love."

Dan Colt was dumbfounded. He would have to talk her out of this crazy notion. But now was not the time. Speaking in a soft tone, he said, "Dorianne, did you mean what you said?"

The girl kept her eyes on Hec Mann. Blinking, she said, "Yes, my darling. I meant it. I love you."

"Uh . . . no . . . I mean that you'd do anything for me?"

"I'm holding the gun so you can escape, aren't I?"

Dan looked down at the marshal. "Tanner, if she gives me the gun and I surrender, will you forget this incident?"

"You have my word on it," came the immediate reply.

"Proffitt?"

"Same here," replied the deputy.

Colt took a careful step toward the girl, extending an open palm. "Dorianne," he said cautiously.

"Yes?"

"Give me the gun."

"I don't want you to go to prison, Dan. I can't let them take you back."

"Dorianne, you said *anything*."

"But . . ."

"Please. Give me the gun."

The beautiful face of Dorianne Kates pinched as tears appeared in her eyes. She laid the Derringer in Dan Colt's big hand and broke into sobs as he folded her into his arms.

Zeke Collier, who had stood in the door unnoticed, let out a loud, *"Whew!"* He and Chester Thompson moved inside.

Quickly Collier knelt where the lawmen lay stiff and uncomfortable. Unlocking the cuffs, he said, "I lost one of the keys in the barn, Marshal. They were both in the shotgun, but when I went to dump 'em out, one of 'em fell in the straw."

"It's okay, Zeke," said Tanner. "We'll look for it in the morning before we pull out."

As Tanner and Proffitt lumbered stiffly to their feet, Dan Colt held Dorianne as she wept. "I appreciate what you wanted to do, little lady," he said, "but there's no way I could let you involve yourself in my problem."

"Oh, Dan," she said between sobs, "I know it sounded melodramatic, but I *do* love you."

Without speaking, Dan handed the Derringer to Logan Tanner. The big marshal spoke to his deputy. "Steve, put the cuffs on Jake before he wakes up. He'll need the belt for his pants."

As Steve Proffitt complied, Tanner wordlessly extended the other pair of handcuffs toward Dan. The tall man helped Dorianne back to her chair. Mrs. Thompson began pouring hot water into the bucket at the girl's feet.

The ratchets gave off their tight, clicking sound as the handcuffs were affixed to Dan Colt's wrists. Looking at Hec Mann, the big lawman said, "Mann, you keep an eye on the prisoners." Throwing his glance at Proffitt, he said, "Steve, I don't know about you, but it sure seemed like we were down on that floor a long time." Heading for the rear door, he added, "I really *do* have to go out back!"

CHAPTER TEN

Morning came, with the heat of the sun intense almost from the moment it appeared.

The team was hitched up and ready to roll. With a good breakfast under their belts, the passengers boarded the stage. Dan Colt was chained to Logan Tanner, Jake Finch to Steve Proffitt. Sam Kates sat in his usual corner beside Tanner. Dorianne was in her customary place next to the deputy, across from Dan.

Zeke Collier came out of the barn shaking his head. Sticking his face through the open window of the coach, he said, "Marshal, it just ain't nowhere to be found. I've sifted and scoured the whole area in there. I don't know what happened to it."

"We'll just have to get along with one key, Zeke," said Tanner. Looking at Proffitt, he said, "You keep the key in your vest, Steve. Since your vest pocket has a button on it, the key'll be safer with you."

Proffitt nodded.

Collier looked toward the river where Hector Mann was leaning over a rail in the middle of the bridge. "See anything?" called the stage driver.

Mann looked toward Collier, cupping his hands behind his ears and shaking his head. The roar of the river, when he stood on the bridge, blotted out all other sounds. Zeke motioned for him to come to the stage, then climbed into the driver's seat.

Hec Mann came toward the coach, disgust on his face. "Can't see that shotgun anywhere, Zeke. Guess it's gone for good."

"We'll get you a new one in Gallup," said Zeke.

"Just hope I don't need it before we get there," said Hec dejectedly.

"You want the sawed-off one? It's in the boot. I'm sure the marshal won't care if you use it."

"Guess I'd better. A handgun doesn't demand the respect a scatter-gun does. I'll get it." Walking to the window next to Dan Colt, Mann looked in and said, "Mr. Tanner, Jake threw my shotgun in the river last night. I can't find it. Would you mind if I keep the short-barreled one up top with me till we get to Gallup?"

"By all means," said Tanner. "It's in the boot next to Jake's harness."

As Hec moved to the back of the stage, Jake Finch threw a sinister look at Dan Colt.

Dan felt Finch's eyes on him. Turning his ice-blues on the outlaw, he said, "Don't stare at me, Finch."

Jake snickered. "Oh, is there a law that says I can't look in your direction?"

"You heard me," snapped Colt.

"I'm gonna get you, blondie," said Finch coldly. "I may have to wait till we get to Yuma, but the day'll come. I'm gonna get you."

Dorianne flashed a hard look toward the outlaw. "It'll take a lot more man than you are, Jake," she said ferociously.

Hector Mann settled into the seat beside Zeke Collier. The driver's familiar, "Hee-yaah!" cut the hot morning air as the whip popped. Chester and Ophelia Thompson waved from the door of the way station as the stage pulled away.

The motion of the vehicle sent a welcome breeze through the coach. Sam Kates ran a forefinger under his collar where the sweat was trapped against his fat neck. The dust began to rise through the floorboards. The stage rocked and swayed over the rough road, to the steady drumming of the horses' hooves and the whine of the wheels.

Dan Colt eyed Dorianne quietly and grinned when their gazes met. Her face flushed. She opened her mouth to speak, then let it pass.

"You were going to say something?" he asked.

"Only that . . . that . . ."

"What?"

"I guess I made a real fool of myself last night, telling everybody my feelings."

"You're a mighty fine young lady, Miss Dorianne Kates," said Dan with feeling. "Maybe when we get to Gallup, the marshal would chain me somewhere so we could talk alone."

Logan Tanner had settled back, tipping his hat over his eyes. Without moving he said, "Since she changed her mind about springin' you last night, I think that could be arranged."

"Good," said Colt, smiling at the girl. "It's a date."

Over an hour passed with each passenger in his own solitude. The heat became more intense. The stage rocked on, rattling and squeaking.

Dorianne broke the silence. "Dan," she said, dabbing at her sweaty brow with a handkerchief.

"Yes'm," he responded.

"I've got it all worked out."

"What's that, m'lady?"

"*I'm* going to find your brother for you."

"You're gonna *what*?"

"I'll get me a good horse and track Dave down."

"And just how would you capture him when you found him?"

"I wouldn't need to."

"Huh?"

"He's wanted, right?"

"Uh-huh."

"Then there must be posters on him somewhere."

"There are," nodded Dan.

"I'll carry some posters with me. When I spot him, I'll go to the local authorities and show them a poster. They can arrest him and contact Marshal Tanner. Once he sees Dave he'll know you've been telling the truth. They'll open the gates of Yuma to you. You'll be free forever!"

Dan smiled and clucked his tongue. "Missy, you sure do have a vivid imagination!"

"Imagination, nothing!" exclaimed the petite female. "I can do it! One thing for sure—I won't have any trouble recognizing Dave when I see him."

"You'll never see him," spoke up Logan Tanner from under his hat. "This alleged twin is the little man who wasn't there."

Ignoring Tanner, Dan said, "Dorianne, you can't be traipsing all over creation looking for Dave. This is wild and raw country. A girl like you would be spotted and chased by all kinds of men."

"I'll disguise myself and dress like a man," she said, as if having already thought it out.

"How tall are you?" asked Dan. "Five feet?"

"Hmmpf," she said indignantly. "I'm five feet two inches, I'll have you know!"

"How many men do you see running around that are that short?"

"Wel-l-l-l . . . some!"

"Besides," said Dan with a grin, "in a man's clothes, you still wouldn't look like a man!"

Dorianne's lovely face crimsoned.

Dan was quiet for a moment. Then he said, "Little lady, I want you to know something."

Her big brown eyes raised to meet his.

"I appreciate the willingness you have shown to try to help a man who just three days ago you didn't even know existed."

"Oh, but that's not true," Dorianne said, shaking her head. "My father used to talk about Dan Colt, the gunfighter. I never heard anything about you allegedly being ambushed and buried in Kansas. I suppose Daddy was killed before that story came out. You were one of his heroes. I remember how he used to say that Dan Colt was like a well-oiled machine: smooth, fast and deadly."

"What was your father's name?" asked Dan. "Where did you live?"

"Henry Kates," replied the beautiful Dorianne. "Mother's name was Linda. We lived in Colorado. Southwest of Denver, about seventy miles. Town in the mountains called Manitou Springs."

"Know exactly where it is," said Dan.

"Daddy was an assayer there. He had a good business with the gold and silver being mined all over that area. Then the Utes went on a rampage and killed both my parents. That was six years ago. I moved to Tucson then to live with my uncle."

Sam Kates wiped muddy sweat and gave the girl a dirty look.

The stage rolled on as the sun rose higher and became hotter. At times the vehicle jolted, swayed and bounced on the rock-studded road. At other times it ran smoothly across flatlands where the dust was usually thicker.

Dorianne stared out the window at the monotonous terrain. Once she saw a diamondback rattlesnake sunning itself on a dark red rock. Another time she saw a lone buzzard eye the stagecoach from its lofty perch on the limb of a dead tree.

The dusty breeze whipping through the coach soon took its toll on Dorianne's upswept hairdo. Little strands began to work loose around the nape of her neck. From time to time she would wet the tips of her fingers with her tongue, attempting to keep the stubborn wisps in place. Finally she gave up and pulled out the long hairpins. Her thick, dark hair fell down in swirls around her shoulders.

Dan Colt had been watching her with interest. Their eyes met as she fluffed the thick tresses with her fingers.

"Traveling isn't the best thing for a woman's appearance," she said with a prim smile.

"It'd take a whole lot of traveling to hurt your appearance," Dan said, running his fingers through his thick mustache.

Just past noon the stage began to slow, topped a rise, bounded through a dry wash and came to a halt in front of an adobe shack. Next to the shack was a sun-bleached barn sided by a pole-fenced corral. Seven horses stood lazily in the sun. One of them nickered as the stage rolled to a stop. The nicker was returned by one of the animals in the team.

"Okay," announced Zeke Collier, "this is the Red Mesa way station. Climb out and stretch your limbs!"

The six passengers worked their way out of the cramped quarters into the bright glare. The sun was fierce, like someone laying a hot metal plate on your head. There was no shade except inside the station house. Quickly they filed inside.

A light meal was provided, which was devoured in relative silence. In the stuffy, heat-filled room it seemed that talking only made a person sweat more. The driver and shotgunner finished quickly and excused themselves. They would hitch up the fresh team, they said, and the passengers should come out in ten minutes.

It was evident that Jake Finch was still nursing a headache. His jaw was slightly blue where Dan's fist had made its impact. The outlaw was morose and quiet.

The ten minutes passed and the passengers moved back out into the blazing sun and boarded the stage. Zeke Collier cracked his whip, let out his unceremonious yell and the coach jerked forward. The Red Mesa station disappeared in the dust behind, and the iron-tired wheels took up their tedious drone. The sun tilted westward and grew hotter. More dust added to the discomfort of the Butterfield passengers.

The day wore on. Dan Colt pondered his predicament. He must find a way to escape from Tanner and Proffitt. But he would have to wait until they took the stage from Fort Apache. It was there that Dorianne and her uncle would take the stage for Tucson, while the lawmen and prisoners would take another one for Yuma.

The dust-covered stagecoach wound its way up the steep grades and over the Continental Divide. The stage stopped for twenty minutes in a little town called Thoreau, to let the horses rest and take their fill of water.

Once again in motion, the passengers mopped brown sweat and rolled with the swaying movements of the vehicle. Time drifted by slowly. At last the sun began to dip behind the long, rock-crested plateaus in the distance. Dorianne Kates peered out the window through the yellow dust haze swirling about the stage. The shadowy outline of Gallup, New Mexico, took form against the orange hue of the sunset.

It was nearly dark when Zeke Collier pulled his stagecoach to a halt on Gallup's only street. The Butterfield office was next door to the Wells Fargo office. The Fargo office was closed.

As the dust settled, a wiry little man came out of the Butterfield office, smiling broadly. "Howdy, Zeke, Hec!"

Both men responded with a friendly greeting.

Dan Colt stepped out first, as usual, linked to Logan Tanner. The big marshal waited while Colt assisted tiny Dorianne. They mounted the boardwalk. Dan squinted down the street through the gathering gloom. His eyes focused on the gun shop. It was in front of the gun shop that he had shot and killed a young greenhorn gunslick who had challenged him. *What was his name? Oh, yeah . . . Cletus Barnum.*

Logan Tanner spoke to Sam Kates. "Mr. Kates, you can take

your niece down to the Casa Grande Hotel. Restaurant has pretty good food. Tell the clerk Proffitt and I will each need a room. I'm gonna bunk Finch and Sundeen at the local jail for the night. First thing I gotta do is roust the Wells Fargo agent out and see if he can get all of us on tomorrow morning's stage."

Hec Mann was on the top of the stagecoach, dropping luggage to Zeke Collier and the skinny little Butterfield agent. Speaking to the little man, Tanner said, "Sir, would you know where I might find the Fargo agent?"

"Yessir, Marshal," replied the little man, eyeing the badge and the handcuffs. "He lives right up there above the office. Name's Harley Beeker. Just bang on the office door good 'n loud. He'll come down."

"Thanks," said Tanner.

As Sam and Dorianne Kates waited for their luggage to come off the stage, the fat man said, "Marshal, we'll only need our small handbags for the night. Would you see that the Fargo agent keeps the rest till morning?"

"Sure will," said the federal man with a nod.

Turning to Steve Proffitt, Tanner said, "Why don't you go ahead and walk Jake down to the jail? Tell the sheriff I'll be along with Dave in a few minutes."

Proffitt nodded and ushered Finch down the boardwalk. A silver-haired man was working his way along the street, lighting the street lamps. He watched with curiosity as lawman and prisoner passed by.

Logan Tanner threw a glance to the lighted window just above the Wells Fargo office. "Tell you what, Dave," he said. "Think I'll cuff you to this here lamp post while I talk with the agent. You may be tall, but you'd have to be at least seven feet to reach over it."

Sam Kates was ready to take his niece to the hotel just as Tanner was linking Colt's arms around the lamppost. Dorianne stepped close and said, "Marshal, you said Dan and I would have a few minutes to talk when we got here. Could we do so right now?"

Tanner smiled. "Yes'm. He isn't goin' anywhere till I get back. Talk his leg off if you want to."

The girl turned toward Sam Kates. "I'm going to be here a few minutes, Uncle. You can go on ahead."

Without comment Kates left Dorianne's small bag on the boardwalk and headed for the hotel.

Logan Tanner hammered on the Wells Fargo door and soon produced agent Harley Beeker. The luggage, plus the sawed-off shotgun, box of shells and leather harness were carted into the Fargo office.

"Why don't you sit down?" Dan asked the lovely girl, pointing to the board sidewalk with his chin.

"I'd rather stand," responded Dorianne. "Been sitting all day."

Zeke Collier approached the couple. "Time to say good-bye," he said in a friendly manner. Throwing a glance to where Logan Tanner stood inside the office, he said, "Just between you 'n' me, son, I think Mr. Big Marshal has the wrong man. I hope you get away."

Dan smiled.

Collier winked at Dorianne. "But I hope *you* catch him, honey."

The girl's face colored, but it was too dark for anyone to see.

The Butterfield stage rattled away. The lamplighter had worked his way toward the couple and with his long pole was igniting the next lamp up the street. Slowly he approached the post to which Dan Colt was shackled. A strange look etched itself on his face as he studied the situation.

"Excuse me," said the old gentleman, pushing the burning tip of the pole up under the lampshade. A spray of yellow light instantly encircled the area. Backing off, the aged man took one more look at Dan's predicament, then said to Dorianne, "Tell you one thing, girlie . . . if'n I was your man, you wouln't have to do that to keep *me* from leavin' ya! Purty as *you* are, I'd stick to you like horse-hoof glue!"

Dan and Dorianne laughed as the old gent shuffled along toward the next lamp post.

Lifting her large brown eyes to the face of the tall man, she said, "Dan, I'm sorry if I embarrassed you last night. I really never intended to let my feelings become public knowledge. I know it wasn't very ladylike. But my emotions got away from me. All of this is so unfair. What a horrible nightmare it must be for you." Taking hold of his arm, she said, "But I do love you."

"Little lady," said Dan tenderly, "you haven't known me long enough to be sure of that. It's just that I came along and showed you some kindness. You have merely responded to that because it is a contrast to the treatment you have received from your uncle."

"The kindness I appreciate," said Dorianne. "But a woman knows her own heart."

Dan bit his lip. "But—"

"I know you loved Mary very much, Dan. I'm sure losing her was the most horrible thing you've ever experienced. But you will fall in love again someday. I would like to be around when you do. Maybe it could be me."

"But Dorianne," protested the handsome man, "I'm a mighty poor risk. What woman would want a life lovin' a man that always has to stay a day's ride ahead of the law?"

"All of that will be over—" Dorianne stopped to watch two rough-looking cowboys ride slowly by. One of them twisted around in his saddle and studied Dan's face. He swore and said something to his partner. Quickly they rode up the street.

"That man acted like he knew you," said the dark-haired beauty.

"Possible," said Dan idly.

"As I was saying," continued Dorianne, "when Dave is brought in, all your law-dodging will be over. You can go back to living a normal life."

Colt grinned weakly. "I'm a gunfighter, Dorianne," he said, looking into her dark eyes. "There's no such thing as a normal life. Gunfighters live and die with the smell of gunsmoke."

"But you had five normal years with Mary."

"Let's just say they were the best years," said Dan, "but they were not normal. Every time a stranger rode onto the place, I cringed, thinking it might be some gunhawk who had found out where I was. I lived with the dread I might have to buckle on my guns again. On every trip into Fort Laramie I feared meeting some greenhorn who would recognize me and force a shoot-out."

"But I thought you had hung up your guns. A man can't force gunplay if you're not wearing a gun."

"There are ways to make a man unhang 'em," commented Dan huskily.

"I don't care how abnormal life would be," said Dorianne Kates. "I would live for our moments together, and if Dan Colt loved me, I would make every moment count."

Dan slowly shook his head. "Dorianne, listen. I'm better than ten years older than you."

A pert smile curled her lovely mouth. "So when you're a hundred, I'll be ninety. What difference will it make?"

Dan snickered. "Little lady, gunfighters don't live to be a hundred, they—"

Logan Tanner stormed out the office door, fuming and swearing. When he realized Dorianne was still standing there, the foul language quickly became euphemisms.

Eyeing the girl, then Colt, he said, "You two through talkin'?"

"Looks like we're through, even if we're not finished," said the girl. "What's the matter, Marshal?"

"Apaches are killin' everything in sight," replied Tanner with disgust. "Wells Fargo is stoppin' all stagecoaches 'tween here and Fort Apache till the army gets 'em stopped."

"Does that mean we stay here?" queried Dan.

"Agent says there's one last stage goin' to Eternity tomorrow. Apaches are expected to hit there soon. Stage has a load of rifles and ammunition that has to get through if the people of Eternity are goin' to make a stand."

"And . . . ?" said Colt.

"Kates and the girl will have to stay here. The rest of us will be on that last stage to Eternity."

CHAPTER ELEVEN

Sam Kates's face was red as the sunrise. "And just why not, Tanner?" he demanded, eyes bulging.

"Because it's too risky, that's why," snapped the big marshal. "I've got enough to worry about just gettin' my deputy and two prisoners to Fort Apache with their scalps intact. I don't need you and the girl to look out for, too."

"We'll look out for ourselves," said the fat man.

"Is Dorianne getting a vote in this?"

"She'll do what I say."

"And you'll do what *I* say," said Tanner with a note of finality. "You two will stay here until this Indian killin' spree is stopped."

"I thought you said the stage was only going as far as Eternity," said Kates caustically. "What's this about Fort Apache?"

Logan Tanner rubbed his mustache. "I had it arranged for a cavalry unit to escort us through Indian territory. Seems that territory has spread its borders. Once I get you out of my hair, I'm headin' for the telegraph office and see about havin' a unit meet us at Eternity and accompany us safely to the fort. From that point we'll go horseback to Yuma."

"If the girl and I were at Fort Apache," argued Sam Kates, "we would be that much closer to Tucson when the stages start rolling."

"That could be some time, Kates," said Tanner.

"I have faith in the United States Cavalry, Marshal," said the fat man with conviction. "They'll have those redskins under control in short order. Now, I've got a business to run and I can't run it sitting here."

"You can't run it if you're dead, either," parried the big lawman. "You're staying here. That's final."

Sam Kates stomped away in a huff. Logan Tanner headed toward the telegraph office.

It was nearly noon when the stagecoach stood before the Wells Fargo office, ready to travel. In the rack on top was a rectangular wooden box containing twenty Winchester .44 seven-shot repeaters and four cases of cartridges. The rest of the rack was empty. The mail sack and Logan Tanner's gear were in the boot.

The driver, a thin little man of sixty, was listening as Sam Kates stood arguing on the boardwalk with the Fargo agent. The lovely Dorianne stood nearby, dressed to travel. Looking up the street, she saw Tanner and Proffitt escorting the two prisoners toward the stage. A wagonbed of Navajo Indians rolled by, its occupants staring at the shiny handcuffs linking the lawmen to the prisoners.

"Looks like Kates is determined," said Tanner, setting his gaze on the scene in front of the office.

"Two bits says they're goin' with us, Marshal," clipped Steve Proffitt out of the side of his mouth.

"No bet," came Tanner's rejoinder. "The man's smart enough to know that everything I've said is a bluff. There's really no way I can stop him."

The shotgunner came out of the Fargo office carrying Sam and Dorianne's luggage. The skinny little driver scrambled up top and began laying them in place as the shotgunner passed the pieces up to him.

The agent had the look of a browbeaten husband. Sam Kates had the light of triumph in his eyes as Tanner approached. Giving the marshal no time to speak, he said, "The girl and I are going, Tanner. I've paid the fare and you have no legal right—"

"Okay, okay!" spoke up Tanner. Turning to Dorianne, he said, "Miss Kates, you don't have to go. You could wait here. I can see to it."

Dorianne set her eyes on Dan Colt and, holding them there, spoke to Tanner, "It's all right, Marshal. I want to."

Dan said, "Dorianne, it's really dangerous. I would feel better if you *would* stay here. Apaches are not kind to white women."

Oblivious of the bystanders, the beautiful girl said, "Dan, I want to be with you as long as possible. I'll take my chances."

"Girl's got grit," spoke up Jake Finch. "Too bad she has to waste her love on a saddle bum like you, Colt."

Dan fixed the outlaw with an icy stare.

The Wells Fargo agent cut in. "Marshal, did you make contact with the fort?"

"Yep," said Tanner. "There's a platoon gonna meet us at Cathedral Rock, 'bout twenty miles north of Eternity. They're bivouacked at Concho right now. Apaches hit Concho yesterday."

"How far is Concho from here, Marshal?" asked Dorianne.

"I'm not sure, exactly," said Tanner.

"Exactly ninety miles, miss," put in the stagecoach driver.

Smiling at the little man, she said, "How far to this Catherdral Rock?"

"About fifty miles, Miss," he smiled back.

Speaking to Logan Tanner, Dorianne said, "Then we've really only got fifty miles of danger between here and Fort Apache."

"It's not that simple," responded the big marshal. "If the Apaches have the numbers, they could wipe out a cavalry escort."

"What are we standing around here for?" asked Sam Kates. "Let's move out."

The driver threw Kates a look of disdain, then extended his bony hand to Logan Tanner. "My name's Early Byrd, Marshal." Nodding at the shotgunner as they shook hands, he said, "This is Larry Fields."

Fields was twenty-three, tall and rawboned. He grinned and met Tanner's grasp.

Introductions made the rounds, with Colt and Finch being ignored. Byrd took note of it and gave the prisoners a toothless smile. "My handle's Early Byrd, fellas. First name's really Earl, but me ole mammy used to call me Early. 'at's cuz I came two months early when I was borned. So it stuck. On'y problem is, some smart aleck's always askin' if I eat worms for breakfast. Truth is, I eats tobaccy!" With that Byrd pulled a tobacco plug from his shirt pocket and broke off a chaw with his gums.

"I'm Jake Finch," the outlaw said darkly.

"My name's Dan Colt," said the blond man.

"Yeah," laughed Byrd, rolling the chaw in his mouth, "and I'm Bat Masterson! Haw! Haw!"

"His name's Dave Sundeen," said Logan Tanner coldly. "Wanted in three states and several territories. Yuma jailbird, just like Finch here."

"Well," said Byrd, "we'd best be stirrin' dust if'n we gonna meet them troopers at Cathedral Rock. Gotta git them rifles up there in the rack to them folks at Eternity!" Five minutes later the stagecoach leaped forward as Early Byrd cracked his whip with a "Hee-yaah!" that sounded just like that of Zeke Collier. Dan Colt smiled at Dorianne and said, "If I didn't know better, I'd swear those drivers all graduated from the same school."

As the Wells Fargo vehicle rocked back and forth and Gallup fell behind, Logan Tanner said, "We might as well make plans in case we encounter some Apaches." Looking at Dorianne, he said, "If they attack, Miss Kates, you dive for the floor. You'll be safer there. You fellas lift your feet so she can get down."

"Seems to me," said Sam Kates, wiping brown sweat already, "we ought to break out those rifles up top. Be better protection than your handguns or my Derringer."

"Wouldn't be a bad idea," agreed Steve Proffitt.

"I'd be glad to use one," said Jake Finch.

"Yeah," said Tanner. "On my back."

"We might be wishin' everyone in here had a rifle," said Colt.

"You two'll play fire gettin' guns," rasped the thick-bodied US marshal.

A half-hour passed. Logan Tanner wiped sweat from his worried features. The swaying vehicle rounded a curve that ran through some high rock formations. The passage was narrow, forcing the coach to slow down.

Suddenly Early Byrd yanked on the reins as four men ran into the narrow path, guns leveled on himself and Larry Fields.

"We ain't carryin' no money!" exclaimed Byrd.

"We ain't after no money!" shouted one of the men. "We want that big blond dude you got on board!"

Fields lifted his empty hands, his eyes scouring the tops of the rocks on both sides of the passage. There were more guns trained on the coach than he cared to count. Quietly he said, "Early, they got an army. Tell the marshal to forget tryin' to resist. They'll cut us down like fish in a barrel."

The man who had spoken out stepped forward. To the toothless driver he said, "Hey, skinny, you tell that big-bellied marshal I'm comin' in to talk. Anybody starts any gunplay, we'll make that coach look like a sieve."

Immediately Byrd eyed the muzzles aimed his way from the rocks and said, "Marshal Tanner!"

Tanner was already pushing Dan Colt through the door, trying to get himself out to see what was going on.

"Marshal Tanner!" repeated Early from his perch up top, "don't start no gunplay! They's a whole passel of guns aimed at us from all directions!"

Tanner scanned the rugged skyline, then turned his attention to the spokesman who approached, gun in hand. The US marshal swore. "What's goin' on here?" he bellowed.

"We're takin' one of your prisoners, lawman," came the answer. "We want that tall dude that's cuffed to you."

Tanner swung a hard look at Dan Colt. "Jake ain't got nothin' on you, eh? You've got your own gang of killers, too!"

"I never saw these birds before," said Colt frigidly.

"You give us Dan Colt, Marshal, and you can ride away unmolested after you and the folks on the stage witness a little quick-draw contest."

Logan Tanner's face knotted quizzically. "What in blue blazes are you talkin' about, mister?"

Waving the muzzle of his six-gun, the hard-faced man said, "Hurry up and get those cuffs loose."

"You're makin' a mistake," said Tanner loudly. "This man's name is Dave Sundeen, not Dan Colt."

"Ain't never heard of no Sundeen, Marshal, but a few weeks ago Dan Colt squared off with a gunhawk up Pagosa Springs way. Outdrew him and killed him dead. That gunhawk was Herb Kline, Marshal. Ever hear of Herb Kline?"

"Yeah," replied Tanner. "Reputation of bein' one of the fast ones."

"He was, Marshal," said the man, adjusting his hat brim against the brilliant sun. "Kline found out Mr. Dan Colt wasn't dead like the story was bein' told. He was alive and campin' outside of

Pagosa Springs. You know how it is with gunslicks, Marshal. Kline had a hankerin' to move up the ladder of fame. He had that green monster eatin' at his gut. Just had to challenge Colt."

Tanner turned to Dan. "This so? You kill Herb Kline?"

"Yep," nodded Dan.

The man continued. "We got another hawk wants to square off with him here and now."

"You're interfering with justice, mister," hissed Tanner, his face florid with anger. "I am a federal officer. This man is an escaped criminal. I am taking him back to prison at Yuma."

"Apparently your hearing is fogged up, lawman," said the outlaw. "I said *off with the cuffs*! Now you can cooperate and make it easy on yourself . . . or you can play stubborn and we'll just shoot everything includin' the horses. Dan Colt is goin' up against my brother fair and square."

"Who's your brother?" asked Dan.

"Man soon to be the undisputed fast-draw champeen of the West," said the outlaw. "Cabe Terrell."

Dan Colt's pale blue eyes registered recognition.

"Ah," said the hard-faced man, "you've heard of Cabe. Name put a little tingle in your spine, does it? Well, I'm Vince Terrell, Cabe's big brother. I'll tell you this, Colt—Cabe's faster'n a gambler's wink. You've dropped a lot of men in their tracks, but today's *your* day to drop in yours." An impatient look crept over his face. "Now, Marshal, you cooperate and be a nice man. After everybody on the stage and all my boys witness Cabe put down Dan Colt, you can take his corpse and tell the world what you saw."

Logan Tanner tensed. Dan touched the marshal's arm with his free hand. "You're gonna have to do it, Tanner," said Dan calmly. "Cabe Terrell has been workin' his way up. He's a big leaguer now. Vince'll keep his word. His brother just wants an audience. If you act stubborn, you'll just get yourself and everybody on the stage killed."

Tanner's feet twisted in the sand. "So what do I do if he kills you?"

"Take my body and head for Eternity . . . I'll already be there."

"This is no time to be funny," snapped Tanner. "My big

problem comes if *you* kill *him*. Then I've got you with a gun in your hand. Huh-uh. There's gotta be another way."

"Enough talk!" yelled Vince Terrell. "Get those cuffs off him!"

"Now look," retorted Tanner heatedly, "you're treadin' on federal ground, Terrell. Now you back off and ride away and I'll forget this ever happened. But if you—"

Logan Tanner's words were cut short by the roar of a Colt .45 from behind Vince. Tanner's hat left his head and sailed to the ground behind him. The six-up team shied, startled by the sound of the gun. Early Byrd held the reins tight and gripped the brake handle.

Cabe Terrell stepped up beside his brother, smoke drifting from the muzzle of his gun. He glared hungrily at Dan Colt.

Dorianne Kates looked wide-eyed through the coach window. The US marshal clenched his jaw angrily. Dan saw it and said hastily, "Tanner, you fool! Okay, I'll give you my word. After I kill Cabe I'll give the gun back to his brother."

"Your solemn oath?"

"Yep."

The big marshal eyed Vince, then Cabe. "I have your word that you'll not harm anyone on this stage if I let you have Colt?"

Cabe Terrell holstered his gun and raised his right hand. "On my mother's grave," he said, a cynical smile twisting his thin lips.

Tanner stared hard at Vince.

"Yeah, same here," said Vince.

"What about when Colt kills Cabe?" asked Tanner.

"*If* he kills me," said Cabe with a laugh, "I will personally see to it that everyone goes free, Marshal!"

Laughter spread among the gang.

"Either way, Marshal, you and the rest of the passengers ride away. Even Dan Colt. Dead or alive. You're not in a bargaining position, but you have my word on it."

Tanner turned toward the coach. "Steve! Get everybody off the stage. Bring me the key!"

Dorianne Kates was first to move. As she stepped to the ground, a series of whistles filled the hot morning air.

"Hey, Charlie!" called one of the gang to another. "She's even a better looker than you said!"

"Maybe we oughtta take her with us!" came an unidentified voice up in the rocks.

"The girl stays with the stage," said Vince to Colt.

Steve Proffitt unbuttoned the pocket on his vest and produced the key. Tanner took it from his fingers and unlocked the handcuffs. Dan immediately rubbed his wrist.

"All right, everybody," said Vince Terrell loudly, "let's walk out in the open area to the rear of these rocks. That includes you, too, driver. And your gunner. Leave your weapons up there."

Tanner and Proffitt were relieved of their guns, which were tossed inside the stagecoach. The men in the rocks scrambled down and trained their rifles on the crew and passengers as Cabe Terrell rounded the tall rocks to where the gang's horses were stashed.

Dan stepped close to Dorianne and said, "See what I mean about a normal life?"

The gunslinger appeared bearing a Colt .45 in a well-used and heavily oiled black holster. The broad matching belt was wrapped around it, thong dangling. "I know you're used to two irons, Mr. Colt," said Cabe, "but you'll have to go with one. We're fresh out of dual holsters."

"'s okay," said Dan. "One'll be enough." Strapping it on and tying the leather thong to his muscular leg, he said, "Mind if I get the feel of it?"

A dozen muzzles were swung on him as Dan whipped the gun from its holster, broke the action and checked the loads.

"It's all on the up-and-up, Colt," Cabe Terrell said dryly. "When I kill the great Dan Colt, I want all these folks to tell everybody it was fair and square."

Turning his back to Terrell, Dan did a few fast draws to get the feel of the holster. The gun was the same model as his own twin Colts. Heft and balance were the same. The gun was used and well oiled. Cabe hadn't been lying. As he turned around, Dan caught a glimpse of Dorianne Kates's pallid face. She was scared.

Dan smiled at the girl, then faced Cabe Terrell. "Okay, Cabe," he said frigidly, "pick the spot where you want to die."

Terrell sneered wordlessly and backed up until the two men stood forty feet apart.

Dan Colt had lost count of how many times he had stood in this same position. Some gunfighters notched their guns. Dan had never bothered. What difference did it make how many men he had killed? The important thing was that he had been the one to walk away.

The tall, blond Colt had never underestimated an opponent. That could get you killed in a hurry. He faced each challenger as if the man were top-ranked. However, Dan was never short on self-confidence. A man had to believe in himself. If he didn't he'd better pack his bags and get out of this raw, savage country real fast.

Cabe Terrell went into a low-crouch stance. Dorianne Kates swallowed hard as Terrell barked, "Go for your gun, Colt!"

"You're the challenger, Cabe," said Dan thinly and waited, right hand dangling loosely over the deadly weapon on his hip.

There was no signal in Cabe Terrell's cold eyes. His hand darted downward. No one saw the invisible hand of Dan Colt until the gun roared.

The .45 slug slammed into Cabe Terrell's chest, knocking him down. His own gun slid from his lifeless fingers as a crimson stain spread through the cloth on his pulseless breast.

Dorianne bounded to Dan, who stood holding the smoking gun. Placing her head on his chest, she wrapped her arms around his slender waist and wept.

Stunned, Vince Terrell and his men silently picked up the dead man, draped him on his horse, mounted and slowly rode away. Not one of them even looked back.

Logan Tanner edged warily toward Dan, who held the gun in one hand and the back of Dorianne's head with the other. While the girl sobbed, Dan eyed the marshal, flipped the gun in the air and caught it by the barrel. As Tanner took it, Early Byrd spoke up. " 'at oughtta convince ennybody in his right mind 'at you are the real genu-wine article, mister! Yesiree! Dan Colt! Whew! Faster'n a mother-in-law's tongue! Ennybody," he repeated, shaking his head. "Ennybody in his right mind!"

Dan eyed Logan Tanner with a frosty stare. "Guess you know where that puts you, Tanner."

CHAPTER TWELVE

Harry Doyle mopped sweat with his shirt sleeve as he spoke to his four partners in the oven-hot jail of Los Alamos. "It'll work, boys. This hick-town marshal doesn't even know which side of the bed to crawl out of."

Doyle, Mulligan and Perryman were crowded into one cell while Elbert and Lewis shared the other one. The small jail reeked with the smell of unbathed bodies.

"Bet Jake'll be mighty glad to see us," said Pat Lewis.

"Yeah, surprised, too!" laughed Tommy Elbert.

"Main thing we gotta do is catch 'em before they join up with them troopers," said Harry Doyle.

A blistering hour passed.

"Ain't he ever comin' back?" asked Skinny Mulligan impatiently.

"He'll be back," said Doyle. "As soon as he hits that door, you stick your finger down your throat."

"Will do," said Skinny. "I used to do this with my breakfast as a kid. Ma sure thought I was sick. Kept me out of school lotsa times."

Suddenly the office door of the jail opened out front.

"Go to it, Skinny!" whispered Harry Doyle.

In the office Marshal Rex Chase took off his hat, wiped his glistening brow and cursed the heat. From the cell area in the back he heard a stomach-churning, gagging sound. The mixed voices of four prisoners began shouting, "Marshal! Skinny's sick! Marshal! Come quick!"

Chase ran back, took one look and hurried to the office. As he grabbed the keys, Dink Perryman hollered, "Hurry, Marshal! Skinny needs a doctor!"

Chase held his nose and turned the key in the lock.

The Wells Fargo stage bounded southwest and soon crossed the New Mexico–Arizona border.

The blazing sun lifted higher in the sky, forcing the temperature up inside the coach. The infernal dust hovered among the passengers like a brown cloud. Dorianne Kates fanned her face with a small fan produced from her handbag. She smiled at Dan Colt. "It was a horrible thing to watch, but you really are something with a gun. You ever think about being a lawman, Dan?"

"I've substituted a couple of times when a town was in need," replied the tall man, "but wearin' a badge just isn't for me."

"Man has to walk straight to be a lawman," spoke up Logan Tanner from under his hat.

"I've known a few that didn't," said Colt.

"By the way, Mr. Tanner," said Dorianne, "you called your prisoner Colt back there."

"That was just for the Terrell brothers' sake," responded Tanner, adjusting his hat over his sweaty face. "Don't bother me. Can't you see I'm tryin' to sleep?"

"He sure whipped out that gun like the Dan Colt I used to hear my father talk about," said Dorianne. "You have to admit Dan is quite a gunfighter."

Logan Tanner lifted his hat and bolted the girl with a hard look. "Dave Sundeen *is* quite a gunfighter, ma'am."

"He had that gun in his hand, Mr. Tanner," pressed Dorianne. "He could have shot you and walked away."

The big lawman lifted his hat again. "He gave me his word."

"Well, if he was an outlaw, like you seem to think, he—"

"Strange as it may seem, miss," cut in Tanner, "even outlaws have a code of ethics."

"But what was there to keep him fr—"

"My dear Miss Kates," blurted the marshal, sitting up and

112

glaring at her, "you may be blinded by love, but I am not! You can call him Dan Colt and write love letters to him while he's behind bars all you want, but all your passionate pleas are not gonna change anything. I'm lockin' Dave Sundeen up in Yuma."

At high noon Larry Fields punched Early Byrd and pointed at the tip of Cathedral Rock jutting upward on the horizon. Byrd smiled and showed his gums.

"Cathedral Rock dead ahead!" shouted Fields to those in the coach.

Dan Colt leaned out the window and squinted against the glare.

"See any sign of the troopers?" asked Tanner.

"Not close enough yet," answered the blond man. "Can only see the top of the rock."

"What do we do if the troopers aren't there?" asked Steve Proffitt.

"We'll keep pushin' toward Eternity," said Tanner. "Sittin' still sure won't help us."

"How do you plan to make it all the way across Arizona with your prisoners, Marshal?" queried Sam Kates. "Won't the Apaches spot you and leave your bodies to the buzzards?"

"Four men on horseback can slip through a lot easier than a dust-ballin' stagecoach, Kates," said the Marshal.

"For your sake and Proffitt's, I hope so," commented the obese man.

A torrid hour passed. The Wells Fargo stagecoach slowed down, then began a perfect circle around the towering red rock formation. The passengers leaned toward the windows, studying the giant, cathedral-shape rock.

Heaps of massive, sun-blistered red rocks lay around its base, evidence that at one time the rock stood even taller. Some primitive shaking of the earth had clipped off its pinnacle and toppled it to the ground, shattering it into hundreds of pieces.

The dust-laden stagecoach completed its circle and hauled up beside scattered boulders in the slender shade of the great rock. Early set the brake and climbed down. Pulling open the door, he

113

said, "C'mon out, folks. Looks like the cavalry's runnin' a bit late. Not even a sign of 'em toward the south."

Logan Tanner followed Dan Colt out the door, growling under his breath.

"Gotta let the animals catch their breath, Marshal," said the wiry little driver. "We'll be here about an hour."

Larry Fields took water from the barrels on the side of the vehicle and watered the horses. The passengers took their fill of the warm liquid from the community canteen and placed it back in the coach. Byrd and Fields drank from the canteen up top.

While Larry fed oats to the lathered team, lawmen, prisoners, uncle and niece sought relief from the merciless sun in the shade of the giant rock. Logan Tanner spotted Byrd climbing a huge boulder, shading his red-rimmed eyes and studying the southern horizon. Then the little man descended to the burning sand and began walking a wide circle around the base of the rock.

"C'mere, Sundeen," said Tanner, leading Dan Colt toward the stagecoach. "I'm gonna chain you to the coach. I want to talk to Byrd."

Reaching the vehicle, Tanner suddenly remembered that there was only one key to the handcuffs . . . and Steve Proffitt had it. Swearing mildly, the big marshal lifted his voice and called toward the spot where the group sat in the shade, "Steve! I need the key!"

As Proffitt started to get up, Dorianne jumped to her feet. "I'll take it to him, Mr. Proffitt," she said, extending her hand. "No sense in two of you getting up when I can go easier."

Proffitt pulled the small key from his vest pocket and gently laid it in Dorianne's hand. "Thanks," he said, managing a dusty smile.

As she walked away, Jake Finch said, "She's gorgeous even when she's sticky and dirty."

"I guess you noticed," said Steve. "I'm Mr. Proffitt and Tanner's prisoner is Dan."

"She ain't sweet on you," said the dark-eyed outlaw.

"Don't I know it," said the deputy. "Lucky Colt has her heart."

"He ain't so lucky. What good'll it do him? Time he gets out of Yuma, she'll be married to some other lucky dude."

Steve Proffitt said nothing to Jake Finch, but there was an unnamed feeling building up inside him. He doubted that Dan Colt was going to reach Yuma. The absence of the cavalry unit was haunting him. He wondered if any of them would make it through this hostile territory without their escort.

The deputy's thoughts were punctured by Jake's gravelly voice. "You really *are* convinced he's Dan Colt, ain'tcha?"

"Huh?"

"You called him Colt a minute ago."

Proffitt snickered, fingering away a trickle of sweat that ran down his temple. "After watchin' him slap leather against Cabe Terrell, I have no doubt of it."

"Then there *is* an outlaw named Sundeen who is Colt's twin?"

"Has to be."

"Then why don't you do somethin' to free him?"

Steve Proffitt thought on Finch's question for a long moment. "It has crossed my mind. But I'd have to hog-tie Tanner, and I'd end up in prison myself for turning Colt loose. I can't prove his innocence any more than he can. So what good would it do?"

"Run off with him. Help him find his brother."

Proffitt set a quizzical gaze on the outlaw. "I thought you hated him, wanted to get even for his runnin' you back to Tanner."

Jake shook his head. "Every minute I'm around the *hombre*, I have more respect for him. He promised Tanner he'd hand over that gun after he killed Cabe. Did it to save our skins. Coulda walked away scot-free. Stood by his word."

"Yeah," agreed Proffitt, "he's some man."

The boiling sun was throwing its steaming rays on Early Byrd as he circumvented Cathedral Rock on foot. His slitted, furtive eyes scanned the shimmering desert, scouring knolls, rocks and bushes.

Logan Tanner caught up to him, his sweat-soaked shirt and vest clinging to his big, beefy body. "See anything, Early?"

"Nothin' but dried-out sand, cactus, rocks and more of it," replied the little man. "But that don't mean a whole lot. 'paches can rise right out of the desert with them wigglin' heat waves."

"You been ridin' this land a long time, Early?" asked the sweating marshal.

"Seventeen years, to be exact."

"You think the cavalry not bein' here is a bad sign?"

"No *thinkin'* about it, Marshal," said Byrd worriedly. "If the wire you got said they were in Concho and were going to meet us here at midday today, we got trouble. Concho ain't that far, and it is now way past midday."

Tanner removed his hat, sleeved away sweat and dropped it back on his big head. "Guess we just push on to Eternity, huh?"

"Yep. Gotta git them rifles to them people there."

As Byrd and Tanner slowly made their circle, Dan Colt stood beside the stagecoach, his wrists handcuffed around the door post. The sun had moved enough since Early had parked the coach so that Dan was now standing in direct sunlight. Dorianne stood next to him, fanning her glistening face.

"Little lady," said Colt, "why don't you go back over there and sit in the shade?"

"Because I want to be near you." The heat of the day and the strain of the trip did not hide the love light in her eyes.

Dan shook his head slowly. "Dorianne," he said in a dispirited tone, "you mustn't let yourself feel this way. There's a fine young man out there somewhere who'll be worthy of your love and affection . . . someone who'll make you a good husband. You saw me kill a man today. If I'm able to get away from Tanner somehow, I'll be on Dave's trail. There'll be more trigger-happy hopefuls along the way with the green monster eatin' out their insides."

"How does a woman change how she feels?" asked Dorianne, misty-eyed. "I love you, Dan Colt. Good or bad, right or wrong, I love you. I'm willing to wait for you to love me, as long as you don't shut me out of your life."

"It's not a case of shutting you out, Dorianne," said Dan tenderly. "Even if I were to fall head over heels in love with you, I'm still no good for you. Can't you see that?"

"Let me be the judge of that, Mr. Colt," she said, lifting a handkerchief to his glistening face and dabbing away the moisture.

Logan Tanner and Early Byrd came on the scene, talking loudly.

Lifting his voice, Tanner hollered, "All right, everybody! Restin' time's over. We gotta head for Eternity on our own!"

Dan was shackled once again to the marshal. The passengers returned to the hot stagecoach. Byrd and Fields stood beside the vehicle, scanning the horizon.

Dorianne set her eyes on Logan Tanner. "Marshal, do you think the Apaches attacked our escort?"

"I don't know, ma'am," answered Tanner. "Somethin' sure has held 'em up. They've had plenty of time to get here from Concho."

Worry etched itself on the girl's lovely face. "Without the escort we're easy prey, aren't we?"

Tanner bit his lip. Anxiety was evident in his steel-gray eyes.

"We'll make it all right, Miss Dorianne," said Steve Proffitt, forcing a note of encouragement into his voice.

"Tell you one thing, Tanner," spoke up Jake Finch. "If them stinkin' savages attack, I demand that you take off these cuffs and let me have a gun."

The big marshal guffawed. "You'll get a gun over my dead body!"

"That's the way I would prefer it," Finch said levelly.

Logan Tanner's face turned to granite. "You don't *demand* anything, Finch."

The outlaw's eyes flashed fire. "I got a right to defend myself!" he rasped.

Tanner's lips pulled tight. "You gave up your rights when you decided to break the law, bucko. Apaches or no Apaches, you're not gettin' a gun."

The coach rocked as Byrd and Fields climbed up to the driver's seat. Byrd released the brake and nudged the team in a tight circle. Harness rattled and wheels squeaked.

A heavy frown pulled at Dan Colt's features. "Tanner," he said blandly, "before this is over, you may be glad to stick *two* guns in his hands."

The stage moved toward the open desert, away from Cathedral Rock and the tumbled boulders.

117

"I can handle a rifle," said Dorianne. "My father taught me when I was twelve. I used to hunt rabbits on the Colorado plains."

"Think you can kill a human being?" asked Dan.

"Who said Apaches are human?" sneered Sam Kates sourly. "They're just savage beasts."

Dorianne brushed her uncle disgustedly with her eyes, then fixed them on the tall blond man. "If it's my life against theirs, Dan, the answer is yes."

"Well, you won't be usin' a gun, Miss Kates," huffed US Marshal Logan Tanner, "unless things get mighty sticky."

Dan eyed the marshal dimly. "She can probably outshoot the whole bunch of us."

Up top, Early Byrd raised his whip as the stagecoach pulled into the clear. At the same instant his attention was drawn to movement among the shimmering waves to the south. "Look, Larry," he said pointing.

Larry Fields breathed a swear word.

Abruptly the whip cracked and the vehicle lurched forward. Byrd was shouting at the horses at the top of his lungs. Suddenly the coach veered sharply, slamming Dan Colt and Dorianne Kates against the side. Steve Proffitt swung into the girl, with Jake Finch hurling solidly against him. The heavy weight of Logan Tanner, backed by fat Sam Kates, crushed Colt.

Logan Tanner swore vehemently. "What's that stupid idiot doin' up there?" he bawled.

As each person struggled to gain his balance, Jake Finch took advantage of the awkward moment to reach around Steve Proffitt and curl his fingers around the butt of the deputy's revolver.

Tanner shouted, "Steve! He's goin' for your gun!"

Before Proffitt could react, Finch had the weapon out of its holster.

Tanner's free hand was his right. He braced his heels against the bottom of the seat and swung his ponderous fist violently. It connected just behind the outlaw's left ear. Lights lit up in Finch's head. He was struggling to bring the gun around when the same fist smashed his jaw again. His eyes glassed over as the gun slipped from his fingers. The thick-shouldered lawman hit him yet again with all his strength.

Finch slumped over Proffitt's lap. The deputy hoisted Jake's limp frame upward, retrieved his gun and jammed it in his holster.

The stage was rocking heavily as it rolled back among the boulders and skidded to a halt at the base of Cathedral Rock. Logan Tanner shoved Dan toward the door. "Let's get out," he said roughly. "I want to find out what's—"

Byrd jumped down, and his scraggly face appeared at the open door. "Injuns!" he shouted. "Couple dozen of them red devils bearin' down on us hard!"

CHAPTER THIRTEEN

Larry Fields was already up on the rack, shoving the long wooden box over the edge. "Somebody take the rifles!" he yelled.

As Early Byrd responded, Steve Proffitt unlocked the cuffs on himself and the unconscious outlaw. By the time he had finished, the others had piled out of the coach. Quickly he dragged Finch across the burning sand and laid him behind a boulder. He yanked off a boot, handcuffed Jake's wrist to an ankle and hurried over to where Early had opened the box of Winchester repeaters.

The four cases of cartridges cracked open as Fields dumped them to the ground.

"Gimme your key, Steve," said Tanner hurriedly.

Proffitt flipped him the key. Tanner unlocked the cuff on his own wrist and said, "Take off your left boot, Sundeen."

Dan's brow furrowed.

"Gonna truss you up just like Steve did Finch," the marshal said through tight lips.

"Tanner," said Colt, eyes wide, "have you gone crazy?"

"Shut up."

"You need me, man," argued Dan. "Didn't you hear the little fella? He said a *couple dozen*!"

The indignant marshal whipped out his revolver. "We can do it one of two ways," he hissed, "easy or hard."

Dan soon found himself behind the same rock as Jake Finch. He watched as Logan Tanner instructed Dorianne how to load the

120

seven-shot repeaters. Early Byrd was barking orders, telling Fields, Proffitt and Kates where to take their places. They were fanning out behind the boulders, positioning themselves to prevent the Apaches from approaching unseen on foot from behind Cathedral Rock.

The thunder of galloping hoofs filled the hot, dry air now as Dorianne crouched behind a large boulder, jamming bullets into a brand-new Winchester. Logan Tanner again gruffly spoke his command for the girl to do no shooting unless he gave the order.

Murderous, savage cries and doglike yapping preceded the bark of rifles as the Apaches drew near. Their bronzed bodies on painted ponies stood out in contrast to the white sand and bleached rocks on the open area.

Nestled among the red boulders of Cathedral Rock, the five men opened fire. Apache bullets whined off the boulders and threw up dirt spurts in the enclosure. Dan Colt tried to work his way up the rock to get a view of the action, but his awkward predicament prevented it. Just then a vicious slug chewed the stone above his head, spraying him with rock fragments.

The six-up team tossed their heads, eyes bulging, and tugged against the brakes of the coach.

Amid the screeching of the circling Apaches and the guns roaring, Logan Tanner bellowed for Dorianne to bring him a loaded rifle. Dan watched the girl dive to the dirt, rifle in hand, and crawl to the marshal. Switching guns with him, she hastened back to answer the same call from Larry Fields.

An Indian screamed with pain, and suddenly they all galloped away.

"I got him!" shouted Sam Kates. "I got him!"

"No you didn't!" argued Early Byrd as the firing stopped. "I got him!"

Kates swore. "You did not! I had him dead center!"

"Aw, baloney!" shouted Byrd. "You couldn't hit a bloated bull in the behind with a busted banjo, Kates!"

"What difference does it make?" barked Logan Tanner. "The savage is dead. That's what counts."

The big marshal stood up and watched the Apaches gather about a half mile away. Steve Proffitt eyed the three dead Indians that lay sprawled on the hot sand.

"Can you bring me a fresh gun, missie?" asked Early. "Them red devils'll be back shortly."

Dorianne hurried to him, cast a glance in the direction of the Apaches, then returned to her place.

Jake Finch regained consciousness, cursing his predicament. His muddled eyes focused on the blond man sitting next to him. "What's goin' on, Colt?"

"Little Apache uprising," said Dan in a neutral tone.

Tanner threw a glance at the distant gathering and spoke to his deputy. "Steve, keep an eye on 'em."

Proffitt nodded, turned and narrowed his eyes against the glare.

The US marshal strode to where his prisoners lay in the sand. "I see you're back with us," he said to Finch.

Jake glared at him malignantly.

"Don't give me that look, bucko," said Tanner crustily. "You try to get your hands on another gun, I'll cave your skull in."

"How many Indians you fellas get, Tanner?" queried Colt.

"Three. None of us even scratched. Did it without *you*, too."

"You're not through yet," said Dan.

"How many out there?" The question came from Jake Finch as he tried to adjust himself to a more favorable position.

"Couple dozen, more or less," replied Tanner. "Whatever the number, there's three less now."

Finch squinted up at the mid-afternoon sun. "That many can wipe out five men before sundown, Tanner. Two more guns could make a difference."

The big lawman was about to speak when the shrill voice of the stagecoach driver pierced the air. "Marshal! C'mere!"

Tanner walked to where Early Bryd stood, his gaze fixed on the cluster of Apaches out on the desert. Tobacco-juice splatterings speckled the rocks nearby.

"What is it, Early?" asked Tanner.

Pointing, Byrd said, "See that big blue roan to the right of the rest of 'em?"

Tanner squinted. "Yeah."

"Savage on his back is Donimo."

"So who's Donimo?"

"You don't know?"

"I've been chasin' outlaws, Early," said the marshal. "My Indian fightin' has been a little sketchy."

"You've heard of Four Fingers?"

Logan Tanner nodded grimly. "Yeah. Old blood-and-guts himself."

"Donimo is Four Fingers's son. The old man and Geronimo are cousins. Four Fingers wanted to name his son after his famous cousin but dared not use the same name. So he settled for givin' it a similar sound."

Tanner nodded.

"Donimo is even more mean and bloodthirsty than his pa," said Early. "He won't settle for anything but wipin' us out, Marshal. We're cooked."

Tanner swore.

"Here they come again, Marshal!" shouted Steve.

Early spit and dropped behind his rock. Tanner made his way to his own position and picked up the rifle. The metal was blistering hot.

The Apaches came, whooping, yapping, screeching. A cloud of yellow dust raised behind the galloping ponies, hiding Donimo, who remained in the distance.

Dan called to the girl, "Dorianne, stay as low as you can when you're deliverin' those guns! First so you don't get hit. Second so the Apaches don't see you! They'll concentrate harder on breakin' through if they know you're in here!"

The girl nodded and managed a weak smile.

Hooves thundered and guns roared as the Apaches took up their incessant circling. Dorianne hunkered low, reloading rifles. Adeptly she thumbed cartridges into each magazine, jacked one into the chamber and began loading the next rifle.

Sam Kates was a short man. He found himself behind a boulder that was a little high when he was up on his knees. He fired and missed several times. Swearing, he looked around for a better spot. His eyes settled on the stagecoach. *Sure*, he told himself, *I could shoot better from the window of the stage. I'd be up higher.*

While bullets sang across the rock-strewn area, the fat man waddled toward the vehicle. Early Byrd saw him go. He shouted above the din, "No! Kates, don't get in there!"

Sam Kates showed no sign of hearing the warning. He plunged

123

into the coach and began firing from the window. His elevated position had no protection. The gun spitting fire from a new place drew the Apaches' attention.

Suddenly the dust-covered vehicle was alive with splitting wood, puffs of dust and holes appearing rapidly.

Sam's gun was abruptly silent. He raised up in spasmodic reaction to the hot lead ripping into his fleshy body and slumped headfirst out the window. His derby hat, punctured with several bulletholes, dropped to the ground. Kates's bloody head and one shoulder hung inertly against the windowsill.

Dorianne watched the scene, eyes wide, hand over her mouth.

While dust rose and the acrid smell of burned gunpowder filled the air, Dan Colt saw an Apache on foot bounding over the rock where Sam Kates had been stationed.

Before watching her uncle die, Dorianne had just jacked a cartridge into the chamber of a rifle. The savage had spied the girl and was headed for her.

"Dorianne!" shouted Dan, stiffening against his manacles.

The girl jerked her head up in time to see the red man coming. She raised the rifle and shot him in the stomach. He rolled over, rising to his knees, trying to lift his gun. Like a veteran, Dorianne worked the lever, shouldered the rifle and put a .44 slug between his eyes. He fell backward, one leg twisted underneath him.

Instantly another Apache leaped over the same rock. Momentarily he stumbled over his dead comrade, giving Dorianne time to work the lever again. The Winchester boomed and the second Apache dropped dead.

In a series of smooth motions the girl picked up boxes of cartridges from one of the broken cases and tossed two to each of the four men. "You'll have to load your own!" she hollered, diving to the spot where her uncle had hidden before he made his move toward the stagecoach. Too short to fire from her knees, Dorianne worked from a crouch.

Dan Colt started to cry out for her to stay hidden, but it was too late. She lined her sights on a yapping Apache in the thundering circle and squeezed the trigger. The savage peeled off his horse and flopped hard to the ground.

Colt and Jake Finch watched in awe as Dorianne Kates dropped two more Apaches in four shots.

Stationed about four yards to the girl's left was Larry Fields. While he lay low, reloading his rifle, he shouted, "Miss Dorianne, where did you learn to shoot like that?"

The girl did not answer. She was too busy.

Dorianne dropped down and reloaded. Just as she raised up to fire again, a bullet tore through Larry Fields's neck. He fell on his back, sightless eyes staring into the blue Arizona sky. The girl felt her stomach roll over. She wanted to be sick, but the nausea passed as another Apache left his pony and charged on foot. Dorianne sighted carefully and fired. The red man was nearly to her when she shot him. He went down hard, his momentum cracking his head against the large rock that was her cover.

Dorianne levered in another cartridge. As she took aim at another painted savage, an Apache bullet struck the rock where she crouched. Stone fragments pelted her eyes as the slug ricocheted off into space, whining angrily. Instantly the girl's eyes pulled shut and began to water. As she blinked against the stinging particles, another bullet whacked the rock and screamed away. Her gun was taking its toll, and the Apaches were concentrating on her position.

Straining to see clearly, Dorianne spotted another Apache moving in on foot. Her gun barked, and the Indian went down. As he dropped, he stumbled into the path of a rider. The pony tripped over him and sent its rider rolling to the ground. Still blinking, Dorianne shot him through the heart as he gained his feet.

All of the sudden the Apaches broke rank, gouged their horses' flanks, and scattered. They quickly faded out of rifle range, and the firing ceased.

Dorianne laid down her rifle and began thumbing her eyes. Unable to walk in his awkward predicament, Dan rolled in the blistering sand to where the girl knelt. Raising up on one knee, he put his free hand to her face. "Dorianne!" he said excitedly. "Are you all right?"

"Yes," she answered, blinking and trying to look at him. "One bullet hit the rock and some pieces flew into my eyes."

Whirling, Dan set his gaze on Steve Proffitt, who was examining Sam Kates's body. "Proffitt," he called, "bring a canteen. She's got rock dust in her eyes."

Early Byrd stood over the lifeless form of Larry Fields. With tears staining his leathered cheeks, he knelt and closed the dead man's eyes.

Logan Tanner watched the Apaches gather around the blue roan in the distance. Satisfied that they were safe for the moment, he walked toward Colt and Dorianne. "She okay?" the marshal asked Dan.

"Got some rock dust in her eyes. I think we can wash it out."

Steve Proffitt arrived with the canteen from the driver's seat of the coach. "Better go easy," he said, handing it to Dan.

Colt eyed Tanner and said, "Would you mind takin' me out of this position so I can help her?"

"Unlock 'em," Tanner said to Steve. "But keep a gun on him. When he's through, shackle him to one of the wagon wheels."

Dan gave him an acrimonious look.

The big marshal turned his attention to Early Byrd, who still knelt over his friend's body. Laying a hand on his bony shoulder, Tanner said, "Sorry, Early. He was a fine man."

Byrd sniffed and wiped tears with the back of his gnarled and calloused hand. "We rid a lotta miles together, Marshal." He sniffed again. "Larry was jist a kid so to speak, but we shore was good pards. Hard to believe he's gone . . . done made his last run."

"At least he went fast," commented Tanner. "Didn't suffer any."

"Yeah," sniffed Byrd. "I'm glad for that."

The big lawman lifted his hat, ran his fingers through the thick mop of wet salt-and-pepper hair and quietly strode toward the bullet-riddled stagecoach. One of the horses stamped the hot earth and blew.

Steve Proffitt stood over Dan Colt and watched Tanner remove Sam Kates's heavy frame from the coach. The marshal stretched the dead man out in the gathering shade of the coach. Casting a long look southward, he noted that the Apaches were gone. Lumbering back to where Dorianne Kates was the center of attention, he commented to the group, "Apaches have flown the coop."

"Don't think so," said Dan, dabbing a wet handkerchief on the girl's eyes.

"Well, they ain't out there," snapped Tanner defensively.

"Just regrouping," said Dan in an even tone. "They'll be back."

"What makes you think so?" queried the marshal stiffly.

"How many'd you kill?"

"I dunno. Dozen or so. Fifteen, maybe."

"How many they have left?"

"Dozen or so."

Dan nodded. "They'll be back. If it's today, it'll probably be that same number. If it's tomorrow, they'll bring reinforcements."

"He's right, Marshal," put in Early Byrd. Looking at the position of the sun, he said, "If we can weather the next attack, we'll hightail it outta here come dark!"

"We're gonna have to," said Proffitt. "The only water we have left is in that canteen. The other one's full of holes."

"I didn't check the water barrels," said Tanner. "Are they—"

"Full o' holes, too," said Byrd. "Dry as bones. These animals can't take us much further without water."

Logan Tanner smacked a fist into a palm and swore. Quickly eyeing Dorianne, he said, "Sorry, ma'am."

"There's a water hole 'bout six or seven miles south," said the Wells Fargo driver. "Soon's it gits dark, we'll pull out and head for it. It's right on the way to Eternity."

Tanner nodded, scanned the southern horizon and bent low over Dorianne. "She gonna be okay?" he asked Dan.

"It's much better now," spoke up the girl.

"That's good," responded the marshal. Turning to Proffitt, he said, "Steve, whyn't you and Early drag those stinkin' Apache carcasses outta here? Since we gotta stay till dark, I don't want to have to look at them."

Proffitt holstered his gun, nodded to Byrd and the two of them moved away.

Tanner unsheathed his weapon, eyed Dan warily and spoke to Dorianne. "Miss, that was some shootin'. I appreciate you jumpin' in without my say-so . . . I was pretty busy at the time. Did you say your pa taught you how to shoot?"

"Yes, sir," replied the girl, enjoying the attention she was getting from Dan Colt. "I figured things were sticky enough so you wouldn't mind."

Tanner worked up a half smile. "Can't jab at the kind of

127

shootin' you were doin'. You're mighty dadburned accurate. How'd you get so good?"

"I told you my father taught me to shoot rabbits on the plains. You ever shoot rabbits, Marshal?"

"Nope."

"They're very small and very fast. If you can shoot a darting rabbit, Marshal, a moving Indian is not too difficult."

"You sure made short order of those devils that came over the rock," said Dan. "You acted like a veteran."

Dorianne hunched her shoulders.

Dabbing at her eyes one more time, the blond man said, "How's that?"

"I'll be fine now," she said with a slight smile. Standing up, Dorianne walked quietly to where her uncle lay dead.

As Dan raised himself to full height, the muzzle of Tanner's revolver followed him. "Look, Tanner," Colt said tightly, "when those Apaches come back, you're gonna need every man here with a gun in his hand. They've set eyes on that girl now. You know they'll come after her, don't you?"

Logan Tanner's face was grim. He nodded, looking at the ground.

Byrd and Proffitt returned. The stagecoach driver threw a glance toward the shimmering southern horizon and said, "We'd better be prepared, Marshal. Ol' Donimo will be back before sundown. I'd bet my boots on it."

Dan Colt's head snapped around. "Early, did I hear you say *Donimo*?"

Byrd spat a brown stream to the sand. "Yep. He's leadin' the pack that jumped us."

Colt's face blanched.

"What'sa matter?" Byrd asked the tall man.

"He's a blood-hungry maniac," replied Dan. "All Apache warriors are savage and brutal. But the son of Four Fingers is a madman. He's probably trying to figure out a way right now to take us alive so he can torture us."

"I know what you mean, son," piped up Early. "Tales that are told across this desert about Donimo's means of torture will shiver your timbers!"

Jake Finch was in earshot of the conversation. "Tanner!" he

yelled. "You gotta let me have a gun! It ain't human to let me face Donimo and his cutthroats without bein' able to defend myself!"

The big marshal set his jaw stubbornly. "You ain't gettin' a gun, Finch. I got enough problems facin' Apache guns. I don't cotton to bein' shot in the back, too."

Finch swore violently, eyes flashing with fire.

Dorianne returned to the group.

"Sorry about your uncle," said Dan softly.

The girl dabbed at the sweat on her face. "Thank you, Dan. I really did not like him. He was a vain, self-centered man." Turning to look at Sam Kates's inert form, she said, "But I'm sorry he had to die like that."

"Bad way to go," agreed Dan.

Scanning the faces of the men who stood in a semicircle, Dorianne said, "What's this talk about a maniac Indian?"

"His name's Donimo," replied Colt. "He's the son of an Apache chief called Four Fingers. The old chief is vicious enough, but his son is a rabid dog. He's—"

"Looks like you might get a chance to meet him," cut in Early Byrd. Pointing southward, he added, "Here they come!"

CHAPTER FOURTEEN

The orange rays of the slanting sun emphasized the cloud of dust stirred by the charging Apaches.

Hurriedly Logan Tanner shackled Dan Colt to the spokes of a coach wheel. Dorianne positioned herself in the spot where her uncle had been at first. Tanner, Proffitt and Byrd spread themselves a little wider to make up for the absence of Larry Fields.

Fifteen of the sixteen thundering horses split into two groups about five hundred yards out. Donimo reined his blue roan to a halt.

"They're comin' at us from two sides!" yelled Early Byrd.

The stagecoach team began prancing nervously, nickering and blowing.

About sixty yards due south from where Dorianne, Tanner, Proffitt and Byrd crouched, guns ready, was another small cluster of large rocks. The boulders were surrounded by snakeweed and young mesquite trees. The yapping Apaches sent seven riders in a wide circle, while the remaining eight pulled to a halt and dismounted at the brush-covered boulders.

"What are they doin'?" cried Tanner to Early Byrd.

Dan Colt twisted against the wheel, attempting to see.

"Trying' to divide our attention," said Byrd. "Watch 'em! They're tricky!"

Taking cover in the bush, the eight savages opened fire. Bullets chipped rock and stirred dust as the Cathedral Rock four returned the fire. Suddenly the seven mounted Apaches formed a single line off to the right and came at a full gallop.

So much lead was coming from the brush-covered boulders, it was difficult for the four to lift their heads. The mounted savages were veering in close. Logan Tanner raised his head to see the oncoming charge when a bullet buzzed within an inch of his ear like an angry bee. Just as he ducked down, the firing stopped at the boulders and the mounted Apaches commenced.

Three of the riders fired toward those who crouched behind the rocks. Strangely enough, the others seemed to be shooting over their heads. Then the truth came home. The Wells Fargo horses were screaming as they were being shot.

At first the team tried to bolt. The stagecoach lurched forward, throwing Dan Colt to the ground. Pain shot through both arms as the spinning spokes twisted the handcuffs on his wrists. The stunned Colt was trying to get to his knees when the coach backed up and shot forward again. Dan felt his feet fly through the air. There was a sudden numbness in both hands. Amid the kicking, falling and screaming of the mortally wounded horses, Dan rolled in the dust and found himself slammed against a rock. It wasn't until he saw both hands in front of his face that he realized he was free.

Though his hands felt numb and the wind was temporarily knocked out of him, Dan scrambled to his feet. Gasping for air, he dived for a Winchester. Seizing the gun, he crawled to where Dorianne was reloading in a cloud of mixed dust and smoke.

The line of mounted Apaches had passed, and now those in the brush-covered rocks were firing again.

Dorianne looked at Dan while shots racketed in the air. Her eyes fell to the broken handcuffs on his wrists, a few links dangling from each one.

Dan took a quick look behind him at the horses. All but one was down. The others kicked and pawed at the twisted harness in the throes of death. A lone Apache rider seemed to appear out of nowhere. He took aim at the last standing horse and fired. The horse screamed. At the same instant two bullets slapped the rock near Dorianne's head. As she dropped low, Dan shouldered his rifle and put a bullet between the shoulder blades of the rider that had just passed. The savage stiffened, threw up his arms and sailed off his pinto.

Abruptly the firing stopped as the Apaches in the rocks ran to their horses, mounted and rode away with the others. Dan watched as they joined the big Indian on the blue roan out of rifle range. They conversed for a moment, looked back, then rode southwest and soon disappeared.

Logan Tanner stood up, saw the rifle in Dan Colt's hands and turned gray. "Sundeen, how'd you—"

"Looks to me like he's as good with a rifle as he is with a revolver," said Steve Proffitt. "I'd swear he planted that slug smack-dab through that dude's *heart . . . from the back!*"

Tanner's steel-gray eyes locked with the ice-blues of Dan Colt. The marshal did not raise his rifle. He spoke coldly. "Lay down the gun, Sundeen."

"Name's *Colt,* Marshal," said Dan just as coldly. "You will notice that the bullet I just fired went in the Apache's back. Not *yours.*"

Dorianne was standing next to the tall man. Slowly he put the Winchester in her hands. Tanner's gaze dropped to the broken manacles on Dan's wrists. The skin underneath was chafed and bleeding.

Lifting them, allowing the chain links to dangle, Colt said, "When the Apaches started shootin' the horses, they tried to take off. I'm sure glad they shot the lead ones first, or I'd be mincemeat by now."

All eyes suddenly turned to the horses as one of them neighed pitifully. Two of the animals were still alive. One lay in a grotesque heap, blood flowing from its stomach, sides heaving. The other cried again, tangled in the harness, lifting its head.

His face twisted in pity, Early Byrd raised his rifle and shot the animal between the eyes. Working the lever swiftly, he lined himself with the other one and did the same thing. Looking in the faces of the others, he said, "Looks like Donimo has got us where he wants us." Casting his eyes toward the sunset, he added, "That savage will let us think about it all night. Then he'll come after us in the morning."

Dorianne bit her lip and looked up at Dan. Cold fear was in her dark brown eyes.

"Don't worry, little lady," said Dan, impelling a note of optimism into his voice. "We'll get out of this somehow."

Sudden sobs shook Dorianne's small body. The rifle slipped from her fingers into the dust. Her hands went up to cover her face. Dan put his arms around her and held her tight. "Go ahead, Dorianne," he said tenderly. "Go ahead. Cry. Let it out."

While the girl sobbed, Early said, "Poor little kid. This has been some day for her. Watched her uncle shot to death. Had to pick up a gun and kill to keep from bein' killed, and now she's trapped, facing the torture of the Apaches."

"There's a way out of this," said Colt firmly. "We've just got to use our heads."

"I hope you're right," said US Marshal Logan Tanner, "but I just can't see puttin' yourself out to get us free of this mess so I can deliver you to Yuma."

"If it's a choice of Yuma Prison or dyin' by Apache torture," said Dan, "I'll take Yuma. But I don't plan on either one."

Tanner's face stiffened. He looked at Steve Proffitt, then back to Colt.

"Because I *am* Dan Colt and not Sundeen the outlaw," said the man holding Dorianne Kates. "I'll make you a deal, Tanner."

"You ain't in no position to make deals," snapped Tanner.

"I think you ought to at least listen to him, Marshal," said Steve Proffitt. "I've got a feelin' we're gonna need him to help us out of this situation."

The big lawman threw his deputy a petulant look, then fixed his gray stare on Dan Colt. "I'm listenin'."

"I saved your life once, right?"

Tanner cleared his throat. "Yeah."

"I could've shot you dead a little while ago, right?"

The marshal pursed his lips. "Yeah."

"If all of us work together, we might get out of this alive, right?"

"Hope so."

"I've got to handle a gun to do my part, Tanner."

Dorianne had stopped weeping and now was listening. Intent on his conversation, Dan was still holding her tight.

The lawman opened his mouth to speak.

133

"Just a minute," said Dan. "I've already proven to you that I'm not out to kill you, right?"

Tanner took a deep breath, pursed his lips again and let it out slowly. "Yeah."

"I want out of this fix, but more for this girl's sake. I give you my word that I'll make no attempt to escape until Dorianne is absolutely safe. If and when I see my chance after that, I will try to get away from you and Proffitt because I can't find Dave while I'm sittin' in prison." Dan bolted Tanner with his ice-blue stare. "Fair enough?"

"The only reason I'm gonna agree, Sundeen," said the big lawman, "is because I know you mean business about gettin' Miss Kates to safety. Okay. It's a deal."

Suddenly Dan noticed that Dorianne had stopped weeping and was looking up at him with bloodshot eyes. "Is there really a chance for us to get out of here, Dan?" she asked, voice trembling.

"As long as we're alive, there's hope," Dan answered confidently.

"What do you suggest?" came Logan Tanner's deep bass voice.

"First thing we've got to do," replied Colt, "is bury Kates and Fields. Second, we've got to get water. Third, we gotta think about something to eat."

"I know where the water hole is, Dan," said Early Byrd. "I can take the canteen and be back in four or five hours. Wish we had somethin' else to put water in, but we don't."

"All right, Early," said Dan, "let's all get us a good drink. Then you head out for the water hole. You sure there's water in it?"

"Always has been."

"Steve and I will bury Kates and Fields," offered Tanner. "We'll let Finch help us. It'll work some of the stiffness out of his joints."

"If I can't have a gun," spoke up Finch from his position on the ground, "I ain't handlin' no shovel."

"If I put a knot on your head first, you'll beg to handle a shovel, bucko," snapped Tanner.

"Then Dorianne and I will cook the steaks," said Dan.

"Steaks?" asked the girl.

"Steaks?" echoed the two lawmen.

Early Byrd chuckled. "Apparently these folks have been cod-

134

dled a little, Dan," he said. "The only food we have in sight, folks, is layin' on the ground."

"You mean . . . *horsemeat*?" asked Dorianne, her hand clutching her throat.

"Mmm-hmm," nodded Dan. "We'll only get one crack at it. Tomorrow will be too late."

While Dorianne was adjusting herself to the idea, Early Byrd fetched the canteen. Returning with it, he sloshed the liquid inside. "There's enough for a good long pull for each of us." Extending it to Dorianne, he said, "You first, honey."

As the canteen made the rounds, Byrd said, "I'd like to say a few words over Larry's grave when I get back, Marshal."

"Surely, Early."

"How about takin' these off my wrists?" asked Colt, shaking the broken handcuffs at Tanner.

The big lawman looked at his deputy. "Take 'em off him, Steve."

Jake Finch gulped his portion of water and handed the canteen back to Byrd. Early carried it to Dan and said, "Your turn, Dan. I'll be last."

Colt rubbed his bruised wrists as the handcuffs came off and ran the back of his hand over his mouth. Circling his dry lips with his tongue, he said, "I'll just take one swig, Early. You'll need the rest of it to get you to the water hole."

"Naw, son," said Byrd, "go ahead and take your share. I'll get by."

Dan took one big mouthful and put it back in Early's gnarled hand. Early shook it and said, "You can have some more.".

"You better get going," insisted Colt.

Byrd took a healthy swig, capped it and slung the strap over his shoulder. "See ya'll in a few hours," he said, and trudged away.

The sun dropped its flaming rim behind the long plateaus to the west, casting a purple and orange afterglow on a few low-hanging clouds.

Horsemeat sizzled on mesquite sticks as graves were dug in the soft earth. Darkness slowly descended over the desert, and the air began to cool. The sand and rocks retained the sun's heat as the group, including Jake Finch, sat down to eat. Dorianne pretended

135

it was beef and was able to take her fill. Several slabs were put aside for Early Byrd.

Dan Colt was asked by Dorianne Kates to say a few words over her uncle's grave. He quoted the Twenty-third Psalm and committed the body to the earth.

The night wind came up, ruffling the flames of the fire. Dan threw on some more mesquite branches. The fresh wood began to snap, and the flames crackled. The group sat around the fire. Jake Finch was shackled to the same wheel Dan Colt had been earlier.

"You have a plan, Sundeen?" asked Logan Tanner.

"It's a long shot," replied Dan, "but I've got one."

"Let's hear it."

"The main camp of the Apaches must not be real close. If it was, Donimo would have gone after more warriors when his pack was cut in half. His killing the horses indicates that he wants to force us out into the open on the desert. He probably has only the handful we saw last to attack us with."

"Probably?" asked Tanner.

"I realize he may come back with a thousand men," said Dan, "and if he does, it's all over for us. But if I'm right, he'll come at sunrise with his fourteen or fifteen and try to take us. If we can cut his ranks to the nub, maybe he'll hightail it homeward and we can head for Eternity."

"That's a lot of *probably* and a lot of *maybe*," said Tanner, doubt edging his voice.

"You have somethin' better, I'm all ears," said Colt.

The marshal ran his fingers through his mustache and stared into the fire.

Knowing the lawman had nothing better to offer, Dan continued. "Our best bet is to fight them right here. If they catch us out in the open, we wouldn't have a chance, even against his handful."

"But we don't have any more food," said Steve Proffitt. "One canteen of water won't last six people very long."

"If Donimo comes at sunup and we can cut his numbers down enough to send him back to camp, maybe we can make it to Eternity," said Colt.

"What if Four Fingers's camp is in the direction of Eternity?" queried Logan Tanner. "We'll walk right into their teeth."

"We have no way of knowing," countered Colt, "but Eternity is the closest hope for our safety. I realize it's a gamble, but we can either prepare for what looks like the most likely event or die for lack of foresight. If Donimo comes back with an army, we're done for no matter what. But if my guess is correct, we have a chance."

"How do you propose we cut down Donimo's braves?" asked the US marshal.

"I didn't get to watch the first two attacks because you had me on the ground," said Colt, "but I assume from what I could hear that the Apaches rode circular fashion around us. It sounded like they were in the open area between us and those rocks out there."

"Right," said Tanner.

"Which side of the clump out there did they come around?"

"The east side," answered the lawman.

"Okay," said Dan, "what if two of us hide out there amid the bush in those boulders and the others shoot from here? If we could get them bunched up between us, we could catch them in a cross fire."

"How would you get them bunched up?" queried Dorianne.

"Apaches, like most Indians," said Dan, "have a deep reverence for their dead. That's why they'll come sometime tonight and take away those bodies out there."

"They will?" the girl said, wide-eyed.

"Yes'm."

"Maybe they'll attack us then!"

"Not likely," said Colt. "We'll keep someone on watch all night, but Apaches, like all their race, are very superstitious. They believe if they die in battle at night, their souls must wander forever in the spirit world, never finding the Happy Hunting Ground. Few are willing to chance it. So they'll slip up in their noiseless fashion and carry away their dead for proper religious burial."

"So what's this got to do with bunchin' them up?" asked Proffitt.

"How far did you and Early drag the bodies that Dorianne killed in here?"

"Laid them just outside these rocks to the west," answered Steve.

"We'll drag two of them back in here," said Dan, "and prop them up right on top of the stagecoach where they can be easily seen. When the Apaches charge around the boulders out there, we'll let them get a good look, then set the dead Indians' hair on fire."

"What will that do?" asked the girl.

"It'll infuriate them," answered Dan. "If my guess is right, they'll center their attention on the burning bodies, at least momentarily." The tall man threw some more branches on the flames and resumed his explanation. "We'll break open some of these boxes of cartridges and run a line of gunpowder on each side of the area, all the way out to those boulders. We'll set the powder on fire at both ends of each line at the same time."

"That'll spook their horses," said Steve Proffitt, catching the idea.

"Right," said Dan. "Then's when we'll open fire on both sides, catch them in a cross fire and cut 'em down."

"Sounds great if it'll work," agreed Logan Tanner.

"It'll work," said Dan with a grin. "All we have to do is get the timing right."

"And one other thing," put in Dorianne. "Pray that they come at sunup with the same group we saw when they rode away."

"Correct," agreed Colt. "If it's the other alternative . . ."

"Let's not even think about it," said Dorianne with a shudder.

CHAPTER FIFTEEN

Plans were carefully made and rehearsed. It was agreed that Dan and Dorianne would be the ones to launch the ambush from the boulders sixty yards away.

Together the group broke open the cartridges of two whole cases and stored the powder in Dorianne's overnight bag. It would not be placed on the ground until just before dawn. The night wind could blow it away if it was strung all the way out to the clump of boulders any sooner.

The bodies of the two Apaches were placed on top of the stagecoach and braced in a kneeling position with mesquite branches. The bands were taken from their heads and their long black hair let loose so it would catch fire faster.

Dan Colt volunteered to take the first watch. Proffitt would take over at one o'clock and go until four o'clock. Tanner would take it from four until dawn.

Taking his place in a comfortable spot on a boulder, Dan levered a cartridge into the chamber of a Winchester and peered into the night. There was no moon. The stars twinkled overhead, filling the dark sky with speckled silver. The fire had dwindled to a few red embers.

Somewhere out on the desert, a coyote howled. The night winds scurried across the cooling sand.

An hour passed. Dan was shifting his position on the boulder when a small figure drew near in the dark. "Dan," she whispered.

"Dorianne," he whispered in return. "What are you doin' up? You're supposed to be asleep."

"I can't sleep," came the reply. "Can I come up and sit with you?"

Dan extended a hand and pulled her up beside him. "You're gonna need some rest, little lady," he said in a mock-scolding tone. "We've got a tough day ahead tomorrow. I'm gonna be dependin' on you to shoot good an' straight out there in those rocks."

"I'll be all right," said Dorianne. "I think I can sleep if I can just talk to you for a little while."

Dan could make out her long, dark hair being ruffled by the wind. She shuddered slightly. "The air is chilly tonight, isn't it?" she said softly.

Shifting the rifle to his other hand, the brawny Dan Colt pulled Dorianne close to him. "That better?"

"Uh-huh," she responded, cuddling as close as possible. "You know what?"

"What?"

"As bad a fix as we're in, I'm not afraid as long as *you're* here."

"Nothin' immortal about Dan Colt, little lady," he said, chuckling.

"But with that . . . that Donimo around, I'd be very much afraid if you weren't here."

"He's a bad one, all right. But if we can cut him to three or four men, he'll give up and go after reinforcements. Then we've got to cut out for Eternity."

"How long will it take us to walk it?"

"In the heat, about a day and a half. Maybe two days. It's a good thing that water hole where Early's gone is right on the way to Eternity. We'll be able to water up at that point."

All was quiet for a few moments. Then Dorianne asked, "Dan, this Donimo and his father . . ."

"Yes?"

"Why are they so vicious? I mean, I know all the Apaches have a legitimate reason for hating the white men . . . but what makes Four Fingers so mean?"

"The very words you just spoke."

"What? I don't understand."

"Four Fingers," said Dan flatly. "That has only been the chief's name for about twenty years."

"Oh?"

"About that long ago, *his* father, Vagondo, was a chief. The Apaches had attacked some white settlers. In retaliation, the settler kidnapped Vagondo's son. At that time his name was Mongo or something like that. He was about thirty years old. Maybe thirty-five. The white men cut off his right hand and the thumb of his left hand."

"Oh," nodded Dorianne. "That's why he's called—"

"Four Fingers," said Dan, finishing her statement. "They sent him back to Vagondo maimed. This was an exceptional tragedy in the eyes of the Apaches because Mongo had been unbeatable in hand-to-hand combat, fast, strong and deadly with a knife. Cutting off his knife hand and preventing him from getting a grip with the other was a thousand times worse than killin' him."

"That's why he's so vicious," commented the girl.

"Sure is," said Dan. "Within a few weeks Vagondo had caught every one of those settlers. Hanged 'em by their thumbs and cooked 'em slowly over red-hot coals."

"Ugh." Dorianne shuddered.

"Four Fingers hates whites with a passion," said Colt, "which he passed on to his son. Only Donimo is worse than his pa. He has a mean streak that's almost insane. Four Fingers taught him how to fight, maim and kill. He's as skillful with a knife as his pa ever was, only more savage. He lives for one thing: to take vengeance on white men for what they did to his pa."

Dorianne tried to make out Dan's angular features by the light of the stars. "If Donimo likes to kill white men so much, why does he stay out of the battles?"

"It's not because of cowardice," replied the tall man. "I've heard stories all over the southwest of his courage in battle. Word is that lately old Four Fingers has ordered his son to lead the attacks but stay out of the thick of things. Donimo will be chief one day. They say that Donimo has invented tortures that even shock his own people."

"He must be a vile beast," said Dorianne.

"He is," agreed Dan, "but to the Apaches he's a god. They worship him almost as much as they worship Four Fingers."

141

"Oh, Dan," she said, gripping his arm, "we just can't let Donimo take us tomorrow. We *have* to carry through your plan."

"We will, Dorianne," he said, sounding more sure with his voice than he felt in his heart. "Now you've got to—"

Dorianne stiffened at the sudden silence of Colt's voice. "What is it?" she whispered.

Keeping his voice very low, the blond man said, "Apaches. Comin' for their dead."

"I don't hear anything."

"When it's Indians, you never will," said Dan. "If you'll study real close, you'll see them moving out there. A few minutes and they'll be gone."

"Won't they miss those two that you put up on top of the stagecoach?"

"They might, but they'll just figure they overlooked them in the darkness. Dark as it is, they'd have to be as close as we are to the stagecoach in order to see them."

Within twenty minutes the figures moving like ghosts on the desert floor were gone. Dorianne huddled next to the big muscular man, saying nothing until his breathing relaxed. She knew, then, that the Apaches were gone.

"I hope Early makes it back," the girl said, breaking the silence.

"He will," said Colt. "Early's a desert-wise old fox." Running a finger under her chin, he said, "Now, little girl, it's time for you to get some sleep."

Pulling close to him, Dorianne said, "I love you, Dan Colt."

Without comment Dan eased her to the ground and said, "G'nite, little lady."

Dorianne Kates dozed periodically through the night, but she was awake at the first light of dawn. As the gray grew lighter, she watched Colt, Tanner and Proffitt lay two thin lines of gunpowder from their rock fortress across the sand to the weed- and mesquite-surrounded rocks where she and Dan would hide just before sunup. The two lines were some sixty feet apart. She noticed that every six feet or so the men were making little piles of powder. These would cause the hissing flashes and billows of smoke to frighten and confuse the Apaches' horses. Timed correctly, the chaos caused by the gunpowder should give the stagecoach party time to pick off a good many Apaches.

Dorianne turned and eyed the two dead Indians silhouetted against the dull gray sky, held upright on their knees by the mesquite limbs. The breeze caused their long black hair to dance freely in the air.

Swinging her gaze around on the ground, Dorianne saw Jake Finch asleep next to the steel-rimmed coach wheel, his wrists shackled to it. Squinting through the gloom, she saw a sleeping form that had to be Early Byrd. Relieved to know he had made it, she breathed a prayer of thanks. "And Lord," she added, "if we somehow are not able to withstand the attack today . . . would you have mercy and let us die quickly? Please don't let them torture us. Especially Dan."

The three men returned and awakened Early. The plan was rehearsed again as the canteen made the rounds. Jake Finch was awake and listening.

"All right," Colt said, finalizing the strategy, "everybody got your matches?"

Each one, including Dorianne, nodded.

"Early, your torch ready to light?"

"Yep," said Byrd, smiling at the tall man. He lifted up a mesquite branch with a ball of dried weeds tied to its end with string.

"Now remember, Early," said Colt, "you light the Apaches up when Donimo's warriors are about fifty yards the other side of the clump out there. That way when they come in close, they won't notice the black lines of gunpowder on the ground."

"Or Dan and me hiding in the rocks," put in Dorianne.

"I've got an idea, Dan," piped up Early. "How about if I stuff some dry weeds down the necks of them dead Injuns and light 'em off at the same time I torch the hair?"

"Good!" agreed Dan. "That'll put out a lot of smoke. Only you better hurry." The tall man threw a glance at the brightening horizon. "The sun's about ready to put in an appearance."

Dan and Dorianne picked up two rifles each and several boxes of cartridges. Looking at the girl, he said, "All right, Deadeye, let's go." Setting his pale blues on the big lawman, he said, "See you when it's over."

Logan Tanner nodded soberly and watched the tall man and the pint-size girl dart across the sand between the two lines of black powder.

"Okay, men," said Tanner, "let's take our positions."

Byrd scurried up on top of the stagecoach with his hands full of dried snakeweed. "Hand me up the torch, wouldja?" he said to Steve Proffitt. The weeds were quickly stuffed behind the necks of the two dead Apaches.

Tanner and Proffitt hunkered in their places, guns ready. The marshal looked up at Byrd. "See anything, Early?"

The wiry little driver was scanning the desert at the time. "Nope," he answered. "Nothin' yet."

"Tanner!" hollered Jake Finch. "It ain't Christian for you to let me face them savages shackled like this! If a man's gonna die, he oughtta be able to die fightin'!"

"I agree, Jake," said Tanner. "But if I'm gonna die in this situation, I want it to be fightin' Indians . . . not Indians and *you!* Now shuddup!"

The fiery rim of the sun appeared on the eastern horizon. For a few moments the desert took on a yellow-orange hue.

Nestled among the boulders sixty yards from the others, Dan and Dorianne watched Cathedral Rock come alive with color. It started at the top and slowly worked its way down.

"You think they'll wait till later in the day, Dan?" asked the girl.

"If they're comin'," replied Dan, "it'll be quite soon. They would rather catch us out in the open, but Donimo is thirsty for blood, so they'll come at us in the rocks again."

"I hope it's just his little handful," said Dorianne heavily.

As Early Byrd peered at the southern horizon, suddenly he saw movement on the broad expanse to the southwest. Watching him, Logan Tanner said, "See somethin'?"

"Yep," responded the little man, squinting. Byrd studied the moving dots carefully.

"Tanner!" shouted Jake Finch. "If you let me die this way, it's *murder!*"

Logan Tanner did not answer. He was intent on Early. The old man spit a brown stream. His lips were moving in a silent count.

"Byrd," said Tanner.

"Jist a minnit, Marshal," said Early without looking down.

A full minute passed.

"It's Donimo, Marshal!" he said excitedly. "Excludin' him, there's fourteen of 'em!"

"Good!" exclaimed Tanner. "No reinforcements!"

Byrd cupped his hands and yelled toward the rocks where Dan and the girl waited. "Dan! They're comin'! Fourteen of 'em!"

Down among the boulders, Dan Colt heaved a sigh of relief. "Okay, little lady," he said, "We've got a chance to come out of this thing alive. Shoot fast and straight."

"I'll do my best, darling," said Dorianne, her large brown eyes adoring Dan Colt.

Uncomfortable under her gaze, Dan said, "Get your matches out."

The gunpowder had been strung to the edge of the rocks so that from their prone positions, they could ignite the powder. With his head low Dan watched Early Byrd through the crevice between two boulders. The little man was kneeling now behind the erect corpses.

A long, tense moment passed.

Then they came. At precisely the same instant the sound of thundering hoofs blended with the Apache war cry, penetrating the early morning air. Dan and the girl could feel the sudden trembling of the earth.

Dan Colt's eyes were riveted on Early Byrd. "Get ready," he said to Dorianne from the side of his mouth.

Within thirty seconds it felt like the Apaches were going to run right over them. Then smoke billowed from Byrd's hand as the weed torch caught fire. Instantly the two Apache corpses were ablaze as thick rolls of white smoke lifted skyward.

Early waved the torch back and forth, screaming something inaudible at the oncoming horde. The yapping savages rounded the rocks and brush where Dan and Dorianne lay. They were just about to divide and ride in the customary circles around the Cathedral Rock fortress when the lead rider skidded his pony to a halt. The others followed suit.

Every dark-eyed savage sat his skittish horse, attention drawn to the flaming corpses of their dead blood brothers. Dan raised his head sufficiently to see that all fourteen riders were inside the two black lines. "Okay," he whispered, "light it!"

Two matches were struck simultaneously. The gunpowder hissed and sped from the rocks toward the long, straight lines. Tanner and Proffitt touched fire to the black lines on their side. The stunned Apaches came to their senses as the racing fire began to reach the piles of powder, flaring and sending off billows of smoke. The frightened horses began to whinny and rear. The Indians began shooting while trying to bring their mounts under control.

Dan shouldered his rifle, sighted in on the nearest Apache and opened fire. Dorianne followed suit. Tanner, Proffitt and Byrd cut loose. Shots caromed off the hard rock surfaces. In the bedlam Apaches were dropping off their horses, filling the air with their death cries. Smoke and dust was everywhere. The confused Apaches were firing in every direction.

Dorianne shot one buck, who fell from his pony, started to get up and was knocked down by a wheeling horse. Another, in the confusion, stepped on his head.

Dan was on his second rifle when, abruptly, the Indians that were mounted bolted for safety. As the dust and smoke cleared, Dan stood up and counted six riders joining Donimo to gallop away.

The riderless horses were scattering as Tanner, Proffitt and Byrd were coming over the rocks. Dorianne stood up and brushed the hair from her eyes. The tall man moved toward her. "You all right, little lady?"

"Yes," she answered weakly, shaking dust from her dress. "But I don't know if I can take much more of this."

"You did fine," said Dan.

Dorianne's hand went to her forehead. "I . . . I just feel a little shaky."

"Here," said Colt, "let me help you." Relieving Dorianne of the rifle in her hand, he guided her to a rock and sat her down. Turning toward the three men who were moving slowly among the scattered corpses, he said, "One of you fellas bring the canteen, will you? She needs some water."

Early wheeled, responding to Dan's request.

Dorianne looked at the scattered corpses with her large brown eyes. The painted faces of the savages were wild and fierce even in

146

death. One horse was down, having caught a bullet in the head. Tanner and his deputy were prodding each body with their rifles.

Early Byrd picked up the canteen from between two rocks, where he had placed it for safety's sake. From his place next to the wagon wheel, Jake Finch eyed the canteen in Early's hand and said, "How about some water?"

"Later," said Early woodenly. "The girl needs it right now." Passing by the hard-faced outlaw, the wiry little man eyed the burned corpses of the two Apaches. They had both toppled off the top of the stagecoach and lay in crumpled heaps. "Shore do appreciate you boys helpin' us out," he said to them.

The sun was lifting and shafting its heat onto the desert. While Dorianne drank from the canteen, Dan looked overhead at two buzzards wheeling against the brassy sky. To the gathered group he said, "Looks like we've got company for breakfast."

"Only the company gets the breakfast," said Early Byrd idly.

Colt looked at Tanner and Proffitt. "Guess we killed eight, huh?"

"Yep," replied the big marshal. "Means Donimo still has six. Whaddya think?"

"He'll probably come at us again," said Dan evenly. "Only next time we won't have the element of surprise . . . and we won't have the rocks for cover."

"You don't mean we're strikin' out for Eternity with those red devils still waitin' to jump us?" said Proffitt.

"We don't have any choice," said Colt blandly. "Time the sun's been on all those dead horses another few hours, we won't be able to stand the stench. We've got to move on."

CHAPTER SIXTEEN

No one could argue with Dan Colt's reasoning. Soon the sickening odor of rotting horseflesh would make the rock enclosure uninhabitable. They would carry one rifle apiece and as much ammunition as they could bear. The remaining rifles would be smashed against the rocks so as to render them useless to the Apaches. Jake Finch would carry ammunition, but no rifle.

The four men gathered up the dead Indians' rifles and smashed them first. As they moved toward the stagecoach to destroy the case of new seven-shot repeaters, intended for Eternity, something caught Dan's eye around toward the back of the towering rock. "Hold it," he said, his eyes fixed in that direction.

Everyone looked toward the tall man.

"One of the Apache horses is hangin' around," Dan said, pointing. "I've got an idea."

"What is it, Dan?" queried Dorianne.

"If we could catch that pinto, she could pull the stagecoach."

"*One* horse?" The voice was that of Early Byrd.

"Sure," said Dan. "The land is level between here and Eternity. That way we could keep the rifles, too."

"Sounds good, son," said Early. "Only thet there animal is for *ridin'*. She'd go wild, you try to hitch 'er to the stage."

"Maybe not," said Colt. "The Apaches use nearly all their horses to pull travois when they move from camp to camp. I'll bet that mare's pulled a load before."

"It's worth a try," said Logan Tanner.

"Next trick is to catch her," put in Steve Proffitt.

"Yeah," said Byrd, "she's used to smellin' red skin. She may not take to yours, Dan."

Easing away from the group, the tall, blond man walked slowly toward the pinto. As he drew near, her head came up, ears pointed. She did not jump.

Watching Dan Colt moving toward the mare, his open palm extended, Early Byrd said, "Two bits says he'll get her."

"If it was a stallion, I'd bet you," said Steve Proffitt. "But that long, handsome dude seems to have a way with the females."

Dorianne looked up to see all three men staring at her. Face reddening, she said, "He's a kind and gentle man. He's no outlaw, either." Her eyes turned to Logan Tanner, who did not comment.

Dan was within ten feet of the mare now, speaking to her in gentle tones. She swished her tail but did not move. The reins of the pinto's rope bridle lay on the ground. Carefully Dan closed in, putting a foot on the reins. Taking hold of the bridle, he stroked the animal's long face. She blew as he lifted the reins and wrapped them around her neck. Quickly he swung aboard.

When Logan Tanner saw Colt hoist himself to the mare's back, he shouted, "Hey! What're you doin', Sundeen?"

Dan laughed, kicking the horse's sides. As she went into a gallop, he guided the mare to the north side of the towering rock and disappeared.

Logan Tanner went into a rage, running toward the east side, swearing. Suddenly Dan Colt rounded the giant rock from the same direction. He was still laughing. "What's the matter, Tanner?" he said, pulling the horse to a halt. "You didn't think I was going to leave, did you?"

"Looked like it!" bellowed the thick-bodied lawman.

"I told you, sir," said Dan, "I won't leave you until Dorianne is out of danger."

Tanner lifted his hat, wiped sweat and turned back toward the others, grumbling. Steve Proffitt wanted to laugh but did not dare.

While Dan and Early were fixing up a makeshift harness, the deputy went to Jake Finch, pulled the key from his button-down vest pocket and unlocked the handcuffs. Jake used the wheel to pull himself upward. Once he was on his feet, the cuffs were snapped on both wrists. "Now I'm leavin' your hands in front of you, Jake," said Proffitt. "But you just *look* like you're *thinkin'* about gettin' tricky and they'll be behind you."

"I thought you'd probably shackle me inside the coach," Jake said sourly.

"Not on your life, Jake," responded Steve. "You're gonna *walk.*"

"Walk?" snapped Finch. "While the rest of you *ride?*"

"You're gonna lead the horse, Jake," said Dan Colt. "She's pulled a travois, without question."

Leathers were already on the pinto's back. She was perfectly calm.

"She wouldn't know how to react to reins from the driver's seat," continued Colt. "She's used to being led when she pulls a load."

"So you're elected, Jake," said Tanner. "That'll keep you outta mischief."

Finch screwed up his face. "I ain't doin' it."

Tanner's jaw squared. "Maybe you'd like your skull caved in," he growled, pulling his revolver.

The outlaw took one look at the determination in the marshal's steely eyes and surrendered. "Okay, okay."

Rifles and ammunition were loaded on top of the coach. Dan Colt and Early Byrd finished hitching the mare to the vehicle. The tall man led horse and coach free of the rocks. Bringing them to a stop, he said, "All right, Dorianne, you climb in. Tanner, you can ride first. Us boys will trade off."

With the reins slung over his shoulder, Jake Finch started the stage in motion. "Straight south, Jake," said Colt. "Keep us out in the open, away from rocks or gullies."

"That's stupid," retorted Finch. "When them savages come, we'll have no place to take cover."

"*You're* stupid," retaliated Colt. "*Ambush* comes from rocks and gullies. If we're out in the open, we can at least see them coming and prepare ourselves."

Steve Proffitt walked on the left side of the coach. Dan was on the right side. Early Byrd took up the rear.

"Keep your eyes peeled, everybody," said Dan. "Donimo may just come back any time."

The sky blazed down on the unprotected party. Progress was slow, and talk at a minimim. A stop was made after a mile or so to sip at the water in the canteen. Dan soaked a large handkerchief and pressed it to the pinto's tongue and lips.

The tall man turned and looked northward. From where they'd come, a dozen or more buzzards were hopping, screeching, flapping their dark, ugly wings. The feast was about to begin.

The day dragged on. Each man afoot squeezed his eyelids to slits, attempting to minimize the sun's painful glare. They must stay alert. Their lives depended on it. Donimo and his six remaining braves could come at any moment.

Dan Colt's red-rimmed eyes swept the desert constantly. Where were the rest of those savages? Why didn't they come? They would be easy prey for the Apaches now. They would have to fight back from under the stagecoach. Swinging his gaze to the rear, he spoke to Early Byrd. "Early, how far do you figure we are from the water hole?"

Before answering the wiry little man took a long look north, then south. "I figger we've come about three miles so far, Dan. Water hole was a leedle further than I had thought. It's better than seven miles from Cathedral Rock. Maybe even eight. Goin' at this rate, we won't make it to the hole by sundown."

A water stop was in order again. After everyone had taken a share, Dan moistened the pinto's mouth, then checked the canteen. They would run out of water after two more rounds.

Jake Finch was given a breather and allowed to ride in the coach with Dorianne. "I'm not shacklin' you to the door, Finch," Steve told him. "When Donimo comes, I wouldn't have time to get you loose." Turning to the girl, he said, "If he so much as moves toward you, ma'am, you sing out. I'll put him back out here and walk his legs off."

Dorianne smiled weakly and dabbed at the sweat on her face. Jake settled into the seat opposite the girl, his face shiny with moisture.

Logan Tanner took Finch's place. Dorianne kept looking out the window, watching the tall man. A long-tailed lizard watched the slow-moving procession from a hot rock.

As Dan Colt walked alongside the bullet-riddled stagecoach, he tried to sort out the thoughts that crowded his brain. Dorianne

Kates. Nice kid. The hand of fate had not dealt too kindly with her. And now she had taken a fancy to *him*. Dan Colt would do his best to see to it Dorianne made it out of this horrendous fix, but then he must walk out of her life. She must have her chance to live . . . and to fall in love with some nice young man her own age.

Another thought edged out Dorianne's plight. It centered on the big sweaty man who now led the Apache horse toward Eternity. Somehow Dan had to mastermind an escape without harming the US marshal or his deputy. *No way to make a plan at this point*, he told himself. *I'll just have to wait* . . .

The sun was hanging low in the western sky when it came Dan's turn to ride in the coach. Byrd and Proffitt had taken their turns. The canteen was now empty. As the tall man moved his weary body toward the vehicle, he eyed the sun's position and spoke to Logan Tanner. "We'd better go till sundown, then rest for the night. One of us can make a run for the water hole after dark."

Tanner nodded, moving in to fill Dan's position on the right side of the coach.

Dan sighed as he lowered himself into the seat across from Dorianne. She eyed him lovingly and said, "Why do you think Donimo hasn't come back?"

"Probably lickin' his wounds," answered the blue-eyed man. "We've gained his respect, too. He'll pick his next spot carefully. But as long as he has six men, I'm sure he'll try it again."

"He must really hate us by now," mused Dorianne. "We've cut a big hole in his ranks."

Early Byrd was now in the lead spot. Finch trudged at the coach's left and Steve Proffitt was at the rear. As the sun touched the tips of the mountains far to the west, Byrd scanned the land in front of him. Something caught his attention off to the left. Straining his eyes in that direction, he studied hard. Nothing. Was the heat getting to him? There were some scattered patches of sagebrush, flat rocks and ocotillo stalks. But nothing an Indian could hide behind.

As the coach moved slowly by the area, Early satisfied himself that the movement had been his imagination. Moments passed. The sun was half covered by the sawtoothed horizon when suddenly an arrow hissed by Steve Proffitt's head and thunked into the back of the coach. Wheeling, he shouted, "Apaches!"

Six bronze-skinned savages seemed to rise up right out of the ground, five of them with rifles blazing.

Dan shoved Dorianne to the floor and dived out of the coach. Early dropped the reins, leaped up on the coach, set the brake and rolled underneath. The Apaches were about fifty yards behind.

Tanner and Byrd opened fire from underneath the coach. Proffitt and Colt flattened themselves on the hot ground off to the west side of the vehicle. Bullets were biting the ground around them when Proffitt let out a yelp.

One of the Apaches took a bullet in the chest and toppled. Instantly the others turned and ran a zigzag pattern to an arroyo on the east and disappeared.

Dan turned his attention to the deputy, who was rising to his feet, holding his left shoulder. Blood seeped through his fingers onto the white sand. The thirsty desert dried it quickly, leaving dull brown spots.

"Is it bad, Steve?" asked Colt.

"Just nicked me," said Proffitt, shaking his head.

Dorianne was out of the coach and reached the bleeding deputy before Tanner and Byrd. "Let me see it, Mr. Proffitt," she said, reaching for the hand that pressed the wound.

The bleeding was already slowing down as the girl examined it. "It's not deep," she said assuringly. "Just caught the corner of the shoulder."

Within ten minutes a piece of petticoat stuffed inside the deputy's shirt had stopped the bleeding completely.

Proffitt rode in the coach till sundown. The weary travelers lowered the coach into a deep arroyo. Sitting down on the incline of the bank, they watched the last rays of the sunset.

"I'm so hungry," said Early Byrd, "I could eat thet there pinto."

"Don't you dare," chirped Dan, trying to lighten the moment. "She's gotta get us to Eternity." As he said it Dan silently wondered if there was anything left of the town by now. If the Apaches had attacked, those people did not have the guns they needed.

Saying no more, the broad-shouldered Colt reached to the floor of the coach where the canteen was kept and slung the strap over his shoulder.

"Jist give me that canteen, son," said Early, standing up. "I know where the waterhole is. I'll go after it."

"I can find it," protested Dan. "What would you say? 'Bout three miles?"

"I reckon so," replied the old man. "But you'll prob'ly not find it in the dark. Better if I go."

Dan succumbed to Early's reasoning, and the old man was up the bank and gone in the hovering gray light.

Somebody's stomach growled. No one commented. It would bring up the subject of food.

Steve Proffitt shackled Jake Finch to the left rear wheel of the stagecoach, under his useless protest.

The other four sat on the incline and watched the stars come out. A cool breeze whipped through the gully. Contrasted to the heat of the day, it raised goose bumps on everybody.

All was quiet for some time; then Dan Colt spoke. "I've got an idea."

"What's that?" asked Logan Tanner.

Dorianne was seated next to Colt. She reached over in the dark and slid her hand inside his arm.

"Those bucks no doubt heard Steve holler when he got hit,"

"I'm sure they did," commented Proffitt.

"They'll examine the ground where we were and see the blood spots, right?"

"I'd bet on it," said Tanner. "What're you gettin' at, Dave?"

"The name's *Dan*, Marshal," quipped Colt. "*D . . . a . . . n.*"

"Hmpf," came Tanner's response.

Dan continued. "Donimo is always within five hundred yards of the battle scene, right?"

"Mmm-hmm."

"They've studied us close enough to know how many of us there are and what we look like."

"Yep," agreed the marshal. "Finch may have confused them a bit today, but we can be sure they've noted each one of us."

"Okay," said Colt, "they know that one of us is hit, but they don't know how bad."

"What's this got to do with Donimo?" queried Proffitt.

"I'm comin' to that," said Dan. "Since we know they're trailin' us, they'll find where we holed up in here."

"Mmm-hmm," hummed Logan Tanner. "Go on."

"They won't attack till sunup. If we pull out while it's still dark and leave a grave in this gully, they'll think the man they hit died, right?"

"You lost me there," said the marshal. "You mean what looks like a grave?"

"Precisely," said Dan. "If when they come at us at sunup, we let them see everybody *minus me*, they'll think I was the one that died."

"Where *you* gonna be?" asked Tanner.

"Sneakin' up on Donimo," said Colt flatly. "If I can grab him and put a knife to his scaly throat, he would have to call off his dogs."

The big marshal's voice lifted with optimism. "That's a good idea, Dan—er . . . Dave."

"You slipped, Marshal," chided Dorianne.

"We'll have to pick our spot," said Dan. "A place with some protection, so you can hold them off long enough for me to locate Donimo, jump him and get him subdued."

"It's a long shot," said Steve, "but it's a good one. Gives us a fightin' chance."

"Let's get the grave dug," said Tanner, standing up and brushing at the seat of his pants.

"We'll have to haul a few large rocks from another area," put in Dan. "Gotta drop the rocks in the bottom of the grave. We won't have to dig real deep. Just enough to make it look authentic."

CHAPTER SEVENTEEN

Just about the time the bullet-riddled stagecoach was pulling into the arroyo, five riders sat silhouetted against the sunset at the base of Cathedral Rock.

"Whew!" said Skinny Mulligan, pinching his nose. "All that putrid red meat would gag a wagonload o' maggots!"

"Buzzards must've come fer miles around, judgin' by this mess," commented Pat Lewis. "Still they left a lotta meat."

"Must've got full," put in Tommy Elbert.

"Harry," said Dink Perryman, "that big lawman sure must have a powerful determination to get Jake to Yuma. From every indication we've saw, him and the folks on that stage have put up quite a fight agin them 'paches."

"If Jake's even still alive," replied Harry Doyle morosely. "For all we know, he could be in one of them two graves over there."

"Mebbe we should dig 'em up and see," said Skinny.

"You think that horsemeat stinks," observed Doyle, "we open them graves, you'll really smell somethin'!"

"If I'm readin' them wheel tracks correctly," spoke up Dink, "it ain't been too awful long since they pulled out. We catch up with that stage, it'll be easy to find out if Jake's still alive."

"Sure hope so," said Pat Lewis. "This gang ain't amounted to a hill o' beans since Jake got locked up."

"One thing I promise all of yuh," said Harry Doyle. "Them two tin stars are gonna die."

"Unless one or both of 'em's in them there graves," said Skinny Mulligan.

"Not a chance," argued Perryman. "If them two marshals is dead, the stage wouldn't still be headin' south."

"Why not?" asked Doyle. "It would just be a matter of survival now. Whoever's alive on that stage may be headin' for Eternity just to *stay* alive."

"Beats me how they're movin' that coach, Harry," said Tommy Elbert. "All six of the team are dead."

"Dunno," said Doyle. "Mebbe they harnessed up Logan Tanner. He's pert'near big as a horse."

"Yeah," said Dink Perryman, "or that big blond dude. He'd make a good pack animal!"

The five outlaws laughed and spurred their horses southward. Once out of range of the horrid stench, they dismounted and set up camp. Darkness enveloped the desert, and soon the stars were winking overhead.

"We'll move out just before dawn, boys," announced Harry Doyle. "Mebbe we can catch them folks on that stagecoach while they're still parked."

An hour before dawn the pinto mare strained in the harness, led by Dan Colt. The stagecoach angled out of the draw and soon was on the level, headed due south. Behind them, in the bottom of the arroyo, lay the somber mound. It was over six and a half feet long and three feet wide.

By the time the sun peeked over the eastern edge of the earth, the stagecoach group had found the spot where they would make their stand. The vehicle was stationed on the outer edge of a mass of large rocks that were surrounded on three sides by mesquite trees and creosote bush.

Dan Colt, with Larry Fields's .44 revolver holstered to his hip and Early Byrd's long-bladed hunting knife in a scabbard on his belt, was hunkered down in a shallow draw some fifty yards to the west. The area was spotted with rocks, draws and clumps of mesquite. Wherever Donimo positioned himself to observe the attack, Dan would have a good chance of sneaking up on him.

Warily Tanner, Proffitt, Byrd and Dorianne Kates stood around the exposed side of the coach. They made as if they were working

157

on a rear wheel. Jake Finch was standing a few feet away, both wrists in the cuffs.

"I know we have to make this look good," said Early nervously, "but I shore don't like bein' on exhibit like this."

"Once they count us and look us over," said Steve Proffitt, "Dan will be free to move in on Donimo. The filthy savage won't suspect a thing."

"The only thing that could mess it up," put in Tanner, "is if they don't inspect that draw where we left the grave."

"Don't you worry none about that," said Byrd. "Ole Dan knows his stuff. Them Apaches will see that set of wheel tracks goin' into the draw but none comin' out. They'll think we're still in there."

"Oh," said Dorianne, blinking her large brown eyes, "*that's* why Dan led the mare for a while in the draw before we came out."

"Keerect, honey," smiled Byrd, exposing his toothless gums. "Thet young feller you've set yore precious leedle heart on is one smart cookie." Byrd swerved his eyes and set them on Logan Tanner. "Much too smart to be a outlaw." There was a bite in Early's voice.

Steve Proffitt scanned the broad expanse of the desert. Nearby Tanner was doing the same thing.

"See anything?" asked the deputy.

"Nope," replied Tanner.

Moments passed.

Steve Proffitt stood up from where he had been bending over by the axle and cast a glance in the area where Jake Finch had been positioned. Dorianne was looking in one direction, Tanner another. Early was concentrating on the wheel. No one had noticed the outlaw slip away.

"Hey!" Proffitt shouted. "Finch has taken off!" The deputy bounded out onto the open flat, eyes darting in every direction. Logan Tanner was on his heels.

"There he is!" yelled Proffitt, heading in Finch's direction.

The outlaw was running for all he was worth. Proffitt dug in and sprinted toward him, hoping that Donimo would not show up at this moment. Tanner was falling behind in the race, cursing Jake Finch.

Finch looked over his shoulder at the oncoming deputy. Proffitt was definitely gaining on him. The outlaw strained to pick up speed, but to no avail. Steve hit him with a flying tackle. After a brief struggle Jake found himself being pushed and shoved back toward the stagecoach.

"You stupid idiot!" bawled Proffitt, pulling for air. "You're gonna get us all killed!"

US Marshal Logan Tanner met them where he had stopped and eyed Finch malevolently. "Where's your brain, Finch?" he snapped. "If you think you can make it alone out on this desert, you're stupider than I thought! Tryin' it with your hands shackled together, you're double stupid!"

Finch did not reply. Stiffening himself, he balked as Proffitt cuffed him to the stagecoach wheel.

"There," said Steve, dusting himself off. "Now you're going to have to hope Donimo gives me time to get you loose when he comes, Jake."

"Better get yore key back out right now!" said Early Byrd excitedly.

Tanner, Proffitt, Finch and the beautiful girl followed Early's crooked finger. Five paint ponies were bearing down on them from the north, at a full gallop. A sixth dropped back to watch. He sat a blue roan.

Quickly Proffitt loosened Finch from the wheel while the others ran to their fortified places where the guns were ready.

"C'mere, Jake," said Steve, leading the outlaw back in the brush. "Lie down right there." The deputy was pointing to a spot behind a rock shaded by a nearby mesquite. Hastily he shackled Finch to the tree.

Apache rifles began barking. Bullets slashed the rocks and ricocheted off into space. Proffitt dived to his place as the others opened fire at the screeching savages. Gunsmoke filled the air, stinging nostrils with its acrid bite.

Fifty yards to the west Dan Colt removed his hat and lifted his head enough to spot Donimo sitting on his roan to the north.

He was somewhat closer than usual. Dan judged him to be only about three hundred yards from the spot where Dorianne and the three men fought for their lives.

Colt breathed a silent prayer for Dorianne's safety and his own success and darted in a crouch for a patch of creosote. Quickly he dodged from bush to rock to gully, making a circle around the proud savage who sat erectly on his mount. Intent on the battle, the Apache did not see Dan working his way toward him.

Finally the tall man lay on the ground behind Donimo, catching his breath, his body weakened from lack of food.

Dan knew he had to do one of two things. He must capture Donimo and hurry him to the battle scene with a knife at his throat. Or he must kill him and let the other Apaches see his corpse. Either would cause them to give up the fight and ride away.

Slowly the blond man crawled toward the Apache from directly behind. When he reached a spot about twenty-five feet away, the blue roan nickered. Dan dropped to his belly and froze. Donimo turned, displaying his sharp-featured Indian profile. He scanned the immediate area, then returned his attention to the shooting.

Dan could easily kill the Indian by shooting him in the back, but there was something in him that would not allow it. Drawing his gun and earing back the hammer, he took a deep breath, preparing to call for Donimo to raise his hands. Just as he gained his feet, the horse nickered again and the Apache whirled. At the same instant that he saw Dan Colt, Donimo came off his horse. He hit the ground and rolled, whipping out his knife.

"Drop it!" bellowed Colt, leveling his gun on the red man.

Donimo hesitated. Dan stepped closer, to within six feet. "Just let the knife fall, Donimo," Dan said through clenched teeth. He had not noticed that the battle-wise Apache had grabbed a fistful of sand with his free hand. His black eyes were like cold bits of marble.

"I don't want to kill you, Donimo," said Colt raggedly, "but I will if I have to. Now drop the knife."

Donimo faked a look of resignation as the guns continued to roar three hundred yards away. He let the long-bladed knife fall to the ground.

Stepping closer, Dan said, "Now turn around. You and I are walking out there, and you're going to call off your yappin' dogs."

The sly Apache started to turn as Dan, eyes fixed on him, knelt to retrieve the knife. Quick as lightning, Donimo flung the sand into Colt's face. For a brief moment Dan was blinded, and the Indian took advantage of it to claw for Dan's gun.

Instantly Dan Colt was aware of why the son of Four Fingers was a great warrior. He was fast and he was strong. Tears flooded the white man's inflamed eyes as the two men wrestled for possession of the gun. Colt was three or four inches taller than his bronze-skinned opponent, but they weighed nearly the same. Dan was weak with hunger. Knowing this would be a fight unto the death, he began to call on his last reserves.

The Colt .44 discharged. Its report racketed across the hot sand but was lost in the noisy barrage coming from the rock enclosure. Suddenly the revolver came loose and sailed through the air. Donimo released his foe to dive for the knife. As his fingers closed around the handle, the lithe white man drove a burly shoulder into Donimo's rib cage, full force.

The Indian grunted with pain, rolling in the dust. But he had a solid grip on the knife with his right hand. As Colt followed, Donimo tried to stab him but missed. With a grip of steel, the blue-eyed man snatched the wrist that held the weapon. The two men rolled over and over, stirring up dust.

Donimo was on top now, trying to force the lethal blade into Colt's muscular chest. Both men sucked hard for air. The savage grunted heavily, pressing downward with all his might. The two men's arms quivered, one against the other.

Dan Colt felt his arms giving in. *Too long without food*, he thought.

The savage's face was twisted in a grin of triumph as the trembling blade slowly edged its way downward. The weary muscles in Colt's left arm screamed for relief.

"White Eyes die," hissed Donimo cruelly.

Overhead Dan saw two black buzzards sailing effortlessly in the Arizona sky. Shots still clattered from where Logan Tanner and the others were fighting off Donimo's bloodthirsty killers. Dan thought of Dorianne Kates. He must do something to spare her. Donimo knew she had killed several of his braves. If she ever fell into his hands she would be raped, tortured and brutally murdered. The thought shot a sudden surge of fresh strength through his body. Donimo's knife hand was abruptly forced back. The wicked grin disappeared from his face. Dan brought a knee up hard against the Apache's groin. Donimo did a somersault but came up quickly, still in possession of the knife. His black eyes were wild.

Colt ran his hand to the knife on his belt and whipped it out. Donimo fixed Dan Colt with a venomous stare. Breathing heavily, he said, "Donimo cut White Eyes real good before kill." With that he charged like a wild beast. Dan sidestepped but felt a sudden thread of fire run along his left forearm. His sleeve was split, and blood appeared instantly.

The wicked grin returned to the savage's dark lips. He charged again.

While the death struggle continued between Dan Colt and Donimo, the yelping Apaches watched one of their number hit the ground. He was dead on impact, a bullet through the heart. Without regrouping or discussion, they charged their horses straight in. It was as if the move had been prearranged.

Steve Proffitt shouted to the others, "Here they come!"

As the four savages rounded the stagecoach, Logan Tanner stood up and took aim at the one in the lead. His rifle spit fire. The Apache jerked as the slug tore into his body but held on as his pinto leaped the rocks. The other three came on fast. In a reckless frenzy the desperate Apaches raced in for the kill.

When the rumbling hoofs landed inside the enclosure, Jake Finch screamed, pressing himself into the mesquite limbs for safety. The small area was suddenly a melee of dust, smoke, bellowing voices, tromping horses and noise like thunder.

The lead Indian, felled by Tanner's bullet, rolled to a stop at Dorianne's feet. He struggled to get up, blood spurting from his chest. The look in his eyes froze the girl in her tracks. She stared in horror.

The savage found his feet, pulling a knife. As he drew back his arm, a rifle boomed. The red man arched his back and stiffened to his toes. He flopped to the ground, stiff as a board.

Dorianne saw Early Byrd's gun smoking. Early smiled and winked at the girl just as another Apache dived from his pony and drove a knife into the old man's side. Almost without thinking, Dorianne raised her rifle and put a bullet in the Indian's spine. He collapsed, rolled over and looked up at her with violent hatred. Swearing at her in his native language, he died. Dorianne ran to Early, who was down in the sand.

A stray bullet smacked into the neck of one of the pintos. It went down with a scream, falling on the Apache Dorianne had just killed.

Steve Proffitt found his rifle empty just as one of the Apaches charged him, knife blade flashing in the sun. Steve's right hand fanned his hip in a flicking draw. The revolver roared and the savage dropped like a wind-bitten cornstalk.

The last of the four savages and Logan Tanner were fighting hand to hand. They were rolling on the rocks, the Apache wielding a knife. Tanner was weakened from lack of food, but his burly frame was too much for the lean-bodied Indian.

The big marshal found the Indian's knife hand, swung him against a tall rock and jammed down the hand until the knife slid to the ground. In a fury Tanner seized the Apache by the hair and violently slammed his head against the rock again and again. Blood jetted across the rock and sprayed the marshal.

Tanner, teeth gritted, continued bashing the bloody mass against the hard surface until Proffitt stepped up and seized his arm. "The man's dead, Marshal," he said calmly.

Tanner paused, eyeing his deputy blankly. Then he blinked and let the lifeless Apache slide slowly down the rock.

CHAPTER EIGHTEEN

Time was swiftly running out, like the sifting sand in an hourglass, or like the blood running from Dan Colt's arm. Sensing Dan's growing weakness, Donimo charged again with a wild yell. The lethal blade sliced through the front of the tall man's shirt, missing the flesh. Dan parried, the tip of his knife raking deeply across Donimo's right bicep. The wounded savage stumbled backward. In desperation Colt lunged again while the Indian was off balance.

The nimble Donimo dodged Dan's blade. Colt's watery legs wavered under him. The angry men clashed again, bodies jarring from the impact. Both were sweating profusely.

The blazing sun had a temper of its own, slamming its blistering fury against the two men as the struggle continued.

The bulging vein on Donimo's right bicep was issuing a steady stream of blood. His cut was much more serious than the one on Colt's left forearm. Now the Apache was losing strength.

Again they were locked together face to face, hot breath commingling. Both men knew that one of them would be dead within minutes, and each was determined to be the victor.

The pretty face of Dorianne Kates flashed into Dan's mind. If this savage beast with black-slate eyes lived, she would die an ignominious death. It must not happen. It *must* not . . .

Suddenly Donimo's knee came up hard at Dan's groin, but the tall man sensed the movement and shifted so the knee struck his hip. The Apache was momentarily off balance, and Colt drove a vicious left hook to the Apache's nose. Donimo staggered, his vision blurred.

As Colt lunged for him, the battle-wise Indian darted sideways by instinct. Dan whirled. Donimo blindly threw a body block and the two bleeding fighters fell in the dust. Donimo's foot flashed out and clubbed Dan on the side of the head. Lights whirled in the tall man's brain. For an instant Donimo cast a shadow over the prostrate Colt, then the Indian was coming down on him like a giant bird of prey.

In that moment Dan Colt swiftly placed the handle of his knife against his own belly, the blade protruding skyward. Flicking the Indian's knife hand to the side as he came down, Dan grunted as Donimo's full weight slammed him. The knife sank into the savage's stomach all the way to the shank.

Immediately Colt felt warm blood washing over his hand. Donimo's eyes bulged. A groan escaped his lips.

Dan pushed the mortally wounded red man off him and struggled to his feet. Donimo's knife lay on the ground. Dan picked it up while the Apache rolled in sand and blood, the knife still in his belly.

The tall man stood over him, shoulders drooping, gasping for breath. Suddenly Dan was aware of the silence over the desert. Turning shakily on his feet, he squinted toward the rock enclosure. No one was in sight. Not even an Indian. *What had happened?*

Breathing laboriously, drenched with sweat and blood, Dan shuffled a few steps where he could see the stagecoach in the hot sun. Abruptly his ears picked up sliding, muffled footsteps behind him.

Donimo!

The indomitable savage had pulled the knife from his belly and was staggering toward Colt with the weapon poised for the kill. There was a wild, unearthly look in his eyes.

Twisting in time to meet him, Dan drove Donimo's own knife into his lower midsection. The Apache gasped, dropped Dan's knife and keeled over. He crawled a few feet in blind desperation, then rolled onto his back.

Colt moved close and stood over him. Only a spark of life remained in the glassy, dark eyes. As the tall man leaned over and yanked out the knife, the chilling sound of the death rattle met his ears.

Still struggling for life, Donimo rolled over, staining the white sand a deep crimson. His face in the sand, he spread both arms and dug his fingers into the ground. Then the Apache breathed his last and lay motionless.

Dan Colt summoned every ounce of strength and staggered in a crooked line toward the rock enclosure. His vision blurred, then cleared, then blurred again. Through the gathering fog, he saw a small, dark figure emerge from behind the stagecoach. Then the ground flew up and hit him square in the face.

"Oh, Dan! Dan!" cried Dorianne, dropping to her knees.

The tall man was splattered with blood. Dorianne eyed the blue roan standing riderless; then her vision fell on the sprawled, lifeless form of Donimo.

Carefully she rolled Dan over. The only wound Dorianne could find was the gash on his left forearm. She assumed that most of the blood on him was that of the Apache. Quickly the girl tore off a long strip of petticoat and began wrapping the bleeding arm.

Steve Proffitt appeared beside the stagecoach. When he spied Dorianne bending over Colt, he ran to her. "How is he?" asked the deputy, kneeling beside her.

"Cut on his arm," Dorianne replied hurriedly. "It's not real bad. He passed out." Pointing with her chin, she said, "Donimo's dead."

"I'll make sure," said Steve, rising. He strode to where the Apache leader lay facedown, fingers clutching the hot sand. One look settled it. The infamous warrior was no more. Proffitt took the reins of the big blue roan and led the animal toward Dorianne. "Here," he said. "You lead the horse. I'll carry him."

"Dan's coming around," said the girl.

Dan Colt's jaw worked as indistinguishable words came from his parched lips.

"Would you get the canteen, Mr. Proffitt?" asked Dorianne. "He needs water."

Leading the blue roan to the stagecoach, Proffitt tethered him and moved in to where Logan Tanner was tending to the wounded Wells Fargo driver. "Colt needs some water, Marshal," he said in a low tone. "He killed Donimo. Got himself cut a little. The girl's with him."

Tanner's lips curled in a half smile. "I'm glad that dirty savage is dead." Carefully the marshal poured a trickle of water in Early Byrd's half-open mouth, then capped it and gave it to his deputy.

Proffitt set his eyes on the colorless face of the wounded driver. "He's not gonna make it, is he?"

Tanner shook his head wordlessly.

When Proffitt reached him, Dan had come to and was on his feet. Dorianne was under one arm, helping him toward the mesquite-covered enclosure. The deputy adjusted himself under the other arm and uncapped the canteen. "Here, Dan," he said, "get some of this in you."

Colt gulped the warm water, spilling some on his blood-stained shirt. He coughed and said, "Thanks, Steve. I'll be all right now. Just pushed myself a little beyond the limit. Almost let that Apache kill me."

"A hot meal will help you feel stronger, Dan," spoke up Dorianne. "We're having horse steaks again."

"Suits me," smiled Colt. "Better'n starvin'."

A little more than an hour had passed before the weary group set their teeth into the horse meat. As they ate, Dan Colt noticed four pinto ponies tied to mesquite limbs on the back side of the rock enclosure. "Somebody's thinkin' pretty good" he mused.

Logan Tanner eyed him casually and spoke around a mouthful of meat. "What's that?"

"Tyin' up those Apache horses."

"Oh. Yeah. Steve's idea. He figured if those horses went home and straggled into camp, the Apaches would know what happened. Might send out a new army."

"Don't know how far the camp might be," said Steve, "but no sense takin' any unnecessary chances."

"That's good thinkin'," said Dan, nodding.

"Of course," put in Dorianne, "the most important animal not to let loose is Donimo's."

Dan's face stiffened. "That's for sure. Let that roan walk into the Apache camp and the whole tribe will be on us. After we bury

167

Donimo and the others, we'll have to take their horses to Eternity with us. We'd best hightail it as quick as possible." The tall man's blue eyes swung to where Early Byrd lay in pain on the sand. A cloth compress covered the deep wound in his side. He looked at Colt with dull eyes and tried to smile.

"I hope Early can take the trip," said Dan.

"He's not good," muttered Tanner.

"Dan," said Dorianne with concern, "you need to wash out that gash on your arm. It isn't real deep, but there is sand and dirt in there that I couldn't get out."

Colt nodded. "It'll take more water than what's in the canteen."

"It's nearly empty," said Tanner. "We've used quite a bit for Early."

"Best thing is for me to go to the water hole," said Dan. "Wash out my cut right there. I'll fill the canteen and head back. We'll load Early in the stage and move on."

"Dan, you're in no condition to do that," protested Dorianne.

"I'll be okay," responded the tall man. "I'll ride the roan and be back in less than an hour."

"Good," said Tanner. "We'll bury these Apaches and be ready to pull out. Diggin's easy in the sand. Jake can help us."

Colt stood up. His legs were still a bit shaky, but already the food in his stomach was renewing his strength. He picked up the canteen and headed toward the roan, which was tied to the stagecoach.

Early called to him, his voice faint. Dan stopped and turned around. As he stepped near, the old man said thickly, "The . . . water hole . . . is jist about three miles from . . . from here. Can't miss it. Right by a double-trunked tree. You . . . might have to dig in the sand . . . to bring it to the surface."

Colt thanked Byrd and headed once again for the roan.

Dorianne rushed over to him. "Dan, be careful," she said. "If any Apaches see you on Donimo's horse, they'd kill you on the spot."

"I'll be careful," he said, patting her shoulder. "And thank you for comin' to my aid."

"Oh!" said the girl. "Just a minute." Stepping away, she turned her back and bent over. Dan heard a ripping sound. She whirled

168

around with another strip of petticoat. "Here's a fresh bandage for your arm."

"Thanks, little lady," said Dan warmly. "I'll see you in a little while."

With a bit of effort Colt swung to the bare back of the blue roan and headed due south. The sun was moving higher in the sky.

Dan held the roan to a steady walk. It was not good to push the animal hard in this heat. Besides, the pain in his arm would only get worse with jostling. The cut had apparently stopped bleeding.

Slitting his eyes against the glare, the tall man scanned the desert around him. He felt tremendous relief. Now they had a chance to make it. A good one, unless they ran onto another war party.

It was high noon when Dan Colt reached the water hole and slid off the horse's broad back. He lifted the sling over his head and pulled the cap from the canteen. Before kneeling, he surveyed the shimmering land in every direction. No sign of life whatsoever.

Satisfied that he was alone, Colt dropped to his knees beside the hole. A thin film of warm water lay over the shallow, sandy bottom. Early was right. He was going to have to dig in the sand to get more of the life-giving liquid.

Lying on his belly, Dan began digging with his hands. Pulling the wet sand toward him in a series of scooping motions, he soon had fresh, cool, clear water bubbling toward him.

First he filled the canteen. Rising to a sitting position, he drank long and deep. He replenished the canteen again and capped it. Then he removed his hat, dipped it in the water upside down and filled it. He carried it to Donimo's horse and let him drink. This was repeated six times, until the roan had enough.

The next task was to peel off the petticoat bandage. Dan took a long look around him, found the desert hot but motionless, and unwrapped the bandage. The cut immediately began to bleed again. Dan knew it had to, in order to get more dirt out. He would have liked to have a disinfectant, even if it was only whiskey. The gash was about a quarter of an inch deep. It ran midway between elbow and wrist, about four inches in length.

Going to his belly again, he submerged the wound, swirling the water in order to dislodge dirt and sand particles. The process continued for a good quarter hour. At last he examined the

169

smarting gash carefully, then reapplied the makeshift bandage. Wrapping it tight to check the bleeding, the blond man knotted it with his teeth. He looked the area over again and swung aboard Donimo's roan.

The sun's early rays pressed against the eyelids of Harry Doyle. He lay slack, his head partially on his saddle. Held loosely in one hand was an empty brown bottle. Three other empty bottles were strewn on the sand.

Doyle blinked at the sun, closed his eyes and groaned. He felt the smooth glass in his hand. With a stiff arm he lifted it upward, then opened his eyes slightly and tried to focus on it. The burning rays stung his bloodshot eyes. He quickly closed them again, but he'd seen enough to know that the bottle was empty. Without looking he gave it a disgusted toss.

The whiskey bottle sailed twenty feet through the air and banged Dink Perryman on the head. Perryman hollered and swore with a slurred tongue. Rolling over in the sand, he sat up. Narrowing his gaze against the glare of the morning sun, he looked around at the other four outlaws, who were stretched out on the ground. Angrily he rubbed his head and yelled, "Who flung that bottle?"

Harry Doyle rolled up to his knees and guffawed. "I flung that bottle, Dink! Now whatcha gonna do about it?"

"I'll show yuh!" exclaimed Perryman, staggering to his feet. With uneven steps Dink scuffed through the sand and piled on top of Doyle. The two outlaws, still feeling the effects of the alcohol they had consumed far into the night, rolled and wrestled on the ground.

The other three were awakened by the noise and sat up, rubbing their eyes and holding their heads.

Doyle and Perryman carried on for several minutes, now laughing playfully like schoolboys. Finally Skinny Mulligan found his feet and hollered, "Okay, boys! That's enough! We gotta get goin'!"

"Yeah," put in Tommy Elbert. "We drank too much and slept too late. That stagecoach is gonna get way ahead of us."

"They ain't travelin' very fast," said Doyle, now on his feet, brushing off the dust. "We'll catch 'em without too much trouble."

170

"I got another bottle in my saddlebag," offered Pat Lewis. "Let's have another shot."

"Save it," said Harry. "I got one, too. We'll use 'em to celebrate after we spring Jake and kill them stinkin' lawmen."

CHAPTER NINETEEN

Dorianne Kates watched Dan Colt's broad back as he rode away on Donimo's blue roan. As she stood motionless, Steve Proffitt climbed up on the stagecoach and tossed off two shovels. The tools bounded and fell against a creosote bush.

"Unlock Jake's wrists, Steve," said Logan Tanner, heading for the shovels.

The big marshal stepped to the spot where the shovels lay and looked toward Dorianne. "Miss Kates," he called. "Would you come and stay with Early while we dig the graves?"

The wistful girl turned and nodded.

"All right, Jake," said Proffitt, turning the key in the handcuffs, "you're gonna help us dig some more graves."

Finch emitted a deep growl and said, "I helped you bury white men. Okay. But I ain't sweatin' my guts out to bury no stinkin' redskins."

Logan Tanner heard the remark. Picking up a shovel, he said, "Clout him one on the noggin with your gun barrel, Steve."

Proffitt slipped the revolver from his holster, looking the outlaw straight in the eye. His face was rigid, determined.

"All right, all right," said Finch, raising his palms.

Proffitt stuck the handcuffs in his hip pocket. "You help the marshal get started, Jake. I'll go drag Donimo's body in."

Dorianne eased herself down beside Early Byrd. The unmistakable pallor of death evident on the leathered old face.

Dabbing at the sweat beads on his brow, she said, "Are you in a lot of pain?"

The dying man nodded, running his tongue over his dry lips. "Yes'm. I . . . I think the blade . . . went half . . . halfway through me."

"We'll get you to Eternity," said Dorianne, trying to sound optimistic. "The doctor there will fix you up."

"Ain't . . . ain't no doc at Eternity," said the old man. "Closest . . . one is at the fort. Fraid I'm . . . I'm gonna be . . . a goner before we ever . . . ever git there."

"Now you just hang on, Early," said the girl. "Dan will be back in a little while and we'll be on our way."

"I'm not gonna make it, honey," said Byrd, his breathing becoming more laborious.

Dorianne took a quick look at the compress on Early's side. It was glistening with blood. She knew he was probably bleeding even more internally. "Oh, Early," she said, tears welling up in her eyes, "if you hadn't taken your eyes off that savage who was coming at you . . ."

"Had to, honey," said Byrd, coughing. "Thet other'n woulda . . . woulda killed you if'n . . . if'n I hadn't . . . shot him."

Tears were now spilling from Dorianne's eyes. "But if it weren't for me, you wouldn't . . . you wouldn't—"

"Every man's gotta . . . gotta go sometime, honey. I couldn't jist stand . . . there and let that . . . Indian kill yuh. If'n I . . . I gotta go a leedle sooner . . . I'm . . . I'm glad it could be . . . for yore . . . s-sake."

"Oh, Early," Dorianne said, wiping away tears. "Please don't die. Please."

The old man's eyes were closed, but his chest continued to rise and fall slowly. The girl continued mopping his fevered brow. She noticed Byrd's revolver was still belted to his waist. She thought about removing it but decided against it. The movement would only cause him more pain.

Steve Proffitt dragged Donimo's corpse to the spot where Tanner and Finch were digging. The dead Apache's heels left a double trail across the sand.

"I don't think Byrd's gonna make it much longer, Steve," said the marshal, pitching dirt and breathing heavily. The sun was almost at its apex and was bearing down hard.

"He's probably sliced up pretty bad inside," responded Proffitt.

"If he's still alive when Sundeen gets back, I doubt he'll last an hour jostlin' around inside the stage."

"Poor old guy," said Steve sorrowfully.

Tanner stopped digging, lifted his hat and sleeved away the moisture on his brow. "How's your shoulder, Steve?" he asked.

"Won't bother me to handle a shovel, Marshal," Steve answered with a tight grin.

"How about me gettin' a rest?" demanded Jake Finch, anger in his eyes.

"You keep diggin'," rasped Tanner. "I'll spell you as soon as I catch my breath."

As Proffitt traded places with Tanner, Finch swung his shovel, striking the marshal on the right arm. With lightning speed he lunged for the gun in Tanner's holster. Just as his fingers closed over the gun butt, Steve Proffitt came down savagely on the outlaw's wrist with the head of his own shovel. Jake howled and grabbed his wrist as Tanner stepped away, rubbing his arm.

Anger sparked in Steve Proffitt. He took two steps toward Finch, eyes blazing. Jake saw the punch coming and tried to raise his hands in defense. But he was too late. The deputy's fist came on his jaw like a savage club. The blow sounded like a flat rock landing in mud. The outlaw's knees buckled and he dropped to the hot sand, unconscious.

Proffitt turned to Tanner, who was briskly rubbing his upper arm. "You all right, sir?"

Tanner swore. "I will be when this quits hurtin'!"

"Did it break the skin?"

"Naw, just bruised it good." Tanner's eyes fell to the outlaw lying in a crumpled heap on the sun-bleached earth. "You really chopped him one," he said, shifting his gaze to the deputy.

"Been wantin' to do it since we left Taos," said Proffitt, grinning. "He just gave me an excuse."

By the time another hour had slipped into history, the Apaches were buried in shallow graves. The three men moved back into the rock enclosure. Jake Finch rubbed his aching jaw. Steve Proffitt dropped the shovels next to the creosote bush. He did not see the slithering diamondback glide smoothly to the base of the bush from between two rocks and slowly coil near one of the shovels.

US Marshal Logan Tanner squeezed his eyelids to a slit, studying the land to the south. The only movement was that of the heat waves rising off the horizon. Tanner ran a dry tongue over equally dry lips. All the moisture seemed drained from his body. Turning into the enclosure, he said, "Wish Sundeen would get back here with that water."

"Yeah, me too," groaned Finch.

"We need to be ready to travel when he does," said Steve, who was standing over Early Byrd.

"How's he doin'?" asked Tanner, drawing near.

Dorianne looked up from her place next to the dying man. Her face was drawn and pale. "I'm afraid he's about gone, Marshal," she said with trembling voice.

"We'll load him in the coach the last thing," said Tanner. "Let's hook up the pinto mare to it, Steve. We'll tie the other horses to the rear."

"Okay," replied Proffitt. He turned to Finch. "You help him, Jake. I'll bring the horses around."

Finch's face was sour, but Steve's punch had taken the sass out of him. The outlaw followed Tanner to the stagecoach like an obedient puppy.

Soon the coach was ready to roll. The marshal cast another glance to the south. No sign of the blond man. "Let's get Early in the stage, Steve," he said. "We'll go ahead and pull out. We're bound to run into Sundeen." His face twisted. "You don't suppose he took off, do you?"

"He gave his word, Marshal," said Proffitt dryly. "He'll be along."

Dan Colt had left the water hole about a half mile behind him when he spotted movement due north. His heart froze. It was a band of Apaches. *Search party.* Looked to be about twenty of them. They were swinging in from the west and turning slowly toward him. He spotted a gully about fifty yards to his left.

As far as he could tell, they had not seen him yet. But they soon would. The big blue roan would be easy to spot against the buff-color desert. Dan knew his only hope was to separate from the horse.

Quickly he slid to the ground. He felt for Larry Fields's revolver, making sure it was in the holster. Adjusting the strap of the canteen, he bellied down and crawled westward toward the gully. The roan watched him idly, then lifted his head, looking at the approaching band of Apaches. The horse nickered and moved toward them at a trot.

Dan slid over the edge of the gully and spun around to watch. The Indians had spotted the roan and were galloping toward him. *Things will get hot now*, he thought. The tall man hoped that since Donimo's horse was coming from the south, the Apaches would start the search in that direction. He must get to the others and warn them. It was only a matter of time until the band of savages would ascertain that Donimo and his men had met their fate somewhere to the north.

Colt moved to the bottom of the gully, which ran snakelike to the north. The heat was like an oven, but he ran as fast as he could. After several moments he paused to catch his breath and eased up the incline to take a look. He breathed a sigh of relief. As he'd hoped, the Apaches were on a course due south, leading the riderless roan.

Sliding back to the bottom of the draw, he ran again. Time was of the essence. *Only a couple of miles*, he told himself.

Dan ran until he came to the end of the gully. It slowly ascended to the desert floor, then petered out. He paused to look southward. The Apaches were gone.

His breath was coming in short gulps. His whole body was soaked with sweat. The gash in his left arm was throbbing. Dan fought the desire to drink from the canteen. He and the others would have to go around the water hole. This could be the last water until they reached Eternity. No, he dare not drink of it now.

Forcing his weary legs, he pressed on.

The ball of fire in the sky seemed to mock him, sucking the moisture from his aching body. On he ran, stumbling and staggering in the direction of the rock enclosure. Now he was crossing the place where the band of Apaches had first been seen. The prints of shoeless horses were cut deep in the soft earth.

Suddenly Dan Colt's head began to whirl. He stopped, trying to catch his breath. A hazy pressure seemed to be building up behind his eyeballs. His mouth was dry as a sand pit. He had to have water. *Better to take a little,* he reasoned. *Without it I'll never get there.*

Dropping to his knees, Colt uncapped the canteen. With shaky hands he raised the spout to his lips. He took one big mouthful of the life-giving liquid and slapped on the cap. He rolled the water around in his mouth, allowing it to slowly trickle down his throat. When it was all gone, Dan lifted his hat and ran a tattered sleeve over his glistening forehead. Slowly he rose to his feet and pressed forward.

The burning sun seemed to scorch his sweat-soaked body. He had only gone a little way when the smoky pressure began to press the back of his eyes again. The whole world seemed to whirl around him. All at once his knees gave way, and Dan sprawled in the dust.

The sun bore down with murderous heat. As the tall man rolled over on his back, it felt as though red-hot spikes were being driven into his eyes. He managed to get over on his belly again. Dan's face dropped into the sand. His mouth touched the hot particles and some of them clung to his lips. Raising his head, he used his tongue to spit them off. The blond man lay still for several minutes, trying to gain enough strength to get up and go again. Silently he pronounced a curse on the elements. It seemed that the relentless sun and the voracious desert had joined forces to devour him.

The pressure behind Dan's eyes seemed to ease up. With effort he was once again on his feet. He had to get to Tanner. These Apaches would be back when they found no sign of Donimo and his warriors to the south.

After falling twice more, Dan finally spied the rock enclosure on the northern horizon. Just as it came into view, the pressure mounted behind his eyes again. This time it brought a filmy blackness, clouding his vision. He was down on the fiery sand again.

Blindly Colt struggled to his feet and staggered on. His vision cleared momentarily and he saw several dark figures moving about. His legs gave out again, and he sank to the ground. He lay

177

there for a long moment, then jerked as a gunshot rang out from the enclosure, echoing staccato-style across the desert.

Dan lay motionless for nearly half an hour, fighting the black fog that was trying to claim him. Another shot cut the hot desert air. A weak moan escaped the blond man's lips. He heard distant pounding hoofs just before a swirl of darkness engulfed him.

Logan Tanner and Steve Proffitt carefully placed Early Byrd on one seat in the stagecoach. The vehicle was not wide enough for him to lie down. They braced him up in a corner, and Dorianne moved in beside him to make the old man as comfortable as possible.

Steve Proffitt moved to Jake Finch while Tanner was doing last-minute checking around the grounds.

Pulling the handcuffs from his hip pocket, the deputy said, "After your little trick with the shovel, I've decided to chain you to me again, Jake. We'll walk together and lead the mare while Mr. Tanner rides one of the other pintos."

"Why can't I ride, too?" snapped Finch angrily.

"Because somebody has to lead the mare, and since you are full of tricks, you'll be shackled to me." Steve turned the key in the cuffs, flipping them open. Dropping the key back in his vest pocket, he said, "Gimme your right wrist."

Glumly the outlaw obeyed. The ratchets clicked as Proffitt tightened the cuff on Finch's wrist. Then he clamped the other one on himself. Looking through the coach window, the deputy said, "You holler if it gets too rough in there, Miss Kates."

Dorianne, still dabbing perspiration from Byrd's fevered brow, nodded and tried to smile.

Logan Tanner was moving toward the stagecoach when he spied the two shovels lying by the creosote bush. He strode to the spot, leaned over and raised one of the shovels with his right hand. Steadying the tool, he bent down to retrieve the other with his left hand.

There was a sudden hiss, followed by a rattling sound. It happened too fast for the marshal to avoid it. A greenish-gray blur preceded a sharp pain on the back of his left hand. The rattlesnake was coiling for another strike, its little forked tongue darting in and out.

Logan Tanner hollered and reacted at the same instant. The shovel in his right hand chopped violently, slicing into the snake's body with the first blow. The stunned diamondback recoiled and struck at the shovel. The second blow severed its head. While the long, scaly body moved and slithered in the throes of death, the marshal looked down at his hand. There were two little red slashes just above the knuckles.

Dragging Jake Finch behind him, Steve bounded to Tanner. He eyed the wriggling snake and the bloody head. "He get you?" he asked, looking into Tanner's face, then at his trembling hand.

"Yeah," said the marshal, trying to keep control of himself. "Get a knife quick and cut it open. I've got to get that poison out of there." The big man was clutching his wrist tight, attempting to stop the venom from getting into the bloodstream.

Suddenly a dark figure appeared between the rocks, gun leveled. "Forget it, deputy!" barked Harry Doyle. His voice was cold as an arctic wind.

"Harry!" exclaimed Finch. "How'd you—? Boy, am I glad to see you!"

The other four outlaws stepped out, guns drawn.

"Howdy, boys!" smiled Finch. "You showed up just in time!"

Logan Tanner dropped to his haunches, his face white.

Steve Proffitt eyed Doyle stonily and said, "The marshal was just bitten by a rattler, Harry. I've got to tend to him."

Doyle let his malignant dark eyes drop to the dead snake. Chuckling, he said, "So he was." Lifting his gun to Tanner, he shook his head. "Tsk. Tsk. Now that's just terrible, ain't it?"

Proffitt started to move. The outlaws poised their weapons.

"You fire those guns, you're liable to bring a whole army of Apaches down on us," warned Proffitt. "We've killed the son of Chief Four Fingers. There'll be search parties lookin' for him. Gunshots will draw them here like ants to a picnic. We'll all die. Now put away your guns. I've got to help the marshal."

"Leave him be!" bellowed Doyle, his face hard.

Proffitt's eyes spat fire. "Doyle, you fool!" he snapped. "If you let the marshal die, it's *murder!* Do you understand that? Now back off. I'm goin' to take care of that snakebite."

"Murder?" heckled Harry Doyle. "Would you like to know what murder is?"

179

The outlaw's eyes were wild. The gun in his hand roared. Steve Proffitt buckled as the bullet tore into the lower part of his rib cage. He grunted and keeled over.

Dorianne Kates screamed. Dink Perryman charged toward Doyle, anger written on his features. "Harry, you stupid fool!" bellowed Dink. "Didn't you hear what he said about them Apaches bein' near? You wanta get us all scalped?"

Dorianne was out of the stagecoach, kneeling beside the fallen deputy. Jake Finch was down on one knee, held there by the handcuff on his right wrist.

Steve rolled his eyes and set them on the girl. He opened his mouth to speak. The words never came. His eyes closed and his body went limp. Dorianne began to weep. Leaping to her feet, she screamed at Harry Doyle, "You dirty beast! You killed him!" While she screamed she lunged at the outlaw, clawing for his eyes.

The girl's attack took Doyle off guard. Her fingernails dug into his eyes, instantly drawing blood. His big fist swung hard, and Dorianne fell to the ground, stunned.

At the same instant that Dorianne lunged for Doyle, Logan Tanner let go of his wrist and went for his gun. His awkward position made him slow. Tommy Elbert shot out a boot and kicked the gun from his hand. Tanner fell to a sitting position and immediately grasped his wrist again.

"Now we'll take care of the big-shot lawman!" said Doyle, turning toward Tanner, thumbing at his eyes.

"No more gunplay!" snarled Dink Perryman. "You think we can fight off an army of Apaches?" Turning in disgust, Perryman ran to the outer edge of the enclosure, scanning the desert.

"He's right, Harry," said Jake Finch. "We don't need them Apaches on top of us!"

"There ain't no need to shoot Mr. Tanner ennyway, Harry," spoke up Pat Lewis. "He cain't hold onto thet wrist forever. When thet there pizen rides the bloodstream to his *ticker* . . . *wham!* He's one dead lawman!"

Harry Doyle guffawed, dropping his revolver into its holster. "You're right, Pat!" he said with a laugh. "We'll just leave him here for the buzzards!" Doyle blinked, his eyes still smarting.

Perryman returned, saying, "Ain't no Indians in sight at the moment, Harry. Let's take Jake and light outta here."

"Okay," responded Doyle. "You find that deputy's key and get him loose."

As Dink stepped toward Finch, the outlaw boss shook his head, holding up a mangled key. "Won't work," said Jake. "Deputy kept the key in his vest pocket. This was the only one."

"Just stretch it out, boss," said Doyle, drawing his gun. "I'll shoot the chain. We can worry about getting the bracelet off later."

"No!" shouted Finch. "Whatsa matter with you, Harry? Are you deaf? There's Apaches roamin' these parts."

Doyle jammed the gun back in his holster. "Well, whatta you gonna do, Jake? You gonna drag that stinkin' corpse with you?"

"Lemme think a minute," replied Finch, wipin' sweat from his face.

Dorianne was sitting up, rubbing her jaw. Shaking her head, she stood to her feet and walked unsteadily to Logan Tanner. "I'll get Early's knife, Marshal," she said softly. "I've never seen a snakebite before, but if you'll tell me what to do, I'll cut it open."

Tanner's face was ashen gray. He nodded.

As the girl turned toward the stagecoach, Harry Doyle barked, "You ain't gittin' no knife! Stay right where you are, girlie!" Touching his eyes tenderly, he snarled, "After what you did to me, I've a notion to kill you, too!"

The veins in Dorianne's temples stuck out like swollen pieces of rope. "If I was a man," she hissed through clenched teeth, "I'd tear you apart!"

Doyle flashed her an insolent smile and looked toward the stagecoach. Speaking to Mulligan, he said, "Skinny, check out the stagecoach."

As Skinny Mulligan complied, Doyle said to his boss, "Too bad about that blond dude. We saw his grave back there in that gully. Apaches kill 'im?"

"He ain't dead, Harry," said Finch evenly.

"Huh?"

The eyes of Perryman, Elbert and Lewis swung to Jake Finch.

"Naw, that grave was just a fake to fool them stupid redskins into *thinkin'* he was dead. Worked, too. Colt slipped up on Four Fingers's son and killed him."

"Where is he now?" asked Tommy Elbert.

"He's ridin' Donimo's horse to get water at a hole due south of here."

Surprise registered on the outlaws' faces. Dink Perryman blurted, "How come the marshal turned *him* loose?"

"He's got a gun, too," added Finch.

Dink's mouth dropped open. "How come?"

Finch cocked his head. "He an' this federal man have some kind of agreement. Colt won't try an' escape till his girlfriend here, is safe."

"How come he went after water?" asked Pat Lewis. "Since y'all was headin' thet way ennyhow, why'nt yuh jist wait till yuh got to it?"

"Colt's got him a bad cut needed washin' out," answered Jake. "Besides, the stage driver's wounded purty bad. Colt's bringin' water back for him."

"He ain't gonna be needin' it." It was Skinny Mulligan's voice. "The stage driver's dead."

CHAPTER TWENTY

A piteous gasp escaped Dorianne Kates's lips when she heard that Early Byrd was dead. Dropping to her knees beside Logan Tanner, she sobbed, "Oh, Marshal, isn't this nightmare ever going to end?"

Jake Finch raised his shackled hand, lifting the lifeless limb of Steve Proffitt upward. "Guess the only way outta this," he said to Harry Doyle, "is to cut his hand off."

Between her sobs, Dorianne heard Finch's statement. She whirled, looking at him in stark disbelief. A chill ran over her body. "No! You're not going to do it!" she screamed.

"Get your knife, Harry," said Finch, ignoring the girl.

Doyle turned coldly and walked toward his horse.

"No!" Dorianne screamed again.

"You're no different than those Apache savages," growled Logan Tanner. "Only uncivilized savages mutilate the bodies of those they kill!"

"Shut up!" snapped Finch. "It's the only way for me to get loose without shootin' the chain. You want us to signal the Apaches where we are?"

"No," said Tanner, "but—"

"Here's the knife, Jake," cut in Doyle.

"Get it over with," said Finch.

As Harry knelt and seized Steve Proffitt's limp hand, Dorianne screamed in sheer horror and bolted for Doyle.

Pat Lewis jumped in and seized her. She fought him, kicking, scratching, biting. Lewis laughed, grasping her wrists and pulling her close to him. In her cramped position she could do nothing.

"You're a reg'lar little ball o' fire, ain'tcha, honey?" laughed Lewis. "How about a sweet kiss for ole Pat?"

The outlaw lowered his grisled, prickly face toward Dorianne's. She waited until his tobacco-stained lips touched her own, then, quick as a cat, sank her teeth into his lower lip and clamped down hard.

Lewis howled. Dorianne tasted blood, but she held on. Lewis howled again. Dink Perryman sprang to Pat's rescue, snatching Dorianne to pull her away. Her teeth held the bleeding lip. Lewis's mouth and head followed. Blood ran as Lewis hollered. Perryman cocked his fist and slammed it to the girl's jaw. She went down in a heap.

Pat Lewis ran to his horse and began dousing his torn lip with water from his canteen.

Soon the outlaws were ready to travel. They would take the four pintos of the dead Apaches. Jake Finch would ride one, Dorianne another. The other two would follow on lead ropes. They left the mare hitched to the stagecoach.

Dorianne was hoisted to the back of her horse, still groggy from being knocked out. A violent headache stabbed her with pain. The lovely face was bruised and her hair disheveled. Her dress was torn, dusty and spotted with blood.

Jake Finch unbuckled Logan Tanner's gun belt and wrapped it around himself. He picked up the revolver, dusted it off and holstered it. He and Harry Doyle stood over the marshal, who still gripped his wrist. The poisoned hand was swelling.

"Sorry you won't be plantin' me in Yuma, Logan," said Jake with a sneer.

"You'll be planted soon enough," retaliated Tanner. "Only it won't be Yuma. It'll be in your grave. You'll hang right along with the others for killin' my deputy."

Finch laughed. "Now just who's gonna be around to testify against us, Logan? You've got to let go of that wrist sooner or later. You'll be dead easy by sunup."

"Yeah," said Doyle, still fingering at his scratched eyes. "We're takin' the girl as insurance for when we meet up with her big tall

184

boyfriend. Once we dispose of him, we'll put a bullet in her head. Won't be one single, solitary witness to no killin'."

"We're goin' to Eternity for food and whiskey," said Finch. Pointing to the remains of the fly-covered pinto, which lay a few feet away, he added, "You can have my share of the horsemeat for supper tonight."

Laughing, the two outlaws walked out of the rock enclosure, swung into their saddles and galloped away. Dorianne bounced and swayed on the pinto's back, only half aware of what was happening.

Logan Tanner struggled against the panic that was rising within him. Nausea was claiming his stomach, and his head was going light. He was trying to remember where Early kept his big knife. It was somewhere in the stagecoach. Gripping his wrist tightly, he forced himself to stand up. His legs were like hot rubber. Slowly he shuffled toward the bullet-riddled stagecoach. He had to find Early's knife.

The black whirlpool seemed to spit Dan Colt from its depths as fast as it had sucked him in. He opened his eyes and blinked against the brassy glare. He did not know how long he had been out, but from the position of the sun he decided it had been only a few minutes.

Pulling his knees under him, he raised himself up and looked toward the rock enclosure. He could see the top of the stagecoach, but the dark figures he had seen milling about before were gone.

Dan took a healthy swig from the canteen and rose to his feet. He would make it now. The pressure in his head had subsided. *Only about three hundred yards*, he told himself. *You can do it*.

Angling in from the southwest, the tall man made his way steadily for the mesquite-covered clump of rocks. The next few moments seemed like a year, but finally Dan Colt stumbled into the rocky area. He took note that the pinto mare was hitched to the stagecoach. The Indian ponies were nowhere in sight. Two more steps revealed the decapitated rattlesnake and the body of Steve Proffitt.

Dan's eyes bulged as they focused on the bloody stump at the end of the deputy's wrist and the lifeless hand lying nearby. He breathed an angry oath, eyes sweeping the area for signs of life.

Suddenly he thought of the girl. Had the Apaches come and taken her and the others? Proffitt's blood-soaked shirt indicated that he might have been dead before they cut off his hand.

Abruptly Dan was aware of a scraping sound from near the stagecoach. He whirled. The door was open. The bulky form of Logan Tanner was half in and half out. Shuffling toward the marshal, he heard the man's heavy breathing.

Colt's eyes caught a glance of Early Byrd's body in a corner on the seat. Hoisting Tanner's head and shoulders from the coach floor, he eased him to the ground. The lawman's face was pallid, bright with sweat.

"Tanner!" Dan said, kneeling over him. "Where are Dorianne and Jake? What happened? Who took them? Where are the Apache horses?"

Logan Tanner looked at Colt with glassy, droop-lidded eyes. Rolling his tongue with effort, he said weakly, "S-snake."

"The rattler? Did it bite you?"

Tanner nodded, swallowing hard.

"Where?" asked Dan, searching with his eyes.

Slowly the poisoned lawman raised his swollen left hand. Colt eyed the two little punctures just below the knuckles. "T-tryin' t-to find the knife," he said slowly.

Dan remembered that whenever Early had used the knife, he had gone up to the driver's seat to get it. The demand of the moment seemed to lance strength into his body. Hastily he climbed up and found the knife in a sheath on the seat. Wasting no time, the desert-wise Colt cut an *x* over each puncture and sucked blood and poison, spitting it into the brush.

Tanner groaned and rolled his head. His eyes were two dark hollows. He swallowed with difficulty.

Dan walked to Proffitt's body and pulled the deputy's red handkerchief from his hip pocket. Wrapping it around Tanner's swollen hand, he said, "Now, Marshal, you have got to remain as calm as possible. Anything that makes your heart beat fast can kill you. Much of the poison is still in your hand. It's gonna make you violently ill, but if you stay calm, you'll live."

Grasping the canteen, he gave the marshal a good drink, then took one himself. "Can you talk, Tanner?" asked Dan, capping the canteen.

186

The marshal struggled to speak. "My . . . my throat is . . . is swelling. But I'll t-try." Working his tongue laboriously, he said, "Finch's men. They . . . broke jail. D-Doyle shot Steve."

"Why'd they take Dorianne?"

"Hostage. P-protection from you. Th-they plan . . . to kill . . . kill her."

Colt's blood ran hot. "Where they goin'?"

"Eternity. Food . . . whiskey."

"Stupid fools," blurted Dan. "They're ridin' straight into a band of Apaches. I had to let Donimo's horse go. They have him now. It won't be long until they head this way. If the Apaches find Jake and his men with those pintos . . ."

The tall man turned and looked at the mutilated body of the deputy. "Why'd they do that?" he asked, face twisted.

"Bullet went . . . right through the pocket . . . where the key was," said Tanner, struggling with his swollen throat. "They . . . didn't want to shoot the chain. Afraid the Apaches . . . might hear the . . . shot. So they cut off—" Tanner could not finish it. "Could . . . could I have some . . . some more water?"

Without speaking Colt gave the sick marshal another pull on the canteen.

"Tanner," said Dan, "did they kill Early?"

The marshal rolled his head slowly. "No. He died . . . from the Apache knife."

"Look," said Dan, "we've got to try and catch Jake and his bunch before they meet up with that war party. I don't care about those outlaws, but Dorianne's with them. I'm gonna put Steve and Early's bodies up top and cover them with the tarp. You can ride in the coach."

"No," said Tanner, choking on the word. "Just get on the mare and ride. Leave me here."

"I can't do that, Marshal. If those Apaches came back and found you here, they'd torture you a long time before you died."

"But pullin' . . . the stage . . . will be too . . . slow."

"I can't just leave you here," said Dan flatly. "I'll ride the mare. The land is fairly level. Maybe if I'm on her back, I can make her trot a little."

After a brief struggle Dan was able to hoist both bodies up on the rack next to the broken boxes of rifles and ammunition. He unrolled the tarp, covering the bodies. The mare was given a drink from Dan's hat. Logan Tanner slouched on the rear seat of the coach. The tall man allowed himself another mouthful of water, then swung to the pinto's back.

The horse seemed to welcome the trot, and the Wells Fargo stage stirred small clouds of dust as it rolled southward. Within a short while Dan noticed a white salt vein zigzagging in a jagged line across the desert floor. He pulled the pinto to a halt, slid off her back and grabbed a shovel. Borrowing Steve Proffitt's hat, he chipped at the salt with the shovel and filled the hat with the sparkling white crystals.

Climbing into the coach, the tattered and blood-specked man untied the cloth from Tanner's swollen hand. Quickly he dumped a handful of salt in the cloth, then tied it back on the lawman's hand. "Marshal," he said, looking into Tanner's bleary eyes.

Tanner eyed him dully. "Yeah?"

"I found some salt. I wrapped the cloth so the salt is next to the snakebite. When the salt is moistened, it will serve as a poultice. The wet salt will draw the poison out. Understand?"

The big marshal nodded.

"I'll leave the canteen here with you," Dan continued. "Keep the cloth moist, okay?"

Tanner nodded again.

"When we get to the water hole, we'll stop and fill the canteen. You'll make it, Marshal." With that Colt slid out of the coach and closed the door. Stepping up on a wheel, he grasped one of the rifles from the rack, checked the load and climbed back on the mare.

The afternoon sun showed no mercy. A couple of times Colt felt the familiar pressure begin to rise behind his eyes, but it did not overcome him this time. Riding was less taxing than walking.

Dorianne Kates glared at the sweat-soaked back of Jake Finch with pure hatred. Every time she closed her eyes, she could see the bloody hand of Steve Proffitt lying in the sand.

Worry clawed at the girl's mind. What had happened to Dan Colt? He was nowhere on the road. When Finch and his men had stopped at the water hole, there were signs that Dan had been there. But where was he now?

The sun bore down with blistering heat. It was as if they were riding through a giant oven. There was no relief in sight. Not a cloud in the boiling sky. They would bake until the sun went down. Jake Finch had said that they would be in Eternity by sundown. Dorianne eyed the desert and thought of the Apaches.

The land between the water hole and the town of Eternity was dotted with squat cacti, with an occasional towering saguaro. Mesquite shrubs flourished amid red rocks and shallow gullies. Greasewood and snakeweed were seen in scattered patches across the cracked desert floor.

Slowly the heavy stench of death met the nostrils of the southbound party for the second time in as many days. "Somethin's dead," said Harry Doyle, who rode next to Jake Finch, just ahead of Dorianne. The others rode behind her. The remaining two riderless pintos brought up the rear.

Finch raised a hand, extending a finger. "Right up there," he said, pointing.

Slowly the scattered bodies of blue-uniformed cavalrymen and their horses came clearly into view. The buzzards had done their work and deserted the scene. The smell of rotting flesh was unbearable.

"There's the escort Tanner was expecting," said Finch.

"Let's get outta here," said Harry Doyle, spurring his mount.

Even the horses seemed glad to leave the carnage behind. They galloped for about ten minutes, then slowed to the usual walk.

"Wonder what happened to Dan Colt?" said Doyle to Finch.

"Dunno," replied the outlaw leader.

The sun was on its downward slant when the riders found themselves winding their way among scattered boulders alongside a deep arroyo that was fringed with mesquite. There was a four-foot ridge on their right. The arroyo made a long gradual curve, forcing the riders to follow its contour.

Dorianne gasped when a dozen Apaches suddenly rode out of the arroyo some forty yards ahead. Finch and Doyle jerked on the reins and wheeled their mounts. The other four outlaws quickly followed suit and found themselves facing as many painted savages to the rear.

"Jake! What'll we do?" cried Dink Perryman.

"Don't touch your guns!" shouted Finch. "There's no way we can shoot our way out. We'll have to *talk* our way out."

The Apaches closed in from both sides. The leader of the pack, on a large pinto stallion, approached from the front. The lateral yellow stripes on his nose, cheeks and forehead added to the menacing look on his granite face. He stopped a few feet in front of Finch and Doyle, his dark eyes fixed on the Apache pony under Jake Finch. Slowly the savage's burning gaze swung to Dorianne's mount, then to the two pintos at the rear.

Dorianne felt something cold move along her spine as the Apache's hard gaze settled on Jake Finch's face. "You kill Apaches," he said with accusing voice. "Kill Donimo."

"No, that's not true," came Finch's nervous rejoinder. "We . . . uh . . . we *found* these horses, Chief. They—"

"White Eyes lie!" boomed the deep voice of the leading savage. "Where you bury Donimo?"

"We don't know any Donimo, Chief," blurted Harry Doyle.

"You have horses of Donimo's braves," said the Indian. Turning and pointing behind him, he said, "We find Donimo's horse. You lose him, no?"

Dorianne's eyes found the blue roan. The last time she had seen Dan Colt, he was on that horse. She was relieved to know that at least the Apaches had not captured him.

"No!" insisted Jake. "We've never seen that horse before!"

Rifles were leveled at them from both directions. The Apache spoke again. His tone was harsh. "Drop gun belts!"

"Do as he says, boys," said Finch.

"But Boss," said Dink Perryman quickly, "without our guns we ain't got a ghost of a chance!"

"*Talk* is our *only* chance, Dink," snapped Jake. "Drop your gun belts and let me do the talkin'."

Several braves slipped from their horses and gathered up the guns.

Dorianne put a shaky hand to her forehead. It came away cold and wet. The savages were all eyeing her, especially the leader. He stared at her intently while his men gathered up the gun belts.

Jake Finch spoke up. "My name's Finch, Chief. Jake Finch. These men work for me. We're traveling on business to Fort Apache." Finch noticed the way the Indian stared at Dorianne.

"Uh . . . this is my wife," Jake continued, knowing that Indians sometimes respected a white man's marriage relationship. Maybe they would all be spared because of the girl.

"What's your name, Chief?"

The Indian sat impassively, the breeze toying with the two feathers attached to his long black hair. "Me no chief," he grunted. "Four Fingers, chief. Me Bondi, friend of Donimo." Bondi's stoical eyes dilated. Through his teeth, he said, "You kill Donimo and his braves. *You die!*"

"No!" retaliated Finch. "I tell you, Bondi, we found these horses!"

The Apache's dark eyes settled on Dorianne again. Jake took note of it. "Look," he said, fear rising within him, "you want my wife? You take her! Just take her and let us go." Jake's chest felt cold and constricted. His heart drummed against his ribs.

Dorianne looked at Finch with white-hot fury. "You filthy coward," she rasped. For the moment her anger overcame the fear within her. "You'd sell me to these beasts to save your own scaly skin." Looking toward Bondi, she said, "This man is not my husband. I was traveling on a stagecoach to Tucson. These men have taken me by force."

Bondi fixed his eyes on Jake. His voice was like the cutting edge of a broken piece of glass. "Your name not Finch. Your name Forked Tongue!"

Dorianne felt her breath coming in short gasps. Her heart felt like it would leap from her breast. Then it froze when Bondi directed two braves with a sweep of his hand and said, "Take woman. She become Bondi's squaw."

Dorianne did a short intake of breath. Her skin crawled as the two braves nudged their horses, crowding Jake and Harry to one side. One of them took the reins from her trembling fingers, looped them over the pinto's head and led the horse toward Bondi. As Dorianne drew alongside the granite-faced Apache, the pinto stopped.

Bondi looked into her frightened eyes. Speaking softly, he said, "You no be frighten. You live. Become Bondi's squaw."

Mixed emotions flooded through the girl's tiny frame. If this Apache planned to marry her, she would not be tortured and she would not be killed. As long as she was alive, there was hope for her escape. Maybe Dan would come for her . . .

Speaking to the two braves, Bondi said, "Take woman to camp."

Jake Finch and his terrified gang watched as the Apache bucks and Dorianne Kates rode away toward the west.

Bondi grunted something in his native language. He wheeled his mount and veered away. The savages to the rear forced the gang to follow Bondi. The Apache led them a mile further south, where both the arroyo and the ridge leveled out.

As Bondi signaled for them to stop, Tommy Elbert began to cry. "Jake," he sobbed. "They're gonna kill us! I don't want to die!"

Dink Perryman suddenly gouged his horse's sides, heading for open space. Three of the Apaches jumped to the ground, dropping to their knees. Raising their rifles, they quickly sighted on the fleeing man. All three guns barked simultaneously. Perryman spun out of the saddle, flopping on the ground before he collapsed like a rag doll.

The other outlaws looked at each other, faces frozen with fear. The Apache leader spoke again in his own tongue. The braves instantly dismounted and yanked the frightened white men from their saddles.

CHAPTER TWENTY-ONE

Bondi threw one leg over the side of his pinto and slid from its back. His men held the outlaws.

Jake looked into the hawklike face of the Apache and said, "Please. Please. We didn't kill Donimo. It was some white lawmen and . . . and that girl. Yeah. She helped 'em kill a whole bunch of Apaches! It was her boyfriend that carved Donimo up with a knife. He's a tall, blond guy. Name's Dan C—"

Bondi took a step forward and cut Jake's words short with a savage open-handed blow on the mouth. The Indian's eyes were like black bits of marble, hot and vengeful. "White Eyes lie!" he hissed. "Any man who lie to save own hide . . . willing to give woman for own life . . . *he lie about kill Donimo*. Bondi no blind. You have horses of Donimo's braves."

Skinny Mulligan swore at Finch. "You jist *had* to take these Apache horses! We coulda done without 'em. Now look what yuh got us into!"

The others were held tight while Jake was flung to the ground. Finch began to weep like a child. "No! Please! Please don't torture me! Please! I didn't kill no Apaches!"

Bondi spoke in Apache to the gathering braves. Instantly three of them ran to a nearby cluster of mesquite trees and broke off limbs. The Apache leader walked the area, searching the ground. Swinging a hand, he grunted and pointed to where he stood. The braves ran to the spot and began digging in the sand, using the large ends of the limbs to loosen the surface. Then, on their knees, they began scooping the soft sand, digging deep.

While the hole was being dug in the sand, Bondi commanded one of the braves to bring him Finch's revolver. Mulligan, Elbert and Lewis watched in fearful uncertainty as the Apaches held them fast. Four bucks pinned Finch to the ground, one at each leg and arm. Tears washed Jake's face. His wild eyes followed Bondi as the Apache came and stood over him.

Holding Logan Tanner's revolver, which Finch had stolen, the malevolent savage pointed it between Jake's eyes. "You shoot my friend Donimo with this gun?" demanded Bondi.

"No!" squealed Jake timorously. "No!"

"Which one of you kill Donimo?" The Indian raked the faces of the four standing outlaws with his hard gaze.

Mulligan, Elbert, Doyle and Lewis broke into a babel of frenzied denials.

"Please!" sobbed Finch. "We didn't do it!"

Bondi released the cylinder of the Colt .45 and turned it slowly with the muzzle pointing skyward. One by one the cartridges plopped in the hot sand. He left one bullet in the cylinder and snapped it shut. Squeezing the trigger just enough to release the cylinder, he gave it a spin. Then he eared back the hammer and aimed the muzzle between Finch's tear-filled eyes.

"Bondi no see where bullet," said the redskin. "White Eyes see? It next to hammer?"

Jake tried to focus on the holes of the cylinder, but his vision was blurred.

"Which one kill Donimo?" Bondi's voice was level and cold.

"None of us!"

The hammer slammed down on an empty chamber. Jake jerked, expecting the gun to fire. The Apache spun the cylinder again. With the black muzzle nearly touching the bridge of the outlaw's nose and the hammer cocked, the question was repeated.

Jake blubbered his innocent plea again. The hammer snapped. The outlaw ejected a wild cry.

This time Bondi did not spin the cylinder. He thumbed back the hammer. Jake saw the cylinder make its partial turn, but could not see clearly enough to make out the lead tip of the single bullet. Screaming in terror, he cried, "I told you—"

The hammer snapped a third time. It was followed with the ominous dry, clicking sound of the gun being cocked again. Shaking violently all over, Jake Finch suddenly realized that the vengeful Apache was going to inflict his wrath on the one man whom he thought had taken the life of Donimo. First he thought of telling Bondi it had been Dink Perryman. Dink was dead. The savage's wrath couldn't hurt him. But the Apache was bent on vengeance. He wouldn't be satisfied until he had unleashed his fury on someone who could feel it.

Finch realized he had one possible chance. If he could get three of the other men to agree on one as their scapegoat, maybe Bondi would let the rest of them go.

Skinny Mulligan had spoken out against Jake only moments before. He would pay for that now.

"All right! All right!" shouted Finch with breaking voice.

Bondi was about to squeeze the trigger again. His hand relaxed.

"Harry! Tommy! Pat!" bellowed Jake. "He's gonna have his vengeance on the one guilty man. We'd better tell him!"

The three outlaws caught the drift immediately.

"It was the skinny man, Bondi," blurted Finch. "He killed Donimo."

"Yeah! Yeah!" said Doyle, Elbert and Lewis in chorus. "It was Skinny!"

Mulligan was temporarily speechless. Fear froze his vocal cords.

Coldly and methodically the dark-faced Apache raised the revolver, pointing the muzzle toward the sky. The big gun boomed when he pressed the trigger.

Jake Finch nearly passed out.

Bondi barked a command in Apache. Skinny Mulligan was jerked immediately to the forefront. The wrathful Apache burnt Mulligan's face with his black eyes. "You die slow, White Eyes," he said evenly.

Four bucks laid hold of Mulligan, dragging him toward the spot where the others were digging in the sand. The terrified little man found his voice and cried, "No! No! They're lyin'! I never killed no Indians . . . *ever*!" Twisting his head around, he eyed Finch, Doyle, Elbert and Lewis with horrific hatred. "You dirty stinkin' rats!" he screamed. "I'll get you! I'll get you in hell!"

Bondi barked another command in Apache. Several other bucks grabbed limbs and began digging four holes at a spot fifty feet from where Skinny Mulligan stood weeping, eyeing the strange hole at his feet.

The four outlaws looked at each other hopelessly, fearing the four holes would be for them. The swarthy, vindictive Apache leader spoke to them with a grating voice. "Man who kill Donimo die slow. You tell Bondi where Donimo buried."

Feeling slight relief and a ray of hope, Jake Finch quickly volunteered the desired information. He described the rock enclosure and exactly which grave held the body of Donimo.

"Bondi thank White Eyes," said the deep-voiced savage, the trace of a smile tugging at the corners of his mouth.

Jake forced a smile of his own. "You're welcome, Bondi." Throwing his gaze past the Apache at the four indentures expanding in the sand, he asked nervously, "You gonna show us mercy? You . . . uh . . . gonna let us go?"

Bondi's trace of a smile broadened. "Show mercy, yes." The smile was not in his voice.

At Bondi's words the outlaws eyed each other, grinning.

The grins quickly disappeared when the Apache added, "But not let you go."

"Huh?" said Jake.

The savage's face went hard. "Your friend," he said gesturing toward the weeping Mulligan, "he die slow. Bondi show you mercy. You die fast."

All four outlaws felt a cold numbness overtake them. Bondi spoke a command to the braves who held them. Instantly they were pushed roughly toward the place where Skinny Mulligan stood trembling.

"You watch beginning," said Bondi heavily. "Then you die."

The speechless victims saw a hole three feet deep in the sand. It was rectangular. Eighteen inches wide. A yard long. The Apaches were filling it with brush and broken mesquite limbs. Skinny ejected a moan as the brush at the bottom was set afire. The dry wood quickly ignited, crackling and releasing billows of white smoke.

Eight bucks struggled toward the hole carrying large rocks, two men to a rock. Jake Finch eyed them, estimating that each rock would weigh at least two hundred pounds. The rocks were laid on the ground while more wood was brought to feed the fire. The Apaches made the terrified outlaws stand and watch until the bottom of the hole was a solid bed of red-hot coals.

Skinny Mulligan screamed as the savages stripped him to the waist, then flung him over the crude oven facedown. His screams gained in volume as they spread-eagled him, placing the large rocks on his hands and feet. He was now suspended over the hole lengthwise, the heat burning him from face to navel.

Finch and the outlaws turned away, struggling against their captors. Mulligan continued to cry and scream as the blistering heat from the coals singed away his hair, eyebrows and eyelashes.

The other frightened outlaws were dragged to the four holes, which had been completed. What hideous, horrible death had the nefarious Bondi prepared for them?

Each hole in the ground was approximately four feet deep and large enough to hold a man. Quickly each man's hands were tied behind him. Then at Bondi's command they were roughly forced into the holes to stand on their knees. They begged and cried for mercy as the sand was shoved in around them. Within a few minutes each man was buried up to his chin.

"Bondi," sobbed Jake Finch, "I beg of you . . . please . . . have mercy!"

The Apache leader stood over him, a formidable tower of vengeance. His mouth drawn into a thin line, he grunted, "Like Bondi say, White Eyes, you get mercy. You four be dead while killer of Donimo still alive. He cook for long time before die!"

In stark terror Finch, Doyle, Elbert and Lewis watched as a dozen of the Apaches climbed on their horses. Each rider carried a rifle. Mulligan continued to scream as the mounted braves trotted thirty yards away and assembled in a straight line. The others led their horses away from the area, including Bondi.

The stone-faced leader pointed at the four buried outlaws and gave instructions in Apache.

Jake was closest to the savages. Next was Harry Doyle, five feet away. Tommy Elbert was the same distance from Doyle. Last was Pat Lewis. The latter called to Finch, "Jake," he said with trembling voice, "what're they gonna do?"

Finch was so frightened he could hardly answer. He twisted his neck to look at Lewis. Weakly he said, "L-looks like th-they're gonna use us for t-target practice."

Suddenly a command was given by Bondi, and two riders detached themselves from the line, galloping straight ahead. One dropped behind the other. They would draw parallel with the four outlaws just inside of the spot where Skinny Mulligan was suffering untold agony.

Wide-eyed, Finch and his cohorts watched as the two bucks took aim at Pat Lewis and fired as they galloped by. Bullets chewed sand on each side of his head. Lewis cried out in fear.

"They're toyin' with us," gasped Elbert. "They missed him on purpose."

Harry Doyle swore. "Jake, they're gonna kill us one at a time!"

Finch started to speak when two more Apaches came on the run. Pinto hoofs thundered, and the rifles barked. Lewis was crying, "Ja-a-a-a-ke!" when both bullets ripped into his head. The sand about him was splattered with crimson.

Hatred boiled inside Jake Finch and became a living thing. Twisting so he could see Bondi, he cursed the Indian, bellowing at the top of his lungs. The Apache leader sent two more horsemen, then slowly strode toward Finch.

Tommy Elbert knew he was next. As the thundering riders drew near, he began crying for his mother. Both bullets bit into the ground on each side of his head.

While Tommy broke into incoherent sobs, Jake looked up at Bondi as the Indian's shadow fell over him. Teeth bared, Finch swore again and said, "You ain't human! You dirty beast. You're worse than any animal! You hear me? You're a dirty, filthy beast!"

The Apache knelt down and said evenly, "Maybe this dirty beast not let you die so soon. Maybe you suffer more than others."

Jake stared holes into his back as Bondi returned to his place. Two more riders were dispatched. Tommy Elbert was still weeping and blubbering indistinguishable words when he died. One bullet hissed by his left ear and bit the ground. The other entered his head through his right eye.

Bondi gave further instructions to his men and sent two more riders. Both outlaws were surprised when they took aim and shot at Jake. One bullet kicked sand in his face. The other one took a slice out of his left ear. Spitting sand and blinking his eyes, Jake felt the warm blood trickling down his jaw.

"You shouldn't have cussed at him, Jake," said Doyle with shaky words. "Now he'll kill you an inch at a time."

Finch did not answer. His fury had been overcome by the fear that now had turned his blood to ice.

Another pair of riflemen charged past the still-screaming Skinny Mulligan. Their rifles cracked. This time they bent their wrath toward Harry Doyle. One bullet ruffled the hair on his head. The other hit six inches from his right ear.

Instantly two more charged. "This is it, Jake!" cried Harry. Just before the guns barked, Jake heard, "Our Father which art in Heaven, hallowed be—"

Harry Doyle died instantly.

The next pair of riders hesitated a moment. Jake looked across the glistening sand at Skinny Mulligan. The little man was moaning weakly. His skin peeled and smoked, filling the hot air with a sickening smell.

Then the two riders bounded forward. They purposely aimed wide. The bullets plowed sand on either side of Jake Finch's head. Finch shook his head violently, launching into a paroxysm of frenzied oaths. Blood flowed heavily from his wounded ear. The riders returned to where the other Apaches were gathered.

Skinny Mulligan was silent. He could be heard gasping for breath.

Bondi spoke to his braves in a low tone. Those on the pintos slid to the ground. Leaving their horses, the entire band walked to where Jake Finch knelt, submerged in the Arizona sand. Fear shone in the outlaw's wild eyes.

The craggy-faced Bondi jacked a shell into the chamber of his rifle. "White Eyes ear bleed much," he said in his deep basso.

The Apaches ejected a humorless laugh.

"Still take long time bleed to death," continued Bondi. "He ask for mercy. Bondi kind savage. White Eyes die faster if *both* ears bleed." The Apache leader, standing twenty feet away, raised his rifle, taking careful aim.

Jake Finch was numb. He could not cry out.

The rifle bucked in Bondi's hands. Finch's right ear was ripped from his head. Blood sprayed the sand. Pain throbbed through the outlaw's head. Without another word the vindictive savage turned and walked away. The others followed.

Dizziness swept over Jake Finch. The departing Indians seemed to swirl in a fuzzy circle. Jake tried to cry out, but his strength was gone. The earth trembled as the Apaches galloped away, heading north.

Except for a slight breeze, the desert was absolutely still. Finch raised his eyes toward the lowering sun. The vicious ball in the sky seemed to taunt him with its burning rays. The outlaw's mouth was dry. Closing his eyes, he tried to roll his tongue. It was useless. No saliva would surface.

Violent leg cramps lashed Jake Finch. He tried to move against the sand. But it was to no avail. The wounds on the sides of his head were throbbing, burning. Warm blood streamed down both jaws.

The outlaw wondered how long he would have to suffer before death would come to release him from his sandy prison. He rolled his smarting eyes toward Skinny Mulligan. Skinny was still alive. The breeze carried the sickening odor of scorched flesh to Finch's nostrils. Mulligan gave no sound, but Jake could see the slight movement of his breathing.

Remorse swept over Finch like an ocean wave. It was his lie that had put the little man to such torture. *You called Bondi a beast*, a voice inside him seemed to say. *Are you any better? Skinny was your friend. You lied and betrayed him. Caused him to be cooked to death, just to save your own hide. And that poor girl . . . Dorianne. You would sell her to those savages to save yourself. If there is a beast on this desert, Jake Finch, it is you!*

Suddenly the outlaw began a dry weep. A mournful wail escaped his parched lips. In a low, choking voice he looked at Mulligan and said, "Skinny . . . Skinny . . . please forgive me! Please, Skinny!"

Skinny Mulligan could not hear Finch's cries. The little man was dead.

Jake twisted his neck, straining to look at the lifeless heads of his partners. "Harry," he sobbed. "Hey you fellas! You heard me, didn't you! I told Skinny I was sorry! *Fellas!* You heard me, didn't you?"

A long, agonizing wail escaped Finch's lips. Closing his eyes, he shook his head till the pain made him stop. Now his throat hurt. It was so dry. A faint word fell from his tongue . . . *"Water."*

A wave of dizziness claimed him. "Water," came the raspy sound again. It seemed to come from someone else's mouth. He clamped his eyes shut against the glare. He was facing due west.

Time ebbed slowly. The sun sank a little lower. Jake opened his miserable eyes. As he did a strange shadow passed over him. He raised his line of sight skyward.

Nothing.

What had made the shadow that flitted by? *Something* had done it. Jake stretched, twisted and craned his neck, but he could see nothing that moved overhead. The wounds were still bleeding, especially the right side of his head where the ear was totally severed.

Then he saw them.

Jake Finch's pallid face became a mask of horror. Two black dots wheeled in the brassy sky. The outlaw's alarmed gaze followed them as they swooped lower and crossed the sun. The brightness was a bludgeon stabbing his haggard eyes.

The buzzards floated downward and touched the ground thirty feet away, flapping their jagged black wings. They were directly in front of him, turning their repulsive red necks. The smell of Jake's fresh blood was in their nostrils.

"Oh, no!" breathed Finch. He had never felt so helpless. Those carnivorous predators would pick his flesh to pieces. Making a guttural sound in their throats, the loathsome birds hopped closer, working their wings. Jake's eyes bulged in terror. He tried to cry out, hoping to scare them off. But he had lost too much blood; his strength was totally gone. No sound would come.

The hideous creatures closed in.

CHAPTER TWENTY-TWO

Dan Colt stood as though his body was carved out of petrified wood. His stomach wrenched and his shoulders drooped as he viewed the grisly scene. Tattered blue uniforms identified the cavalry detachment that had been sent to meet the Wells Fargo stage. The buzzards had taken their fill and left the remains to the sun and the small desert animals. The stench of rotting flesh hovered in the hot air.

The tall man opened the coach door and looked at Logan Tanner. The marshal's face was pale and drawn. His hand was cold, swollen and sprinkled with icy sweat. Dan could see no visible results as yet from the salt poultice.

Tanner rolled his hazy eyes toward Colt. "What's that . . . that awful smell?"

"It's the calvary unit that was to meet us at Cathedral Rock," replied Colt heavily. "Apaches slaughtered 'em."

Tanner nodded wordlessly.

"Nothing we can do here," said Dan. "We'll keep movin'. Want some more water?"

The marshal nodded again.

As the tall man swung aboard the pinto mare once again, a bolt of pain stabbed through his wounded arm. Worry tugged at Dan Colt's mind. If infection set in, he would be in trouble.

The afternoon wore on. Dan studied the ground, following the obvious tracks of the Jake Finch gang and the riderless Apache ponies. Panic struggled to rise within him. Dorianne was in danger. *Real* danger. Those heartless outlaws were capable of killing her. Dan would have to take them by surprise to rescue her. The tracks indicated that they were traveling slow, but he wondered if he was gaining on them. Maybe he *should* leave Tanner and ride on ahead.

As the blazing inferno in the sky sucked moisture from his body, Colt thought about the situation. Logan Tanner was in no condition to fight off Apaches. If Dan left him and they showed up, the marshal was a dead man. On the other hand, Dorianne was already in the hands of her potential killers. If she wasn't rescued soon . . . Dan shook his head as if to reject the ugly thought.

Instantly he made his decision. Logan Tanner would have to take his chances. Dan would find a place to park the stage, hide it as much as possible and ride after the gang.

At the same moment Colt's line of sight fell on a deep arroyo coming up on his left. The gully was lined with a thick stand of mesquite trees. Dan figured if he could find a gradual slope into the arroyo, the coach would be well hidden. A passing war party might never see it.

As he threaded the vehicle among scattered boulders alongside a four-foot ridge, Dolt noticed a sudden change in the tracks on the ground. The pattern of hoofprints was abruptly disturbed by the presence of a great number of unshod horses. Lifting his eyes quickly, the blond man saw the outlaws' horses clustered together among the mesquite. They were taking advantage of the growing shade as the sun sank lower.

Thumping the mare's side with his heels, Dan forced her to hasten. The bloody scene met his eyes all at once. His gaze flicked from the four blood-covered heads protruding from the sand to the two hideous black buzzards that were dancing about, pecking at Jake Finch's mangled ears.

Bounding from the pinto's back, Colt picked up rocks, hurling them at the birds. "Heeyah!" he shouted at the top of his lungs. Startled, the giant beasts flapped their wings and lifted themselves skyward.

Dashing toward Finch, Dan's eyes darted among the heads of the outlaws. It was a shocking, dreadful sight. They looked like some strange kind of creatures that had erupted in a weird manner throught the earth's crust.

Quickly Colt's line of sight raked the area. He saw the lifeless, half-baked torso of Skinny Mulligan hanging limply over the smoking hole. The absence of Dorianne Kates told its own story. *She was in the hands of the hellish Apaches.*

A cold sick numbness settled over Dan Colt. The poor girl would be sexually assaulted by any number of bucks. If she survived the ordeal, they would torture her to death.

The tall man dropped to his knees. It was evident Jake had lost a great deal of blood. The sand around his neck glistened with the thick red fluid.

"Jake!" said Colt.

Finch bobbled his head torpidly and set his languid eyes on Dan's sweaty face.

"Jake! It's Dan Colt! Where's the girl?"

The dying outlaw's tongue ran over his colorless lips. "Colt," he croaked weakly. "Give . . . me . . . water . . ."

Stumbling to the stagecoach, Dan flung open the door. Tanner was asleep or unconscious, he could not tell which. Seizing the canteen, he shuffled back to the outlaw and poured the soothing liquid into his mouth. Dan had to lean close as the outlaw breathed out his words, "Apaches . . . took . . . her."

"Jake, did they give any hint as to where their camp is?"

Finch licked his lips. "No."

Taking a swig from the canteen for himself, Dan gave Finch more water. Choking momentarily, the outlaw coughed and said, "One . . . one of . . . the 'paches is . . . is gonna make . . . her . . . his sq-squaw."

"What?"

"Yeah. Name's Bondi. He . . . was leader . . . of . . . bunch that . . . did . . . this."

"Bondi?" echoed Dan.

Finch nodded. "Sent two bucks . . . took her to . . . camp . . . before they did this."

Dan threw a glance to the west. He was familiar with Apache customs. The wedding would probably take place immediately. If so, the lengthy ceremony would begin at sundown. The drums would beat all night while the people danced around a giant fire.

Having no choice, Dorianne would become the savage Bondi's wife at sunrise.

Somehow Dan Colt would have to get her out of there, although some of this news gave him cause for relief. With one of the Apache leaders taking Dorianne for his wife, none of the others would lay a hand on her.

Another worry picked at the tall man's brain. His physical strength was at a low ebb. In spite of his weakness, he must find the Apache camp and save the girl. But first he had to dig Jake out of the sand.

With effort he went to the stagecoach and procured a shovel. There was doubt in his mind that he had enough strength to extricate the outlaw from his sandy prison. "Jake," he said with a heavy sigh, "I'm gonna try to dig you out. But I haven't eaten for a long time. Strength's about gone."

Finch said in a hoarse whisper, "Food . . . in . . . saddle-bags."

Colt's eyes shot toward the huddled horses. Dropping the shovel, he stumbled to them. He found hardtack, beef jerky, Mexican beans and whiskey. Quickly he popped a handful of raw beans into his mouth and washed them down with the fiery liquid. The whiskey burned his mouth and left a trail of fire all the way to his stomach. His eyes watered immediately. Within ten minutes he had wolfed down the jerky and two slabs of hardtack. Following it with more whiskey, he then unwrapped his injured forearm.

The wound was showing signs of scabbing, but it was ridged along both sides with swollen, red skin. *Infection!*

Dan braced himself against one of the horses and took a deep breath. Tilting the whiskey bottle upward, he poured a generous portion of its contents into the open wound. The arm came alive and burned like brimstone. The tall man's knees went watery. Clutching the bottle in his right hand, he used the same hand to grasp the saddlehorn. The desert seemed to whirl. His head went light.

Dan thought he was going to pass out, but he retained his senses. Moments passed. The pain in the wound began to subside. Steadying himself, he took another gulp of whiskey and poured the last of it onto the wound. The sensation was weaker this time.

Colt wrapped his arm with the same cloth, tied it with his teeth and walked back toward Jake with a glance at the setting sun. He felt strength surging back into his body.

Leaning over, Dan grasped the shovel handle and said, "Jake, I'll shovel the sand away from you and—"

Jake Finch's head lolled to one side. His mouth lay open. His sightless eyes stared downward at the ground.

Dan took another look westward. The sun was almost gone. A few puffy clouds were stained in a brilliant array of orange and red. He placed the shovel in the coach and examined the snakebitten hand of Logan Tanner. A bulbous yellow mass had gathered around the bite.

"Good," breathed Dan. "Poultice is working." Tanner was unconscious and feverish. His clothes were soaked with sweat. The tall man cleaned away the poison and resalted the poultice. Quickly he poured water on it and forced some of the liquid down the marshal's puffy mouth.

"Hate to leave you, Tanner old boy," said Colt to the unconscious lawman, "but duty calls."

Dan tied the pinto mare to a mesquite and tethered the other horses where they stood. He led Harry Doyle's horse to the stagecoach and took one more look at Tanner. Then checking the loads in the revolver on his hip and sliding one of the new Winchester repeaters in the saddle boot, he swung aboard. Riding a wide circle, it took Colt three minutes to learn that the bulk of the Apaches had ridden north. Three horses had gone west.

The desert-wise Dan Colt followed the westbound trail in the orange rays of the setting sun. He had ridden for an hour in the diminishing light when he descended into a shallow valley, surrounded on three sides by great soaring cliffs of red granite. The red stone was now a dull gray. Butting up against the cliffs were huge spiraling stone monoliths, towering against the darkening sky.

At the base of the monoliths, small fires were winking and casting yellow light on the white-skinned tepees.

Squinting against the gloom, Dan descended into the valley. He rode to a spot thick with tall brush and dismounted. Tethering the horse, he set out, rifle in hand, toward the camp. As he drew within three hundred yards, the rumble of drums filled the valley.

At the first sound of the drums, Dan thought the long night of the wedding ceremony was beginning. But the rhythm of the beat soon told him different. It was the slow, methodical beat of mourning. This meant one thing. *They had found Donimo's body.* Such ceremonies were only held for the death of a chief or the male descendant of a chief.

Bondi's marriage to the white girl he had chosen would be postponed. Encouragement washed over the tall man. Maybe in their grief over Donimo, the Apaches would let their guard down. Perhaps fate was finally going to smile on Dan Colt.

Carefully Dan crept closer, keeping a watchful eye for sentries. Slipping among the rocks and brush, he was pleased by the absence of any posted guards. The entire camp was assembled around a stilted platform that stood seven feet high. The body of Donimo lay on the platform. Six small fires ringed the stilted structure.

Standing at Donimo's head was a stately Indian with a black robe draped over his shoulders. His long gray hair flowed freely in the breeze that swooped through the valley. Wailing pitifully the man raised his hands over his head. They confirmed Dan's suspicions. This was the revered Four Fingers.

The entire camp echoed the chief's mournful wail. The medicine man, who stood at Donimo's feet, shouted a series of wild oaths. Four Fingers wailed again. The Apaches followed with their echoed cry. This was repeated over and over again in heathen fashion, to the background of slow-beating drums. A chill danced on Colt's spine.

Where is Dorianne? he asked himself.

Cautiously Dan crept around the perimeter of the circled tepees. The men were closest to the center of things, while the women stood on the fringe, attending to restless children. Then something caught Dan's eye. One Apache brave was detached from the others, standing in front of a tepee. Seated at his feet was Dorianne Kates.

Bondi.

By the light of the fires Dan could see that she had been washed up. Her hair was combed, and she was dressed in the colorful apparel of an Apache squaw. The girl was distinctly distressed and wept like a child lost in a dark place.

Dan Colt knew the Apaches. With the wedding taking place

later, the bride-to-be would sleep alone in a tepee of her own. The groom would not set foot inside the white tent until they were husband and wife by tribal law. Dorianne would be safe for the night.

Customarily the mourning ceremony would last only an hour or two. A wake would be set up until dawn. At that time Donimo's body would be carried to its final resting place. As the sun lifted over the earth's edge, Donimo would be lowered into its surface.

Dan Colt pondered the situation. It was just him against the whole camp of wailing Apaches. Donimo had been killed by a white man. Though they did not know that the man who ended Donimo's life was only inches from their grasp, they would brutalize *any* white man to his last breath. If he was caught trying to free Dorianne, he would die an unthinkable death.

Dan felt the Winchester in his hands and ran the tips of his fingers over the worn butt of the Colt on his hip. He had faced death more times in his thirty-odd years than he could count. The two weapons he bore at the moment would not suffice in this situation. He would die for sure if he tried to break Dorianne out with his measly arsenal. He had to have an equalizer. There was no way he could hope to get Dorianne out of there unless he gave himself an edge in the situation.

While the tall man watched the ceremony from the deep shadows, he saw Bondi bend over and speak to the weeping girl. Then the formidable Indian lifted his arm and swept back the flap. Dorianne entered the tepee and pulled the flap shut. Bondi turned his attention back to the death ceremony.

Dan studied the other tepees, wondering which belonged to Four Fingers. Dorianne would know. A plan was taking form in his mind. He suddenly acknowledged to himself that his equalizer was in the stagecoach. Pivoting into the saddle, Dan made fast tracks across the desert by the pale light of the rising moon.

Logan Tanner was awake but violently ill when Dan Colt arrived at the stagecoach. He was in a cold chill, but his body was extremely hot. He retched severely with dry heaves, while his teeth chattered uncontrollably.

Dan gave him water and bathed his face, trying to make him as comfortable as possible. "You're reaching the crisis, Marshal,"

Dan said with a level voice. "Just hang on. The poultice is working, but a good deal of the poison got into your system. You're going to make it. You'll be better by morning. It'll take a couple of weeks to get back to normal, but you're gonna be okay."

Tanner eyed Colt in the pale moonlight. "I . . . h-hope you're r-right," he chattered. "Wh-where's th-the g-gang? Th-the g-girl?"

"The gang's dead, Marshal. All of 'em. Apaches killed 'em. Kidnapped Dorianne. I've been gone for nearly four hours. I trailed 'em and found the camp. They've found Donimo's body. Havin' a wailing ceremony tonight."

Tanner threw his head back, doubled over on the coach seat and retched again. As he settled down, Dan said, "Have you understood what I've been telling you, Marshal?"

"Y-yes," said Tanner, breathing painfully.

"I'm going back after her, Marshal. If we haven't shown up by nine o'clock . . . and you feel up to it by then . . . take one of the gang's horses and ride for Eternity. If you can somehow make it into the saddle, you ride, okay? Those savages will be back. You understand?"

Tanner nodded weakly.

"The canteen's right here beside you, Tanner," said Dan. "I have to go now. I've got to be ready to break Dorianne out of there right at dawn."

Tanner nodded again.

Dan backed out of the coach, then stuck his head back in. "When you're up to it, Marshal, there's food in the saddlebags."

Quickly the tall man dashed to the boot of the stage and rummaged around until his fingers closed on the stubby barrels of Tanner's sawed-off shotgun. Reaching in again, he found the box of shells and the leather harness Jake Finch had worn. Quickly Colt checked the loads in the big gun.

He jammed his pockets full of shotgun shells and stuffed his mouth full of jerky before he mounted up and galloped away.

CHAPTER TWENTY-THREE

The Apache camp had settled down for the night by the time Dan tethered his horse and crept in again. One small fire remained near Donimo's body. Five braves sat hunched around the dancing flames; Four Fingers was not among them.

Colt made his way to the tepee that harbored Dorianne Kates. He hoped she had not been taken elsewhere.

Patiently he waited until the eastern horizon turned a dull gray. When his plan went into action, the Apaches must be able to see clearly.

Colt's heart thundered in his breast as he crawled to the front of the tepee, shotgun and halter in hand. A quick glance at the five Apaches told him that as yet he was undetected. He must get through the flap and cover Dorianne's mouth fast enough to keep her from crying out. It would be too dark for her to see his face.

Cautiously Dan fingered the edge of the flap and found it swinging free. Like a cat he sprang inside, straining to see. Dorianne was alone, but only dozing. He heard her suck in a breath, preparing to scream. Instantly Dan's hand clamped over her mouth. "Dorianne," he whispered, "it's Dan Colt!" Without removing his hand he said, "Dorianne . . . did you hear me?"

Dan felt the girl nod her head. At the same instant warm tears touched his hand. Slowly he pulled his palm from her lips.

"Oh, Dan," she whispered shakily, "I knew you'd come. I knew you would!"

"Do you know which tent is the chief's?"

"Yes."

"Is anyone in there with him?"

"No. He's alone."

"Good. Now you tell me which one Four Fingers is in. Then wait in here until I call for you. We're gonna walk out of here."

"But how—"

"Don't have time to explain. Just come runnin' when I call."

"I can't."

"What?"

"My hands and feet are tied."

"Oh." Quickly he fumbled in the darkness, pulling at the ropes. "There."

"I'll be ready."

"Good. When we walk, stay close to me."

"I will. It's three tepees to the right as you go out. Has a spear stuck in the ground right by the flap."

Dan peered through the opening. The five braves were still huddled morosely around the fire. The flap waved and he was outside.

Throwing a glance eastward, he noted that things were moving on schedule. The sky was growing light.

Without hesitating Dan made a dash for the third tepee. The spear was there, just as Dorianne had said. He tested the flap and found it loose. He plunged inside. There was enough light to make out the Apache chief lying on his side on a pallet. The slight noise caused Four Fingers to stir and open his eyes. Dan braced himself and chopped the Indian with a rawboned fist to the jaw.

Four Fingers's head snapped back, but a cry escaped his lips.

Suddenly there were rapid footsteps coming toward the tepee. Dan stuck his head out the opening and saw the five braves running toward him. Moving out and standing up, he reacted quickly. Dogging back both hammers of the sawed-off shotgun, he leveled on the closest Apache and pulled one trigger. The gun roared and the charge caught the savage square in the chest. A hole the size of a man's head appeared. The impact drove him backward into the other four. One look at the hole in his chest and they quickly retreated.

Abruptly Dan caught movement out of the corner of his eye.

Bondi was charging at him full speed, a big knife in his hand. Colt swung the double muzzles and pulled the other trigger. The shotgun boomed. Bondi's face disappeared. He flopped backward, the smoking, meaty mass fully visible where his face used to be. Other savages, coming on the run, stopped dead in their tracks. Horror framed their faces.

When they looked up, Dan had vanished into the tepee. While he reloaded the shotgun and trussed the groggy Four Fingers in the halter, he shouted, "If any of you come in here, your chief gets the same thing!"

The gathering Apaches, stirred by the two blasts from the shotgun, gripped their weapons and waited. They dared not fire into the tepee for fear of hitting Four Fingers.

Inside, Dan strapped the chief tightly into the halter. Lifting Four Fingers to his feet, he steadied him and slid the awesome weapon upward through the leather loop. He pressed the cool muzzles tightly against the Indian's square jaw. It took the blond man a full minute to get the wrist strap in place and buckled, but Four Fingers needed the time to get his head cleared.

While heavy voices spoke excitedly outside, Dan eared back both hammers. The Indian's eyes were wide.

"Now, Chief," said Dan with no uncertain edge in his voice, "I just shot a big hole in the chest of one of your bucks and blew away the face of the one called Bondi. Your men have had a good look at what this gun can do. You and I and the white girl are going to walk out of here."

"You not make it, white dog," said Four Fingers through his teeth.

"You see this strap on my wrist?" snapped Colt.

"Mmm," nodded the granite-faced chief.

"If I so much as stumble, both triggers will go. They'll never find a trace of your head. If you even jerk, Four Fingers, you'll never see another sunrise."

"Four Fingers die, white dog, you and girl die, too."

"I don't want to harm you, Chief," said Colt evenly, "and I won't as long as your people let us walk out of this valley without interfering. So you'd better explain how touchy this shotgun is . . . and that I mean business. If you're tired of livin', then you go ahead and tell them to kill us."

212

Colt pushed the venerable Apache chief through the opening and halted. A full circle of wild-eyed savages surrounded them. Murder was written vividly on their faces.

"Tell 'em, Chief!" barked Dan.

Suddenly the tall man's gaze settled on Dorianne Kates as she was held between two bucks. One of them pointed a knife at her throat, a malignant fire in his eyes. "You let Four Fingers loose, White Eyes," the knife-bearing savage hissed, "or girl die!"

"Tell 'im, Chief!" bellowed Colt, shoving the Apache's jaw upward with the twin muzzles.

With his head twisted grotesquely, Four Fingers spoke calmly with a neutral tone in his native language.

Dan Colt knew this was the crucial moment. He watched the expression on the buck's face. The Indian's brow knotted as he slowly lowered the knife. Both Apaches released Dorianne. Dan felt instant relief. Four Fingers loved life like any other man.

Dorianne scurried to the tall man's side, fear on her lovely face. "Dan," she breathed heavily, "they'll never let us out of here!"

"We're walkin' out, honey," said the determined Colt. "Four Fingers is more than their chief. He's their god. They worship him. He just told them how easy this shotgun could go off. I showed them what it can do a few minutes ago." Speaking to the silver-haired Apache, Dan said, "All right, Four Fingers, let's go."

The stolid, sun-burnished face of the proud chief showed no expression as the trio moved forward into the orange-flared sunrise. Dan Colt steered, setting a direct course in the direction of Harry Doyle's tethered horse. Dorianne stayed so close to Dan that he could feel her every move.

As they reached the circle of hard-faced savages, the Apaches slowly gave way. Their dark eyes glared at Colt, then studied the strange apparatus on Four Finger's body. Squaws stood in the background, gripping the children that crept close. A dark, ominous silence prevailed.

The squinting gaze of Four Fingers did not waver.

Black eyes of savage warriors stared with unconcealed hatred, fingering rifles and knives in eager hands. Old men watched from the doorways of the tepees. Heavy breathing was evident as the camp of Apaches hinged at the point of violent reaction.

Jaw squared, Dan Colt moved Four Fingers eastward, raking their angry faces with his sweeping gaze. One young brave emitted a low growl and stepped into their path, brandishing a cocked rifle. Suddenly another brave saw the foolish move and lunged for him, swinging the butt of his own rifle wildly. As the wooden stock connected with the young Apache's jaw, he went down. His rifle fired, sending the bullet harmlessly into the dust.

The report of the rifle caused Dorianne to jerk with fear, her fingers digging into Dan's upper arm.

The unconscious Apache was quickly dragged out of the way. Now braves lined the path on both sides. Heavy silence cloyed the early morning air as Colt steadily moved the small procession between the two walls of dark-skinned savages. The stillness seemed to emphasize the icy contempt that leered from so many hate-filled eyes. The slight sounds of feet scuffing the sand broke the silence, every step carrying Dorianne Kates and Dan Colt closer to safety.

They were now at the edge of the camp. Dan stopped the procession and said to Four Fingers, "Tell them not to follow us. When we reach a designated place out there on the desert, we'll turn you loose. No harm will come to you if they do as I say."

The stone-faced chief stood with his head cocked sideways, pressured by the twelve-gauge muzzles. He spoke briefly with short, choppy words.

"All right, Chief," said Dan, "let's move out. Watch your step. If you stumble, it's *good-bye world*." Looking down at Dorianne, he spoke softly, "Okay, little lady, follow old Dan."

"I'd follow you to the ends of the earth," said the girl with conviction.

The tone of her voice made Dan nervous. The moment was drawing near when he would walk out of her life. He hated the thought of hurting her, but it would be best for Dorianne in the long run. Someday she would understand.

The angry crowd of Apaches watched helplessly as the trio threaded its way across the sandy earth and disappeared into the mesquite thicket.

The sun was midway up the morning sky when Dorianne sighted the stagecoach nestled in the brush. She was on the horse as Dan and Four Fingers walked alongside. From time to time she had cast a backward look. There had been no sight of the Apaches since leaving the camp.

"I see the stagecoach, Dan," Dorianne announced from her high perch.

"Good," said Dan, smiling. "Still no one following us?"

"No."

"They will not come," said Four Fingers levelly. "They have orders."

"That's wise, Chief," commented Colt. "I mean to keep my word. You'll have a long walk home, but you'll still have your head."

Four Fingers gave the tall man a disdainful look from the corner of his eye.

As they drew near the bloody scene, Dan said, "Dorianne, I want you to head straight for the stagecoach. Don't look over to the left. It's a sight you don't need to see."

"All right," the girl agreed.

Dorianne was tempted to look toward the forbidden scene, but she kept her eyes on the stagecoach. As she slipped from the saddle, Dan saw that none of the horses was missing. "Check on the marshal, will you?" he asked the girl.

Dorianne opened the coach door. Colt caught a glimpse of Logan Tanner collapsed on the seat as he eased down the hammers of the shotgun. Working rapidly, he released the weapon from the halter.

"You're going to stay with us till we're safe in Eternity, Chief," Dan said flatly. "I'm leaving the halter on you just in case some of your boys decide to go against your orders." The face of the Apache chief seemed to be chipped from dark stone.

Logan Tanner was still racked by fever. He was awake but groggy, and often babbled deliriously. Waves of nausea were still washing over him periodically. Dan cleaned the pus from the swollen hand and freshened the poultice.

Dorianne rode in the driver's seat of the stagecoach to keep watch for Four Fingers's braves. The silver-haired chief was placed in the coach with the ailing marshal. Dan rode Harry Doyle's horse, leading the pinto mare that pulled the stage. The other horses trailed behind, tied to the vehicle.

The sun beat down as the day wore on. The canteen went dry just past noon. Dan assured them that they would be in Eternity by four o'clock.

Time dragged by slowly, but the moment finally arrived when Dorianne squinted against the lowering sun and peered through the heat waves dancing on the southern horizon. "I see the town, Dan!" she cried.

"Good!" responded the blond man, lifting his flat-crowned hat and sleeving away the moisture on his brow.

An hour later the bedraggled travelers drew near the sun-blistered town of Eternity. A cold feeling washed over Dan Colt as they rode down the dusty street. The town was totally deserted. The afternoon breeze banged an open door against its frame.

"Dan," said the girl with a timorous voice. "What do you think?"

"Somethin' mighty strange," replied the tall man. "Let's pull over."

Colt pumped water at a horse trough and gave the animals as much as they would take. The canteen was filled and passed around. The Apache was surprised that the tall white man gave him an equal share of water. Logan Tanner was only semiconscious but still drank a good amount of the life-giving liquid.

Filling the canteen again, Colt eyed Four Fingers and said, "Well, Chief, I guess you've got to ride with us all the way to Fort Apache. This town is deserted."

Four Fingers remained silent.

Abruptly the jingling sound of cavalry gear came to their ears. At the same time a horse blew. From the south end of town a blue-suited patrol rode toward the bullet-riddled stagecoach.

Dan breathed a sigh of relief and smiled at Dorianne. "You're safe now, little lady."

The chief's face was grim as Dorianne smiled back at Dan. Colt stood at the forefront, waiting for the patrol to reach them. Dorianne eyed the tall, handsome man who had risked his own life to break her out of the Apache camp. *I love him more than ever,* she told herself. *Oh, Dan, someday you'll love me, too.*

"Howdy, Lieutenant," spoke up the blond man. "My name's Dan Colt."

Dismounting and extending his hand, the young officer said, "Lieutenant Clifford Jennings at your service, Mr. Colt."

"What's happened here?" queried Colt.

Jennings threw a hard glance at Four Fingers, then replied, "Apaches massacred the whole town. The people were practically unarmed."

Throwing a thumb over his shoulder, Dan said, "We were bringin' them rifles and ammunition. Donimo and his warriors pinned us down. No way we could get here in time."

"I understand," said the lieutenant. "This is a burial detail. We just finished the gruesome job." He looked past Colt and glared at the Apache again. "That's not—"

"Sure is," cut in Dan. "Old Four Fingers himself."

The chief was instantly taken into custody as Dan told Jennings the whole story, omitting the part about himself being Logan Tanner's prisoner. The big marshal, in the throes of his fever, was still babbling incoherently. Dan was in no danger at the moment.

Dorianne Kates was introduced to the lieutenant and stood by as Dan said, "I must head back for Taos immediately, Jennings. You will see Miss Kates safely to Fort Apache?"

"Of course," smiled Jennings, drinking in her beauty.

"She'll be heading for Tucson as soon as stagecoach traveling resumes."

The lieutenant nodded. "She'll be well cared for, Mr. Colt."

"And you'll see that the marshal gets proper medical attention?"

"Sure will. There's a good doctor at the fort."

"If you could spare some rations and a little antiseptic and fresh bandage," said Dan, holding up his injured arm, "I'll be on my way."

CHAPTER TWENTY-FOUR

The lowering sun cast the long shadow of Dan Colt on Eternity's dusty street as he finished stuffing the saddlebags on Harry Doyle's horse.

The tall man took one final look at the feverish Logan Tanner as four troopers carried away the bodies of Early Byrd and Steve Proffitt for burial. The marshal was getting medical attention from a big sergeant. Dan strode to the lieutenant and shook his hand. "Much obliged for your kindness, Jennings."

"My pleasure, Mr. Colt," said the young officer with a smile.

The tall man turned and set his pale blues on the small girl who stood a few steps behind him. Sadness clouded the usually bright eyes of Dorianne Kates. Tears were evident on her cheeks.

Dan's heart grew heavy as lead. This was a truly exceptional and wonderful young woman. It grated his soul to hurt her, but there was absolutely no choice. Nervously he moved toward her.

Before he could speak, she said, "Dan, earthly language has no words to express my gratitude. You risked your life to come to that camp after me. If they'd caught you, they would have tortured you to death. How can I ever—"

"You don't have to express it, Dorianne," the towering figure said tenderly. "Just to see you alive and unharmed is enough for me."

Suddenly she rushed to him, wrapping her arms around his slender waist. Her head pressed to his muscular chest, she wept for

218

several minutes. Clutching her shoulders, Dan held her tiny frame tight.

As her sobbing subsided, Dorianne spoke, her voice tremulous with emotion. "Dan . . . please tell me that we will see each other again."

The tall man paused, then spoke softly. "It would only be an injustice to *you*." Dorianne's head was still pressed against his chest. Dan continued, "You will meet some fine young man someday, honey. Someone nearer your own age. Someone who is free to settle down and give you a home."

"But Dan, after you find Dave and clear yourself—"

"Dorianne," cut in Dan, "that would be no good even if there were no reservations on my part. No one could ask you to wait around on such an indefinite *maybe*."

"You wouldn't have to ask me. I'll volunteer."

"Little lady," sighed Dan, "you must understand. I'm still carrying the image of Mary Colt in my heart. I'm not ready to change that yet."

Dorianne was silent for a long moment. Pulling her head back and looking him in the eyes, she said, "Oh, Dan, you must think I'm a brazen hussy."

"What do you mean?"

"The way I have so boldly declared my love for you."

"No," he said, a smile tugging at the corners of his mouth. "You're just a lonely, beautiful girl. I understand. Now you go back to Tucson and everything will work out for the best."

Dorianne's brown eyes were swimming again.

Placing a finger under her chin, the tall man tilted her face upward. "I'll never forget you," he said. "You are some little lady." He pressed his lips to hers in a brief but tender kiss.

Without another word he turned and mounted the horse. Dorianne wiped tears with the back of her hand to clear her vision. Dan Colt rode north without turning around.

The weeping girl watched his broad back as the horse carried him forever out of her life. She watched until horse and rider became a small black dot in the low brown haze that lifted out of the sun-baked land.

A firm hand pressed her shoulder. She turned to look at

Lieutenant Clifford Jennings's face. "Miss Kates," he said softly, "we're ready to move out."

Dorianne nodded, then turned to look northward one more time. The black dot on the horizon was gone.

DELL'S ACTION-PACKED WESTERNS

Selected Titles

- [ ] **THE RELUCTANT PARTNER**
  by John Durham $1.50 (17770-7)
- [ ] **BOUGHT WITH A GUN** by Luke Short $1.50 (10744-5)
- [ ] **THE MAN FROM TUCSON**
  by Claude Cassady $1.50 (16940-2)
- [ ] **BOUNTY GUNS** by Luke Short $1.50 (10758-X)
- [ ] **DOUBLE-BARRELLED LAW**
  by D. L. Winkle $1.50 (11773-9)
- [ ] **THE KIOWA PLAINS** by Frank Ketchum $1.50 (14809-X)
- [ ] **LONG WAY TO TEXAS** by Lee McElroy $1.50 (14639-9)
- [ ] **LOCO** by Lee Hoffman $1.50 (14901-0)
- [ ] **LONG LIGHTNING** by Norman A. Fox $1.50 (14943-6)
- [ ] **DIL DIES HARD** by Kelly P. Gast $1.50 (12008-X)
- [ ] **BUCKSKIN MAN** by Tom W. Blackburn $1.50 (10976-0)
- [ ] **SHOWDOWN AT SNAKEGRASS JUNCTION**
  by Gary McCarthy $1.50 (18278-6)
- [ ] **SHORT GRASS** by Tom W. Blackburn $1.50 (17980-7)
- [ ] **DERBY MAN** by Gary McCarthy $1.50 (13297-5)
- [ ] **YANQUI** by Tom W. Blackburn $1.25 (19879-8)

At your local bookstore or use this handy coupon for ordering:

Dell | **DELL BOOKS**
P.O. BOX 1000, PINEBROOK, N.J. 07058

Please send me the books I have checked above. I am enclosing $ _____
(please add 75¢ per copy to cover postage and handling). Send check or money
order—no cash or C.O.D.'s. Please allow up to 8 weeks for shipment.

Mr/Mrs/Miss _____

Address _____

City _____ State/Zip _____

The continuation of
the exciting six-book series that
began with *The Exiles*

The
SETTLERS

WILLIAM STUART LONG

Volume II of *The Australians*

Set against the turbulent epic of a nation's birth is
the unforgettable chronicle of fiery Jenny
Taggart—a woman whose life would be torn by
betrayal, flayed by tragedy, enflamed by love and
sustained by inconquerable determination.

A Dell Book $2.95   (15923-7)

At your local bookstore or use this handy coupon for ordering:

 DELL BOOKS   THE SETTLERS $2.95   (15923-7)
P.O. BOX 1000, PINEBROOK, N.J. 07058

Please send me the above title. I am enclosing $ _____
(please add 75¢ per copy to cover postage and handling). Send check or money
order—no cash or C.O.D.'s. Please allow up to 8 weeks for shipment.

Mr/Mrs/Miss _____

Address _____

City _____ State/Zip _____

The magnificent saga
that began with *The Exiles*
and *The Settlers* continues

The TRAITORS

by WILLIAM STUART LONG

Through heartbreak and tragic loss, a generation
of exiles forged a home out of a barren wilderness.
But their trials were not yet over. Treacherous
forces defied King and country—and threatened
to test the courage of the settlers to their very limit.

THE TRAITORS $3.50   (18131-3)

Order the other books in this exciting series:

THE EXILES $3.95   (12374-7)
THE SETTLERS $2.95   (15923-7)

At your local bookstore or use this handy coupon for ordering:

DELL BOOKS
P.O. BOX 1000, PINEBROOK, N.J. 07058

Please send me the books I have checked above. I am enclosing $_____
(please add 75¢ per copy to cover postage and handling). Send check or money
order—no cash or C.O.D.'s. Please allow up to 8 weeks for shipment.

Mr/Mrs/Miss _____

Address _____

City _____ State/Zip _____

"A magnificent novel...scintillating... vibrant...expert." —*Washington Post*

KING RAT

JAMES CLAVELL

author of *Shōgun* and *Noble House*

Here is an epic novel that strips human beings down to the most naked passion and elemental survival needs, as all distinctions between East and West fade before the all-conquering force of one man's thrust for personal empire.

"James Clavell is a spellbinding storyteller, a brilliant observer, a man who understands and forgives much." —*The New York Times*

A Dell Book $3.95 (14546-5)

At your local bookstore or use this handy coupon for ordering:

Dell

DELL BOOKS   KING RAT $3.95   (14546-5)
P.O. BOX 1000, PINE BROOK, N.J. 07058-1000

Please send me the above title. I am enclosing $_____ (please add 75c per copy to cover postage and handling). Send check or money order—no cash or C.O.D.s. Please allow up to 8 weeks for shipment.

Mr./Mrs./Miss_____

Address_____

City_____ State/Zip_____